SERENITY HOUSE

Also by Christopher Hope

FICTION
A Separate Development
Learning to Fly and Other Tales
Kruger's Alp
The Hottentot Room
Black Swan
My Chocolate Redeemer

NON-FICTION
White Boy Running
Moscow! Moscow!

POETRY
Cape Drives
In the Country of the Black Pig
Englishmen

FOR CHILDREN
The King, the Cat and the Fiddle
The Dragon Wore Pink

CHRISTOPHER HOPE

SERENITY HOUSE

MACMILLAN
LONDON

Lines quoted from 'The Exiles', taken from
W. H. Auden Collected Poems edited by
Edward Mendelson and published by
Faber and Faber Ltd

First published 1992 by Macmillan London Limited
a division of Pan Macmillan Publishers Limited
Cavaye Place London SW10 9PG
and Basingstoke

Reprinted 1992

Associated companies throughout the world

ISBN 0-333-56982-2

A CIP catalogue record for this book is available from
the British Library

Phototypeset by Intype, London
Printed and bound in Great Britain by
Mackays of Chatham PLC, Chatham, Kent

In Memory of 'Max' Klein

CONTENTS

1	Think of a Number	1
2	Max Strikes a Bargain	16
3	A Spider in the Bath	35
4	The New Boy	48
5	An Inspector Calls	61
6	From Tranquillity to Serenity	69
7	Tales his Mother Told Him	77
8	Jack Goes to Market	87
9	Jack Goes to London	100
10	How Albert Got the News	109
11	Jack Gets a Job	120
12	Max and *The Broad Pelvis*	128
13	Innocenta to the Rescue	140
14	Albert Puts his Foot in It	153
15	Fee fi foh fum . . .	162
16	Problems	174
17	The Joy of Passing	181
18	The Great Escape	191
19	Pat Dog Day	203
20	Kingdom Come	221

fascist pl.-s, -ism: whether full anglicization of the words is worth while cannot be decided till we know whether the things are to be temporary or permanent in England.

A Dictionary of Modern English Usage,
H. W. Fowler Oxford 1937 (with corrections)

'Our rooms are ready, the register signed,
There is time to take a turn before dark.'

The Exiles,
W. H. Auden

CHAPTER ONE

Think of a Number

Max Montfalcon lay in bed and tried to remember how many people he had killed. If one understood the question correctly, it seemed very much a question of number.

Beside him, exuding heat and steam, a moistness almost palpable, a damp gust from some peculiar English tropic, he could feel the perspiring presence of Albert, his interrogator. That long ago a fat young man should have stolen one's daughter and become one's son-in-law was bad enough. It was pretty bloody rum when one's son-in-law turned interrogator. Max's eyes were closed and he liked them that way. He heard the distant church clock strike seven, the chimes carrying a mile or more in the evening air. By such sonic rituals Max had marked out his days and nights at Serenity House since that day in early November 1990, when he had gone 'inside'. The church clock clear at seven of an evening. The call for 'lights out' at nine. The electric milk van at dawn. In summer the boys at the prep school across the road were in the cricket nets. In winter their voices grew shriller. Leaping and darting like midges they batted the hard ball back and forth across the fives courts. Roofless concrete sheds lit by fierce electric lamps. Leather glove meaty as it struck the ball; the scramble for the pepper. Eton Fives on a winter evening. Thank God for England!

One had been exposed to bores before. But Albert took the giddy biscuit.

Even the paucity of possessions in Max's room irritated Albert. One blue chair and a table in similar hue, almost sky blue. French blue. Continental. Serenity House seemed to have been furnished from second-hand shops and bankrupt hotels. This was Cledwyn Fox's doing, Albert decided, Welsh tat and French look-alikes, so dismayingly foreign. A broad-shouldered cupboard, oak, five foot tall, bronze facings and a silver lock. Fitted by the locksmith in Highgate Village, Max told him proudly, and 'guaranteed against all but the most professional burglar'. Where Max kept his bits and pieces. 'A few mementoes. Pre-war,' Max had said. 'My treasures.'

Until recently Albert had taken no notice. Now, he was not sure he wanted to know what Max locked in his cupboard. Upon the bed a cover decorated with a map of Corsica embroidered in gold. Why Corsica, for Christ's sake? Well, simply because that was the only map available in old Maudie Geratie's embroidery kit, supplied by her art therapist, a pale girl named Jaci who had been 'carried away by the Campari' old Maudie told all and sundry, as if some evil foreign wind, like the föhn or the mistral, or some modest but fatal European malady, had robbed her of her art therapist. Before Jaci had been carried away she had also taught Maudie French-knitting and the red woollen pixie cap hanging behind Max's bedroom door was another gift. Mixed, mismatched entangled shoes, and shabby slippers, badly bruised, heels trodden flat, lay beside the bed. Sometimes Max would look at the shoes and weep. Not because he had ruined them, walked them into the ground, but because, he told Albert and Lizzie, 'shoes are hell to get rid of! Always two of them to one of you.' Upon the bedside table towered Max's beloved magazines: *Monarchy*, *Majesty*, *Blue Blood*, *Homage* and, of course, on top of the pile, Max's favourite, *Fealty*.

In a reedy, rusty voice, without opening his eyes, Max murmured: 'Think of a number, any number . . .'

Whereupon Albert had heaved himself to his feet. 'I'm not interested in playing silly games with you, Max. You don't want to talk to me? Fine! Suit yourself. But I'd have thought your family deserves a bit better. Lizzie loves you. And she's beside herself. She sits around waiting for the heavens to fall. And then there's Innocenta.'

Albert's voice was tight. But something else too? – got it – terrified!

2

Lizzie loved him? Well, perhaps, once. But that was before they made their bargain and Lizzie broke it. The midnight knock on the door. The iron gates closing behind him. Time to pack a single suitcase.

And Innocenta? His darling granddaughter. Yes, she was going to help him. He had an idea that Innocenta was going to help him catch a mouse.

Albert was crashing around the room, preparing to walk out. But Max preferred to listen to young Dr Tonks, the visiting geriatrician, talking to Night Matron down the corridor about a recent leaver.

'Before we got a rhythm going, she suffered badly, dear old Elsie. I had to time my shots to catch the pain at onset. Mostly I think I got there before it took a real hold. When did you say she left?'

'Night before last, Dr Tonks. Around three in the morning.'

'Anyone see her off?'

'I'd looked in a little earlier. With Imelda. We like to look in if we know guests are leaving. First to know she'd gone was Jack. He's so quick is young Jack. I have no fears for the small-hour leavers.'

'Admirable. Last-minute problems?'

'She was as good as gold.'

'It gives one hope, Matron. Pain control. From onset. Then swift peaceful departure. That's my prayer. And lots of good soldiers like Elsie Gooche, with the good sense not to hang about.'

That's when Albert had walked out of Max's room. He had walked out the way people walked out of the United Nations. And meetings about Northern Ireland. Got to his feet and stomped out, muttering, 'I don't give a bugger. Suit yourself, you stupid old bastard. If you think this is bad, wait till the real questions start!' And then bang, bang, bang, slam. That was Albert walking out like Arabs and Israelis walked out of peace conferences.

Max had discussed Arab–Israeli walk-outs with Major Bobbno, who said: 'Didn't expect you to like Israelis somehow, Monty.'

Major Bobbno would call him Monty. Or sometimes Brigadier. 'The Israelis know that you get nowhere being nice. Peace talks are about power. Look at Versailles.'

'Look at Munich.'

'I do. Munich. I say. Precisely! Nineteen thirty-three. So don't be weak – nail the bastards' balls to the wall. Then talk. That's what the Israelis do. D'you admire the Israelis, Monty?'

'I admire the Israelis, Major.'

'Same here.' Major Bobbno lifted iron-grey eyebrows, two hairy mudguards over rubbery eyes. 'Between you, me and the gatepost, Monty, it's Jews who get on my wick.'

'We might have done better to nail their balls to the wall.'

'Whose balls? The Jews'?'

'The Israelis'.'

'Pardon my ignorance, Monty – but why should we want to nail the Israelis' balls to the wall?'

'Not now. In forty-seven,' said Max. 'When we had the mandate in Palestine and the Stern Gang bombed our hotels and killed our chaps. That way maybe we would have stopped the long decline. We ran out on the Middle East, Major. After Palestine, came Aden . . . '

'And India. Don't forget India, Monty. Then Rhodesia.'

Both men suddenly stopped talking as Jack came by. Jack the American helper. The boy with the thick blond hair and the large smile. 'What you guys saying then? Anybody join?'

'We're discussing the usefulness of nailing balls to the wall,' said Major Bobbno. He waved his plastic hand-reacher at Jack. 'Now clear off, before I have you shot!'

'Eigh! But I love you guys!' said the boy Jack and waltzed off down the corridor shaking his head and muttering delightedly, 'What are you talking about? Whose balls you're going to nail to the wall!'

He went on his way, stopping every so often to wave his hands in some kind of American dance, and shake his hips to some internal music and pray out loud in his savage, incomprehensible way, groans and whistles, to whatever American gods he worshipped. A prayer of thanks for bringing him, a poor boy from a trailer home in Florida, to the great good place of Serenity House.

'Are you sure he grew up in a caravan?' Major Bobbno asked Max as they watched him go. 'Mr Fox swears he comes from a decent home. University lad.'

'How many times has Mr Fox been to America?' Max demanded.

'Once a year. To New York.'

'And you know why?'

'He takes friend Bruce to that nancy parade. Chaps in frocks.'

'Exactly. So what does he know about Jack? One day I'll tell you Jack's story. You'd be amazed . . . '

'He told you his story, the boy Jack?' asked the Major.

Max grinned. Shapely yellow teeth above a full lip. 'The boy's an illiterate. He couldn't tell me if he tried. I wouldn't listen if he did. But I know Jack's story better than he ever will.'

Time passed. Max's room was dark. Behind his closed eyelids it was darker still. The signal for lights out sang in Serenity House. A plangent electronic bleeper, not too harsh, *no*, pro-grammed to mimic the call of the turtle-dove. When Cledwyn Fox, director and sole proprietor of Serenity House, first fitted the device its call was that of a distant ambulance. In the early days of its installation, before Mr Fox muted it, its urgent summons had carried off two occupants of Serenity House. The elderly are susceptible to such alarms and have learnt *never* to ask for whom the ambulance calls for they know it calls for them.

Though lights out rang at nine, guests were free to choose their own bedtimes. 'Remember this isn't *my* home, it's *yours*,' Cledwyn Fox told each new arrival. But most of the elders heard and obeyed the command. Most of the bedrooms were dark soon after nine o'clock. But not silent. Cries and monologues. Abrupt, tearing coughing attacks – so alarming to those who heard them for the first time, but to the veteran strangely reassuring in their recognisable timbre and regularity, rather like the familiar striking of great, chesty clocks – spilled from the darkened bedrooms. The night staff, the ever-alert carers, would pause on their rounds, and identify the calls, just as hunters in the African dark learn to know the cries of animals that hunt and die by night. Bedtime by consensus, a sense of an ending, said Cledwyn Fox. His dove-grey brochure spoke plainly of its merits: 'North London's Premier Eventide Refuge. Four hundred and thirty pounds a week, plus VAT. Trained and kindly staff. Colour televisions in certain rooms.' A congenial regime.

Regime was a lovely word. Max rolled it around his tongue. In the warm darkness of his room, it tasted of salad oil and iron; assertive yet not unpleasant. Serenity House offered all that might be asked: private medical treatment and physiotherapy. Little Lois Chadwick with the limp dropped in once a week for hairdressing with her portable driers and her little box of 'curlers and crimpers'. And the chiropodist, Edgar, wearing the tiniest gold ring through his left nostril, with his inflammatory views on the future of Europe. He dropped in on Tuesday with his little box of 'clicks and sticks'. 'Eurobugger – and Proud of it!' said his pink lapel badge.

'When we go into a united Europe envisaged by the Brussels bureaucrats, we will be taking a fast train straight into the buffers,' Edgar intoned, stripping the wrapping from a corn plaster and examining the yellow, flaking soles of old Maudie Geratie who suffered terribly with her feet. On Maudie's bedside table stood a photograph of a lovely girl in a large ivory frame. This, Edgar knew, had been old Maudie, once – old Maudie young. A coquette, a lissome, large-eyed, flighty dancer whose lovers had gasped, strained, and even died for her. Chiefly, a Brazilian baritone named Arnaldo, famed for his interpretation of Mozart, who had perished in the war. Which war? Edgar could not say – probably the Great War for old Maudie was well into her nineties – but after a certain age which war it had been really didn't matter.

It was one of the few boons of old age – you forgot about your wars. And your dead friends and lovers who seemed so dead then, were now alive and kicking all around you, while the living seemed ghosts from another world.

6

Edgar sighed as he centred the corn plaster. Old Maudie giggled and glanced around her room. 'This is a *lovely* apartment. You don't often get them this size, in Paris.'

Paris! It gave Edgar a sharp pain. Only Brussels caused him more pain. Bunions, whitlows, in-grown toe-nails, warts, corns – excrescences upon the fair face of humanity – these were the secret names Edgar gave to France, Germany, Italy, Holland. Only Mr Montfalcon understood and sympathised with Edgar's fierce sense of Englishness. Only Mr Montfalcon deplored the fall of the Berlin Wall. 'Germans, all over again,' he said, as Edgar treated him for a particularly painful infected toe-nail. 'Overbearing. Over the top. Only a matter of time and they'll be over here.'

'The Channel Tunnel', said Edgar, manipulating a disinfectant swab with gentle concern, 'will be a death trap.'

'Fire?'

'Rabies! Mark my words. The first rabid dog or cat or bat to make the crossing will have "Made in Germany" stamped on its tongue.'

And Edgar's left nostril twitched and the little gold ring caught the light like a star. When this happened old Maudie would smile brilliantly, for her eyesight was still amazingly keen although her other functions had failed one by one. 'Look! The evening star!' old Maudie chirruped when Edgar's nose ring flashed light, and she clapped her hands and would have gone on clapping them until the palms were raw had not Matron One arrived to calm her. Matron One, Mrs Trump, also known as Day Matron, was a kindly lady.

Night Matron, an ex-Rhodesian nurse, Mrs S, known to the Manchester Twins as Rudolpha Hess, but to everyone else simply as Matron Two, regulated the evening and nighttime hours – 'or at least as many hours as are left to us, one and all, for we know not the day nor the hour,' Matron Two liked to say being religious, and so saying sometimes made Agnes cry copiously. Poor young Agnes ('I'm just the right side of sixty-seven'), one of those belonging to a group known, not unkindly, with that soft, understanding smile, which is often the only compliment the young and healthy pay the elderly, as the Five Incontinents, leaking as she sometimes did from both ends.

Max thanked his lucky stars that, with rare exceptions, he

7

leaked from one end only. In bed now, he pressed his thighs together, strengthening the pelvic muscles, feeling his incontinence pad fitted snugly into his underpants. It took you back, to things done as a boy, as a baby and surely best forgotten. To have your own body wake you with its liquid, to have the old man that you knew you were not, go and leave his little wet calling card on you, that was awful. Better the pad, even though it was sometimes uncomfortable to sleep on and, if it ever got any worse, then it would have to be the catheter. Yes, he *would* have the catheter. What did the Arabs say? *Bukra il mish, mish*: 'Tomorrow the apricots!' No apricots for Max Montfalcon – but tomorrow, perhaps, the catheter.

Toileting was one of the major achievements of Serenity House. Guests were toileted regularly. Pads and catheters and commodes on request in the bedrooms and strengthening exercises and attention to diet. As indeed there had to be. For if Agnes leaked from two ends, there were guests who leaked from three. Couldn't keep a thing down, nor in, nor up. On a bad day the Five Incontinents could ruin an entire carpet. Cledwyn Fox *would* have carpet on the floor. And Serenity House would do its best to cope.

' . . . Drycleaning, personal telephone in some bedrooms – not all rooms. Not bloody likely' – since, as Mr Fox explained, the apparently pacific Lady Divina had proved herself to have immensely strong wrists and homicidal ambitions for she had one day tried to strangle Edgar the chiropodist as he knelt to deal with a particularly nasty bunion and it had required the combined efforts of both Matron One, Dr Tonks, Mr Fox and the little Filipino nurse-aide, Imelda, to rescue the dainty Euro-hater from Lady Divina's telephonic garrotte. Afterwards Mr Fox had said: 'From now on, she uses the pay phone.' And who could blame him? Edgar wore the welts of his near strangulation clearly visible on his neck for some weeks afterwards as he arrived at Serenity House in his little van with the sticker in the back window which read angrily 'Fl-EEC-ed!'

The brochure for Serenity House, written in the early eighties, and never revised in the light of more sensitive recommendations by the District Health Authority, was direct and factual. 'Serenity House. North London's Premier Eventide Refuge offers complete care for long and short terms in respect of convalescence. Post-operative. Geriatric. Terminal. Holiday . . .' Plain, perhaps, but free of 'superfluous imbroglio,' declared Cledwyn Fox in tones of some satisfaction, 'and coming from a Welsh-man,' he liked to add to prospective guests, 'you can't say fairer'. The small print, mind you, had to be watched pretty carefully. It laid down conditions for the governance of drink and tobacco and placed their dispensation firmly in the hands of the Director and staff. 'Interest', the brochure warned, 'will be charged on late payment of board. Incontinence damage will be charged directly to the incontinent in question.' Because this ran to replacing top quality carpet – Mr Fox always insisted on good carpet, 'none of your bloody industrial weave around here,' – it could be pricey. Then there was the 'behaviour clause' modelled, according to Mr Fox again, on 'similar exclusion clauses found in public schools'; to wit, the right of the Head to boot out any trouble makers, but, naturally, excluding unconscious mental afflictions, whatever they were, or relatively harmless acts of insanity where the person in question really couldn't help her-self. 'In the evening' – Mr Fox usually spoke only about 'the evening' expecting one to fill in for oneself the obvious conclusion 'of life' – 'in the evening,' said Mr Fox, 'acts of insanity are bound to occur, especially when dealing with dementia and' – here his dark, lively little Welsh face took on a gnomic, almost a pixie-like expression – 'even due perhaps to the inconsolable anguish of great age. Yes indeed!'

Speaking these words as if delivering them at an eisteddfod, thus did Mr Fox indicate both his sympathy and his spirit of discipline. There had to be rules, hence the catch-all killer clause in the contract: 'At all times the patient shall not cause a nuisance or annoyance to the staff of the nursing home or other patients therein.' And finally, there was help with funeral plan-ning. Serenity House had its own scheme to which guests might contribute or they could, if they wished, make use of the scheme run by Age Concern. 'It is something that families in particular appreciate,' Mr Fox explained to the relatives of incoming guests. 'People are able to leave clear instructions as to what they want done. Not to put too fine a point on it, that way there is always the cash to cover the casket.'

*

Who was it who heard Max counting aloud that night, after Albert's ferocious interrogation? It was Matron Two, moving slowly down the corridor, hearing something outside her range of nocturnal reference, a man counting slowly and firmly in a low voice: '. . . one hundred and eight, one hundred and nine . . . ' interrupted now and then by what sounded like choking but turned out to be, she discovered as she listened carefully, not the sounds of asphyxiation – thank heaven! – but only dry, barking sobs.

'Now then, Mr Montfalcon,' said Matron Two, as she slipped into his room and sat down beside his bed, 'it's just a dream you're having.'

So silently she moved, did Matron Two, down the corridors, the crêpe soles of her brogues making no sound, the blue night-lights soft on the dark down of her upper lip, that some of the guests supposed that it was Matron Two whom Lady Divina meant when she kept announcing the closeness of the 'Angel of Death'.

'Numbers were never taken,' Max murmured. '*Never*. So many who came into the place, simply left again without being noted.'

'And where did they leave for, these visitors of yours?'

'Not mine!' Max raised himself in bed, turning on a bony elbow, sharp as a school compass. 'I had nothing whatever to do with the missing numbers. This is hard to understand. I know that. People who weren't there cannot understand. Ever.'

'You're dead right, Mr Montfalcon. That's what I say about Rhodesia. Not all whites were monsters who ate little black babies. So don't you fuss. You can tell me, if it makes you feel better – I'll understand.'

But Max had sunk back on his pillows and said nothing. Matron Two gave him two sleeping pills – her little 'bombs' – and a sip of water. A few minutes later he was snoring.

Dear Mr Montfalcon. He was a nice man and not half so demented as he liked to pretend. Probably did it just to get that dreadful family off his back. She did not know who was worse. The obstreperous son-in-law with the round, pink face and the loud voice, or his stuck-up daughter with all the blonde hair, or that ghastly granddaughter who came at night sometimes, dressed up in her robes and painted eyes. Was she a witch, a druid, or the follower of one of those silly gurus who collected Rolls Royces and cheated on their taxes? *Poor* Mr Montfalcon. The visit from the son-in-law earlier that day had clearly upset him. They could hear the shouting from E-wing.

Max Montfalcon was a fine, sensitive man. Matron Two thought him head and shoulders above most of the intake of 1990, though, as Mr Fox said, times were tight and beggars can't be choosers and what the hell, so long as their cheques don't bounce. But *really*! He didn't have to nurse them, did he?

All the elders in Serenity House were supposed to retain at least the vestiges of health and reason. Or they should be in geriatric wards somewhere else. Yet there were some who, when the doctors arrived on visits, quite visibly pulled themselves together, stood up straight and nodded, and tried not to dribble. Much as she admired Cledwyn Fox, he connived at the deception. Some guests in the House really weren't up to it any longer. Some weren't 'there' at all. And amongst some of the very frail and elderly, even when they were 'there', like old Maudie, or Beryl the Beard, she knew, somehow, that they wished they weren't.

And now a man with a loud voice and pink, shining face, hiding under the pseudonym of 'son-in-law', came into the House and terrorised one of the better guests. It really was too much. Matron Two did not like Members of Parliament. They were always so damned sure of themselves. Perhaps it came of always having to pretend they knew what they were talking about and having to say it in five minutes flat before the chap in the wig shut them up. Visits from MPs usually spelt trouble: just look what had happened when parties of British MPs began visiting Rhodesia – it had been the beginning of the end.

It had to be said that Max Montfalcon was quite a fellow. 'Uncontainable!' Cledwyn Fox said proudly. 'A free spirit' – when he had turned up that afternoon on the arm of Sergeant Pearce, after going missing for a full five hours. Whether sitting in his electric wheelchair or moving in his extraordinarily slow but determined way down the corridor, or out of the front door, his height, his kind of tall, stiff stillness made him memorable.

The dark blue barathea blazer with its single ivory button was thirty years old if it was a day, but style is style, even in a foreign kind of a way, even if it possessed the stylishness of crinolines and bustles and frockcoats, the sorts of things that hung in faded opulence, in pleats and ruffs and elaborate cross-stitches in museums and theatrical outfitters' windows. Max often liked to wear a grey silk shirt washed so thin it seemed transparent, and he would knot a dark blood-red tie around the loose creased flesh of his thin neck, a great Windsor knot of tie that was slung like some woollen anchor beneath his bobbing Adam's apple. Yes, Max Montfalcon was what Cledwyn Fox would once have called 'a gentleman', with his fine good grey hair carefully swept back over the ears, and his light blue eyes, even now with a tendency to water, still imposing and rather beautiful. His height and bearing, at eighty-one, made Max Montfalcon a handsome man, with his rather sad little habits – the elderly red tin of rolling tobacco in his inside pocket, shreds of the stuff lodging in the folds of his clothes and often in the folds of his facial skin, the distressing habit of walking with his heels flat, refusing to lace his shoes properly and turning left and right foot sideways as he shuffled along, walking on his feet but not in his shoes. How he kept them on was a mystery. Yet he never lost a shoe, did Max Montfalcon, even when he went on one of his little 'wanderings' and had to be brought back from the park or the woods, or the heath where he'd been found like some stray dog or picked up like a lost ball.

Once he was returned to Serenity House by Mrs Marcos, the Cypriot tailor, into whose shop he had strolled one afternoon and discussed, to her intense surprise, the vagaries of the English hyphen, while rolling a cigarette. He declared that, in the matter of the hyphen he, Max Montfalcon, preferred to follow the great Fowler and 'wallow in uncertainty'. He said 'vallow' with a little sharp bark. It was one of those words he never ever pronounced correctly, just as he always insisted on tea and 'bisquits' and studied the television programmes in something only he called the 'bulletim', choosing to express the first syllable as if it rhymed with 'dull'. Little Soti Marcos, just eighteen months and safe in her grandmother's arms, looked into Max's pale blue eyes, saw his upper dentures fix upon his lower lip as he proceeded to give velocity to his 'vallow', and howled her head off.

What Max had actually gone on to say to little Soti, if anybody could remember it, if anybody could understand it, and of course he did not now remember it, was: 'I hate the use of the hyphen in the term "German-born Jews". As Fowler pointed out with a similar example of the cumbersome hyphen in the term – "South African-born Indians" – what we should simply say is "Jews born in Germany".'

Why should this example have sprung to mind? If asked at the time, he would not have been able to say. It really didn't matter, certainly not as far as Mrs Marcos and her little granddaughter were concerned. On that afternoon, when the sight of Max's strong yellow false teeth descending on his lower lip had made little Soti Marcos weep like the monsoon, Mrs Marcos had taken him back to Serenity House, wheeling him along like some elderly bicycle on very flat tyres.

But most often it was Sergeant Pearce of the Highgate Police who led him home. The handsome village bobby who stood on the corner of Archway Road watching for the 'amber gamblers', the motorists who jumped the yellow on the Archway traffic lights.

There were some ways in which Sergeant Pearce reminded Max of young von F. Something in the height, the blue eyes, the uniform? No, *not* the uniform. He supposed young von F had worn a uniform, but that would have been after he returned to Germany. Serve him bloody well right. At that time, anyone who returned to Germany ended up in a uniform. What could young von F expect? Seen from the side, Sergeant Pearce's dark hair curled in his nape in much the way that Cynthia Pargeter had found irresistible! What on earth had happened to Cynthia? He'd not seen her since the day young von F (damned fool!) sailed for home.

'Got someone here who I think belongs to you,' Sergeant Pearce would say, on arriving at Serenity House, unfurling his dental flag – his slow crooked smile that had passing housewives blushing like schoolgirls – for the benefit of the goggling nurse. It was the opinion of everyone who knew him that Sergeant Pearce was far too good-looking to be a policeman. And indeed he wasn't much of a cop. He never caught an amber gambler, or ticketed a car, but he nabbed Max Montfalcon on more than one of his little walks.

Perhaps there was something about Max which positively invited arrest. Who would not have been struck by the slow rocking shuffle of the old man in his blazer and red tie and his ruined shoes, proceeding at an achingly slow pace down the uneven pavements of Highgate? Children clutched their mothers' hands, wide-eyed at his agonised progress. Busloads of inquisitive Chinese negotiating the hilly heights, in search of the tomb of Karl Marx, stared at the immensely tall thin old man who teetered on the kerb and waved a fist whenever he caught sight of them. 'Slitty-eyes, slitty-eyes!' Max would yell, borrowing the insult from Philip, Duke of Edinburgh, one of his great heroes (after Earl Mountbatten – now there was an Englishman for you!). Or he would glare at the pale-faced and rather furtive Russians hiding out in their trade mission on the edge of Highgate West Hill, their closed, alien and somehow abstracted expressions reminding him of beings from a planet well beyond our solar system.

They all saw the old man from time to time, buffeting the air like a bather entering a high, cold sea and making barely any progress. For he moved like a tightrope walker fighting a gale-force wind that hit him face on. It could take him five minutes to cross the road; the length of a single block took anything up to half an hour. Anyone watching him closely would have seen that although he always appeared to be moving, he often only went through the motions of walking, lifting his left leg and then seeming to forget the purpose of the movement, freezing it there while his hands, long white hands, with veins so thin yet clear they might have been drawn in blue ballpoint pen, described frantic little circles by his sides, cyclones of effort.

'Do you have daughters?' Max demanded of Sergeant Pearce.

'No, sir.'

'Good. Don't. Daughters are ingrates. Take your money – throw you to the wolves. I made a bargain with my daughter, Lizzie. And my granddaughter, Innocenta. She talked of "granny flats" and "free spirits". But she's young and believes in Buddha or Odin or someone. I am *not* a granny. My suite of rooms in my daughter's house was not a "flat". We had a bargain. My money in exchange for a safe haven. Hadn't been there for two minutes and they shipped me off to the scrap heap.'

'I think we're getting nowhere fast, sir,' Sergeant Pearce said, steering Max in a gentle circle to face the way he had been walking.

'Story of my life. I wonder what you feel about the hyphen, Sergeant? If we follow Fowler, we can dispense with the hyphen altogether. Fowler illustrates this very clearly using the term "South African-born Indians". Fowler suggests in its place that we use "Indians born in South Africa".'

'Really, sir?'

'We transpose this. And instead of the ugly hyphenated German-born Jews, we get: "Jews born in Germany". See what I mean?'

'Yes, sir. No hyphens.'

'No Jews either,' said Max.

'See what you mean,' Sergeant Pearce nodded heavily as the justice of this observation was borne home to him, 'when you put it like that.'

'Like what?' demanded the walking windmill at his side, as the policeman and his charge walked slowly home to Serenity House.

CHAPTER TWO

Max Strikes a Bargain

One February morning in 1990 Max had noticed that his mansion in Hampstead Garden Suburb echoed more than usual. He had been humming snatches of an old song he couldn't remember why he remembered: 'That's How We Live Everyday . . . ' sang Max in his rusty baritone. How very strange! Where had that come from? Was it perhaps something he had danced to years ago in dear old Harwich? Pale winter sunlight shone on the crystal candelabra in the big house, empty but for him and the gardener, Kevin, a pleasant youth burnt mud-brown and wearing a pony-tail.

Two Portuguese maids, Elisabetta and Katerina, came every day and even if they cleaned the place twice, found there was never enough work to fill the time. So they'd polish the very tusks on the blue elephants painted on the cream tiles in the third bathroom and admire their reflections in the taps and talk of Lisbon. Max enjoyed talking to Kevin about the reckless ambitions of some politicians for European Monetary Union. 'The snake lay down in the basket of currencies and brought forth the EMU. It's a German racket!' Kevin preferred to talk of flowers and frost, though he showed himself well aware of the issues Max raised. 'You either go to the country with a referendum – Ask 'em: do you, or do you not, want to be hitched up to Madame Europe? Or what you've got is your elective dictatorship,' said Kevin. And Max could only reply 'Bravo! m'boy!' and marvel that a gardener could see what Her Majesty's Government and Opposition remained blind to.

On the morning his house echoed more emptily than ever Max began to think of disposing of his assets. Max discovered that he had been, in his younger days, something called an 'asset-stripper'. The thought began occurring to him: if asset-stripping takes its toll, perhaps asset-disposal puts some time back into the system? Maybe it was the moment to move.

'Assets', as the great Fowler truly observed, is 'a false form'. Use of the word is merely a journalistic short-cut, and takes the place of other, longer, words reporters can't remember or have forgotten how to spell: words like possession, advantage, resource. An asset is an asset is an asset. Always singular, never plural. He planned to cash in his 'asset' just as he had once abandoned teaching.

Somewhere in the middle fifties, his wife, Angela, would look at him in those brief years they were together and see him as a very tall, temporary teacher of English, loathed by his colleagues in Occam College, a very minor public school not far from Oxford.

'But I adhere to the King's English,' Max would protest to her, in their tiny bedroom in the small rented house across the road from the huge oval cricket field upon which the mist came down like some terribly patient, softly hostile, divine reproach. Elizabeth the baby moved in her mother's arms and looked at Max with his own blue eyes.

'I wouldn't say "adhere", darling.'

'But why?'

'Wallpaper adheres. Or believers adhere to a religion. But not you to the King's English. It sounds—'

'Funny?'

'Well, odd.'

In the single year they spent at Occam College Angela learnt how a man's wife will take on his characteristics in the eyes of others. She heard herself described by the common-room wives as 'the foreign woman', and this despite her blonde hair and her light-green eyes and her very English air. She took on her colour by way of Max's manner, bearing curiously formal, somehow always rather stilted. He could not for the life of him imagine why his fellow-teachers had regarded Angela as foreign. Born in Hove, educated in Cheltenham, the daughter of a prebendary dean and a mother who came from one of the oldest families in Brighton. Strange.

Nineteen fifty-six? Yes. In the little green kitchen Angela had told him that she was ill. She held Elizabeth tightly and the child sucked her thumb. On the wireless a man sang of a white sports coat, a pink carnation and a dance.

They had rented a little house in a village built of brown stones. It was modern and ugly and known, for reasons Max could never fathom, as a 'bungalow'. When it rained the stream which had been diverted when the house was built returned to its old ways and the house would flood. The rental was high: three pounds a week. 'We get five for our caravan in the south of France,' said the landlord, a fierce, florid man called Cowgill. 'I'm a banker!' he would say angrily. As he might have said: 'I am an assassin!'

Max moved around the kitchen, lifting the salt cellars, smoothing his hair, trying to force into his head the information she'd given him. Lifting one great foot and placing it softly on the scuffed, dark-green kitchen lino, he looked, thought Angela, like a walking tree. A broad, strong face. Slightly grey but bright skin, birch-like skin. The long nose and deep-blue eyes seemed natural features, almost accidental markings on the bark of the tree, which unexpectedly came together to make a face.

Max remembered little more of that particular day, though it was there somewhere just beneath his scalp. He'd only to lift his hands to his head and touch his still thick grey hair and the pain of it came back. That horrid little school with the bad sherry, the tight-arsed masters where he had once endured a whole year and lost his wife. Angela's ways had always been light, slight but exquisite. She could hardly have been said to have sickened, instead she grew quieter, paler, smaller, weaker. 'I feel like the Cheshire Cat, fading from view,' she told him as she lay in the hospital bed, seemingly relieved at last to be allowed to stop everything and simply lie down. 'I'll only leave my smile behind.' And she had: his daughter Elizabeth had her mother's smile. Of those years only certain sharp memories came back, like splinters beneath the finger-nails.

He did remember a boy named Hoskins. Small and furtive, he smelt of unaired cupboards and very faintly of cheese. Max never liked Hoskins though, for some reason he couldn't follow, Hoskins attached himself. His face was too narrow and covered with freckles, his thick, dark hair looked unclean and dull and Hoskins was stealthy, Hoskins hung about, he had a habit of drawing his breath in sharply and when he did Max saw his teeth were white and sharp. There was something intense, shamelessly cruel about Hoskins but there was something even more disconcerting – he made no attempt to hide the friendly admiration with which he regarded Max Montfalcon. And it had been Hoskins who caught up with him. One day not long after Angela had died. He carried a hockey stick over his shoulder as if it were a rifle.

'Do you like rabbit, sir?'

'I've never tried, Hoskins.'

'Killed five, sir. Myself, sir. That was yesterday. I go out on the estate for a bit of hunting.'

'You use a gun?'

'Ferrets, sir.'

Later that afternoon Max discovered the rabbit on his doorstep. A film of dried blood connected the three whiskers like a very delicate ruby fan. Its eyes were open, fur cold. He brought the stiff body indoors and laid it on the kitchen table and, for some unaccountable reason, he felt an urge to take a pair of callipers and measure its skull.

He also remembered a boy named Touche. Or was it Tooth? No, it couldn't have been Tooth. A boy with burnished skin, deep chestnut hair and eyes so dark they were almost black. He seemed the perfect androgyne. There was nothing particularly girlish about him. He was very much a boy but equally there was about him no hint at all of anything particularly masculine. He fell outside, and within, all of those categories and, in a class of pleasant fifteen-year-olds, his beauty was unearthly. Touche watched Max silently from the centre of the room – it was, Max realised, the fixed and almost blind gaze of a very young child, a baby.

But it was his own reaction that so astonished him. He felt himself hardening. Max had never had an erection in an English class – he had never felt the slightest sexual stirrings towards persons of his own gender. He didn't like it. He didn't approve of it and yet there it was, pressed achingly against the lip of his desk in the middle of the afternoon while he attempted to explain to the sleepy class the difference between 'factitious' and 'fictitious'.

'Let me take an example. Perhaps you'll see the difference then. Let's say I know a man to be an Anglican. And I go over and say to him – "You're a Jew, aren't you? I can tell by looking at you. You are of the Jewish faith." Then I'd be making a factitious argument – something made up for a particular purpose. For the sake of an argument. Or a controversy. Or an insult. But, on the other hand, if I happened to tell you that I was a secret agent planted here in Occam College to supply a foreign power with the secrets of the English educational system, then I would be telling a fictitious story. Do you see the difference?'

'Sir – what did you do in the war?' Now why was it that this question, coming so unexpectedly from the usually unnaturally silent boy Touche, should have caused such hilarity amongst the back desks of his class on that afternoon? He hadn't answered it at first because he couldn't look up, couldn't look at Touche. His ten fingers were extended on the table, the edge of the table now hurting him, yet he was so hard that he had to continue to press himself against it. Slowly he lifted his fingers and saw on the polished surface of the desk his finger-prints etched in sweat. The class waited.

'Nothing much – I'm sorry to say. An historian, my interests were culture, language, ethnic groups. My practical interest was anthropology. To tell the truth I spent the war in a research department.'

'Did you kill anyone, sir?'

'Measurements,' said Max as evenly as he could. He had to lean forward and ball his hands into fists and then lean again on the knuckles till he could have cried out with the pain. 'I'm sorry to disappoint you.' He could feel Touche's dark eyes on him and he hated the boy and he hated himself, above all he hated the involuntary, irresistible, treacherous sign of his own outrageous weakness. 'Statistical investigations. It was all very boring I can tell you.'

Then, at last, someone asked him a question he could answer. Touche was the boy and his question was simple: 'How much do you earn, sir?' In his relief at the directness of the question, Max told him, down to the last penny. There was a long, shocked silence in the classroom. Never before in their lives had these boys heard an adult reveal his salary. There seemed something indecent, obscene even, in both question and the flagrant, exhibitionist response. No one said a word – except Touche.

'My father earns more than that each week.'

When he looked back he knew that was the moment when 'the word' reached him. What gave Max the impetus, the rage to succeed, was a small word that blew up from nowhere, hit his mind the way a fly hits the windscreen at high speed and explodes in blood and wings. And stays there. Stuck. Max's response, the answer to the answer Touche gave him one morning, and which he now could not remember, did not need to remember, because he had gone out and done it, was condensed into a single syllable.

When Max moved from teaching (when *had* he moved from teaching? – some time in the late fifties, had it been?) he'd fled the tight world of the common-room. Certainly after Angela's death – an event which had undoubtedly contributed to his decision. But more than that, he had fled the questions – though precisely what the questions had been, he could not now exactly remember. Except in his dreams. He woke feeling he had been summoned for searching interrogation by persons unknown. And he sometimes found himself repeating, though he did not know it, that one little word that was the making of Max Montfalcon – 'kill!'

One had gone into business, on one's own account, as one used to say. 'Montfalcon Holdings'. The initial capital came from a sale of personal assets. Mementoes, trinkets. He had begun in a modest way by acquiring a pie and pastie firm in the West Midlands, firing the management, installing modern equipment, simply because all these things seemed logical and then, by Jove! a chappie came along and offered to take it off his hands at almost twice the price he'd paid for it! After that there was no holding him.

Montfalcon Holdings – 'what he has he holds,' they had said of him in the City. And someone once called him the 'piranha

of the boardroom'. The boardroom bit was wrong. He had no
board, no staff, no successors, no confidants. He bought and
sold. Max's line of business was to become fashionable in the
seventies and eighties, but in the sixties it had no name. It was
simply business. And when he did what he did the word went
round in the small circles where these things were done that
Montfalcon had made a 'killing'. He had owned, in his time,
a tiny brewery in Northampton; an edible oils concern in
Coventry; a drop-forge and iron castings plant in Solihull; a
sanitary towel factory outside Cheltenham and, finally, a small
hotel chain in Dorset.

The last had caused him most astonishment and given him
most pleasure. For it was blindingly obvious to Max, who stayed
once in one of the group's lodging houses in Poole, that anywhere
else it would be the guests who should be paid and paid hand-
somely by the owners for enduring a night in these grimy, sad
reservoirs of the lost and the ill-fated. That the customers did
not demand to be paid, that they seemed almost pathetically
grateful for a roof over their heads and that the owners failed
to make money from this stunning display of resignation,
decided him. When Max began in the hotel business guests
calling for room-service were greeted, when they were greeted
at all, by an incredulous, guttural 'yer-wah?' By the time he
was ready to sell they were answered instantly with: 'Hello, I'm
Sharon, your in-service manager. How may I help you?' He
calculated further that a small investment in a new kitchen, and
modest refurbishment, a waiter who shaved, and clean sheets
at least every other day would seem like a revolution to the
travelling public. Indeed it did. *The Hotelier* announced – 'Poole
Leads the Way!' and *The Caterer* went even further with – 'Dorset
Looks to Twenty-first Century!'

He got out as quietly as he bought in. And all that time no
one asked him a single question. Silent, successful, invisible and
small. Max had no interest in growth. He simply liked to see
things work. And everybody left him entirely alone. God, the
freedom of it! It made you proud to be an Englishman.

When his son-in-law to be (oh, dreadful prospect!), one Albert
Turberville who, for reasons he could make neither head nor

tail of, Lizzie decided to marry, plucked up the courage to ask him: 'What is it exactly that you do, Mr Montfalcon?'

Max replied simply: 'Did.'

'Very well. Did.'

'A bit of this and a bit of that.'

Albert, despite years of exposure to the noisy theatre of the House of Commons, remembered enough of his former life to know he was being told to mind his own fucking business. Albert who was dogged – you had to give him that – tried another tack. He tried his wife. 'Where does he come from, your dad?'

Elizabeth paused and thought this over. She had inherited from her mother her blue eyes and golden hair, a soft peachy texture. Of Angela she remembered very little. There had been always and only her father in her life. A school, she recalled dimly, years ago, somewhere in Oxfordshire. And then a large house in Henley, with river frontage. There she had grown up. After that the mansion in Hampstead Garden Suburb with the garden far too large and the two Portuguese maids. Home had been where her father was. But he was a secretive, intense, demanding, dreamy man and perhaps in her heart she longed for something else. Perhaps that was why she had fallen for Albert. So pink and round. Uncomplicated, untroubled, settled. Bright, certainly. The youngest MP in the House, just twenty-eight and one for whom the newspapers forecast 'a brilliant career', as if brilliance were something you predicted like the weather, like an unusually hot June, or a fine December.

'Daddy comes from Harwich.'

Albert threw back his head and roared. 'Go on!'

'What's so amusing?'

'Harwich!'

'You remind me of a seaside comic. Say "Wigan!" and everyone falls about. I don't see what you find so terribly funny about Harwich.'

'I'm not expert on the dialects up that way. But Norwich, Ipswich or Harwich. I hardly think they speak like that.'

'Like what?'

But Albert's only reply was to growl with laughter and hold his belly.

'Are you implying that my father isn't British?'

'Lizzie, for God's sake – are you seriously saying you never noticed?'

'He's as British as you are, Albert Turberville.'

'My family came over with the Conqueror.'

'Well, there you are then. Mongrel French. Daddy went to prep school in London. He was up at Oxford in the thirties. If you're going to make cheap, silly, xenophobic jokes about people who to your tin ear sound strange, then you can go to hell. I suppose you also do a nice line in Pakistanis?'

'Now hang on!' It was Albert's turn to be outraged. He prided himself on his race relations record. He stuck to his guns. Not for nothing was he known in one of his early parliaments, thank God now forgotten, as 'Dogbert – Hound of the Turbervilles'.

On his wedding day he threw Max a curved ball, collaring the old chap in the corner. They eyed each other carefully across their flutes of champagne. All through the ghastly service Max had kept telling himself that this was a bad dream. That Elizabeth would change her mind. That he would wake up and the large pink man by the side of his beautiful girl would have vanished.

'I believe you had a stint as a teacher, once?' Albert gave one of his warm approving smiles, as if teaching, like charity work or famine relief, was a worthy thing. 'Is that right, sir?' He threw in the 'sir' for added spin, more mileage.

'For my sins,' said Max. 'I taught English.'

'English.' Albert nodded owlishly.

'You seem surprised. I had a particular interest in usage. I was, I am, a student of the great Fowler. Have you read him?'

'I don't believe I have.'

'I recommend him.'

'I'll look him out.'

'Do. I'm sure they must have a copy of his *Modern English Usage* in the House of Commons Library. Though judging from the parliamentary reports I read in the newspapers, he's not much consulted by MPs.'

'I suppose – sir – you came out of teaching because the game just wasn't worth the candle. Not enough reward?'

'Not at all,' said his new father-in-law. 'Too many bloody questions.'

What a collection turned up for the nuptials! The Hon. Mrs Angus Watts, little and liverish, who carried everywhere a furious Peke beneath her arm in the manner of a bagpipe. She whistled when she spoke and was said to be a distant cousin of the Queen; several of Albert's parliamentary colleagues including Jimbo Mandeville in old Carthusian tie which clashed alarmingly with his ruddy complexion, one of those florid, malleable English faces which appears to have been delivered from a jelly mould; and that Labour woman, Erica Snafus, in a little black Chanel number and large white teeth. Several friends of the bride and groom, wearing uniform moustaches, broad lapels – girls in very short skirts or very wide trousers, flowery ties. Like *Gastarbeiter*, thought Max, who have fallen to earth from some strange planet and have no idea how silly they look to the natives.

And then it was Albert's turn to register amazement. For who was Max Montfalcon greeting so warmly? Talking to so animatedly? None other than old Ralphie Treehouse. A legendary figure in political circles. Amazing to think he was still alive! Treehouse – the Foreign Office star. Minister in three administrations. Lecher, classicist, homosexual. And what were he and Max talking about so intently? Recalling young von F – a mutual friend of their student days. And after that? They'd talked about Max's success. And Albert, drawing near, heard Treehouse speak warmly of 'abroad'. Max replied that abroad had never been his cup of tea. But he'd sometimes thought of retirement somewhere in Wales. Treehouse shook his massive head and pursed his full lips. Wales, he smiled, might not be far enough. When people started digging, Wales simply would not do. Abroad would be best. Best not to leave it too late. Max looked puzzled: 'You know, I've never got on with abroad. Can't think why.'

And Treehouse, eyeing Erica Snafus talking easily of

'contradictory forecasts for the final quarter', said mildly: 'Can't think why you can't think why.'

But Max stayed put. Retired in the mid-seventies to his big house and sat out the eighties, experiencing a growing sense of something lost, and strangely homesick. From Oxfordshire and Hampstead Garden Suburb, from Harwich, from all the places where once he had started a new life, Max turned away feeling, increasingly, that it was time to go home. He had become a stiff old man who had trouble walking. A long way from the pirate entrepreneur, the 'corporate raider' as that type of predator was called nowadays with quite a radioactive glow of admiration. A longer way from the teacher of English he had once been. And how much further still from careers he felt sure he had pursued successfully long ago, but lost now in the mists of his mind.

So he had called young Jeb Touser of Touser and Burlap, and asked about the feasibility of his plan. Could he cede his assets? 'I want to hand them over to my daughter. Can I do it? Should I do it?'

Jeb Touser favoured camouflage colours, green, tan and black. Hair grew out of his ears like the fine filaments of light-bulbs. 'You could do it, Mr Montfalcon. Whether you *should* do it is a moral decision only you can take.'

Max called a Monday morning meeting at Elizabeth's house. Albert turned up looking grumpy. Innocenta was there in her purple robes announcing her to be a daughter of the Bhagwan Shree Rajneesh. At least they were supposed to be purple but had turned a faintly pinky-brown because the drycleaners dyeing department, bloody expensive as it was, never did a good job and times were tight in the Clerkenwell squat where she had been living with a boy named Nigel whose family owned several thousand acres of good land in Lincolnshire. Nigel's people were respectable but impoverished. Nigel was also a cult member, but an increasingly fainthearted one. The arrest of the Bhagwan in the mid eighties had dented his faith. Lately, in the manner of the young, he had turned from rebelliousness to extreme orthodoxy overnight. He wished to marry Innocenta and carry

26

her back to live in Lincolnshire. Innocenta had opened her leafy-green eyes with their coppery tints.

'Live on *what?*' she had demanded.

As if to underline her rejection she wore that morning a pair of Doc Martens, the heavily scuffed toes of which showed beneath her robes giving her a clumpy, rather dangerous look, like a hobbled hawk. Albert sat on the chesterfield in a dark blue suit and red tie; his black brogues were highly polished. They seemed to share the same brittle impatience of their owner to be up and away. He was very morose. He couldn't imagine why Elizabeth's father insisted on the meeting. It could only mean trouble, of that he was sure. He wore a blue striped shirt with white collar and cuffs. He was supposed to be attending a meeting at Central Office where he chaired a little committee studying unemployment in the marginal constituencies and its impact on the Government's chances at the next election. Elizabeth, trim and cool, sat on the piano stool. In blue jeans and a silk top of pillar box red with a high collar, she thought her father looked very well for his eighty plus years. A little too thin perhaps, but then he had never carried much weight on that lanky frame. With his silver hair he was still a handsome man. There was something almost regal about Max Montfalcon. She noticed the way he hooked his thumb into the waistband of his trousers and tapped, absentmindedly, on his fly, but she put this down to one of those vague little tics the old acquire. She did not know that he did it because he had begun to be troubled by a slight incontinence – 'Intermittent incontinence' his GP called it, 'or leaky tap syndrome'. Max tapped because that way he could be sure the pad of tissues he'd wedged in between the two pairs of underpants he was wearing was securely in place.

Max kissed his granddaughter and she twined her fingers in his.

'Grandpa, this is Nigel. A friend. Do you mind if he sits in? He wants to marry me and carry me off to Lincolnshire where his poor sisters live and his mother and their horses. What will we all eat? Grass?'

'He may be in for a pleasant surprise,' said Max.

He introduced Jeb Touser. Willow-green silk blouson and

black woollen trousers. 'Accountant.' Albert grimly noted the Raybans and Italian loafers. More like one of the bodyguards seen accompanying fiery American preachers. He carried a brief-case, flipcharts and a selection of day-glo markers in pink, green and yellow.

During his presentation of the figures Max sat beside Elizabeth and held her hand. His son-in-law grew no more attractive over the years. Looking at Albert in his House of Commons back-bench slouch, head back on the sofa, the skin beneath his chin had softened and slackened and swayed when he moved his head. He went in several directions did Albert. How could a man so corporeally indecisive seem so sure of just about everything? Uncertain as to the shape it wished to assume, his body had given up.

Touser explained the proposition lucidly and economically. Max had decided to divest himself of his assets. He showed them the figures. 'My estimate is a total sum of around one and a half to three-quarters of a million.'

Max interrupted. 'I'm tired of the big house, you see. I'm tired of living alone.'

'So he has a proposition to put to you, his family. He will make over this sum to you. Everything but for a small amount which will be paid to him each month.'

'Tobacco money,' said Max. 'That damn place in Hampstead is just too big, sweetheart.' He squeezed Elizabeth's hand and smiled into his daughter's blue eyes. 'And this place you've got here, well – it's very pretty and so on. But really it's rather uncomfortable. So why don't we, as a family, pool our resources?'

'Pool – Daddy?' Elizabeth said. 'I don't understand.'

'He's suggesting moving in with us, if I'm not very much mistaken,' Albert was sitting upright now. 'Is that a million and a half clear?'

'Net of tax,' Touser confirmed. 'And then there are the pro-ceeds of the houses. Say another million. These numbers are on the conservative side.'

'Houses?'

'You can hardly go on in this house when I live with you,' Max explained. 'Take the money and find somewhere big and pretty. Perhaps up Highgate way. I get a wing, or a section of the house. Self-contained, separate entrance, a kitchen. Everything. We live together but not on top of one another.' He turned to Elizabeth. 'I want to come home, Lizzie. I want to be together with you again.'

'Tax obligations, capital gains, et cetera. All high on the lump sum,' Touser intoned. 'Less though than overall death-duties. Some further tax leeway is visible by virtue of the two-way split.'

'Split? What's this?' Albert demanded.

'I'll only come if you want me to come,' Max stroked Elizabeth's hair. 'That's the heart of the bargain. Common consent. We must all want it.'

'How can we tell if you want it, Grandpa?' Innocenta's question rang with disbelief.

She began rummaging in her bag as if she might find in it a warning flag or klaxon with which she could sound the alarm. Max heard her fear but he put it down to her sense of her own insecurity. Away from home, between the devil and the deep blue sea. Even her clothes had a refugee look about them. Threads and patches. He would have to speak to her sometime about the dangers of refugee status. He felt strangely moved. He had found a way of saving Innocenta.

He knew how to do this. Some old talent revived. His to give, theirs to receive. Providing they met the requirements for selection. Just like old times.

Max surveyed the room. Lizzie, trembling, trying to smile through her tears. Albert, his black shoes buffed to a military gleam. So proud of his full head of thick auburn hair. 'Rapunzel', the opposition benches like to shout at Albert when he tossed his head. Albert's was a body that missed a uniform. Max remembered bodies like his, the nip and tuck of waist and breast, the curiously girlish posture of the close-fitting tunic, the shining footwear. There was something Nordic about Albert. No, not Nordic exactly – Teutonic. How very German the English could be – even when they claimed to be Norman French by origin. Blood will out.

'I propose to ask each of you whether you really want me back with you.'

Innocenta took from her Peruvian indigo shoulder bag a red

triangular Tattva card and studied it. She drew in the glowing astral doorway until it hung invitingly before her eyes. Large enough to walk through. Red for fire. Red for danger. 'Poor Grandpa. They'll eat you alive.'

'Ask away then,' Albert spoke briskly. The committee man.

'We're getting a teeny bit ahead of ourselves,' said Touser. 'Let me explain the division. Mr Montfalcon proposes that the sum involved be divided equally between his daughter, Mrs Elizabeth Turberville, and his granddaughter, Innocenta. The arrangement being dependent on the condition.'

'Condition?' Albert's voice rose in alarm. Albert crossed his ankles. His shiny shoes clashed softly like sharpened knives.

'Happy with the division, Mr Montfalcon?' Touser asked.

Max nodded without glancing at Albert.

Nigel, the boy from Lincolnshire, turned on Innocenta in her ruddy robes and her big black boots a look of rapt devotion. She replaced her Tattva card in her bag. She wiped her eyes. He couldn't for the life of him see what she was so upset about. Her arms were folded, eyes fixed on a large painting of a North Sea oil platform which hung on the wall opposite, a present to her father by a grateful consortium of Norwegian speculators. Her chin was tilted, her eyes frozen. Nigel had never seen a millionairess before, certainly not a millionairess who only hours earlier could not afford the tube fare from Clerkenwell to Belsize Park. That morning he would have married her stony-broke. But he had to confess to himself, not without a twinge of distaste at his swift commercial corruption, that for a million and a half he would have walked across burning coals for her. Innocenta must have read his thoughts. Interrupting her fierce study of the oil platform, lashed by mountainous seas as green as her eyes, she leapt to her feet.

'Now just hold it right there. You're crazy, Grandpa! You've got your house and your freedom. You're loaded with money and all of a sudden you want to hurl it all in and go home? Home? Where is that? A granny flat in a damp basement and your treat of the week a trip to the post office to collect your pension?' She crossed to where Max sat, stiff and fierce, fell to her knees, reached up and took his face in her hands. 'You're a free spirit, Grandpa. You're an eagle, a wild thing. You're my best person in the world. Because you come and go as you like. Because you can't go home. There isn't a home to go to.'

'What's the condition?' Albert asked.

Max took Innocenta's hands and gently pulled them away from his face. 'That you want me. We're all going into this with open eyes. That's the bargain, the grand bargain. You get my asset and I get a home.'

'Assets I think,' Albert said firmly.

'Asset, asset, asset! Singular always. See Fowler,' the old man muttered.

' "Which of you shall we say doth love us most?" ' Innocenta addressed her question to the piano.

Max ignored her. 'Sooner rather than later Max Montfalcon will die. You and I could be said to have grown up together, Lizzie. Why shouldn't we spend a little time, last days, together again? But you must want it too. Want me. Well, Lizzie, what do you say?'

Jeb Touser, commando accountant, pointed his day-glo marker at Innocenta. 'Hey! Love us most? That's *King Lear*.'

'I'm afraid so,' said Innocenta.

On the piano stool Elizabeth wept. She made no effort to wipe away her tears. She shook her head helplessly and her blonde hair slowly lifted and fell. Max loved to see it doing that. Eventually she quietened and sighed deeply. 'Yes, Daddy. Yes. We can do it. If that's what you want. We'll find a place where we can live together.'

'Can I suggest a formal agreement? I'm sorry it sounds calculating.' Albert did not look sorry. 'But these things are best in writing. So we'll know where we stand.'

'The papers are ready. Once you find a common abode and move in the transfer of assets is triggered,' Jeb Touser said.

Max looked at his son-in-law with palpable distaste. 'You've got the order all wrong, Albert. First – where do we stand?'

'Well.' Albert's word weighed the matter. The judicious chairman of a hundred small committees choosing his words carefully. 'I certainly don't see why it shouldn't be made to work. If we all put our backs into it. Yes. Well, I mean – why not?'

Max leaned forward and kissed Innocenta in the middle of her forehead. 'And now you, my darling?'

Innocenta simply shook her head.

'We won't get far on silence,' Max urged. 'Try again.'

Innocenta got slowly to her feet. She appeared deep in thought. Then she crossed to Nigel.

'OK.'

'OK what?'

'I'll do it.'

'Sorry. You've lost me. Do what?'

'Lincolnshire. The rich acres, and all that. Your mother and sisters. The horses. In a word – yes.'

'Now wait a minute.' Nigel put his hands on her shoulders and looked in mute appeal over her bowed head at Max.

'I see.' Innocenta's lips were thin and icy.

'All I'm saying is – think it over. It's up to you to choose.'

'I am thinking. What I'm thinking is that you're a real drag, Nige. Out for everything. You were happy to take me as I was when we came here today. Now the sight of a million pound notes fertilising the fields of Lincolnshire has blown your mind. Choose? To see my grandfather rolled over a cliff? You're a colossal idiot, Grandpa. Don't you see what you're doing? Delivering yourself into the hands of people who don't love you or understand you. They don't' – and here she shot a significant glance at her father – 'even like you.'

'I don't think, Innocenta, you're in any position to give lessons in love,' Albert was almost enjoying himself now, 'standing there in your boots and old tablecloth looking like some washerwoman on the loose, and pontificating.'

Innocenta glanced at her feet. 'Boots? What boots? You're removed from the world, Daddy. You walked out on it. Your soul has gone critical. You're in melt down.'

'Choose or lose,' Max snapped at his granddaughter.

It was Jeb Touser who unexpectedly intervened now. 'Your granddaughter is at least consistent: you've got to give her that.'

'I don't have to give her anything.' Max was on his feet now, pointing a shaking finger at Touser. 'And I'd remind you that I'm paying you – which I don't have to do either.'

'Mr Montfalcon, cut her out of the bargain and you're still

holding half your assets. How will you resolve that?'

'Simple,' snapped Max. 'I'll give them to Lizzie. Yes. She gets the lot.'

Touser replaced the tops of his day-glo markers with stubborn, precise clicks of defiance. 'There is a slight logical contradiction here. One minute your granddaughter's the apple of your eye. Dammit, she loves you, sir! And the next she's dead in the water.'

'Enough! Another word and you can collect your cards!'

'Collect my – Jesus wept!' Touser yelled. 'My cards! It's all too much.' Young Jeb Touser who in all his few years as an investment adviser had never rejected a brief or contradicted a client and was said by all to be destined for the very pinnacle of the LLL business – little old people, low life expectancy, lovely large estates – turned smartly on his heel and said goodbye to, oh, twenty thousand's worth? if a penny. All because, as he told his friends later at the Drum and Monkey, Threadneedle Street, a girl had the greatest green eyes he'd ever seen, 'like frozen Irelands, I tell you'; and a girl to boot who looked like a refugee from the Hare Krishna place off Oxford Street, only not so pale.

And Innocenta? Well, she was cut out of the bargain. Her mother said it didn't matter as everything she owned would be Innocenta's one day. Her father said it was a sharp lesson to her.

And Nigel? Well, he got the thousands of acres in Lincolnshire. And his mother and his sisters got a reformed son. Gone was all that Eastern mish-mash.

Max got his nice big wing in a great house in Highgate.

Elizabeth got her father back again.

And Albert actually believed, for about a month, that things were looking up.

Indeed, once settled into Greyacres, the Georgian residence on Highgate Hill, Albert went so far as to warm to what he called 'a good deal all round' over a celebratory glass of Cognac in Max's splendid new quarters: bedroom, kitchen, sitting-room, two bathrooms, one *en suite*; the wallpaper was silver chevrons against a dark blue ground; the furniture steel and glass and somewhat severe for Albert's taste, but elegant, certainly, in a faintly aggressive way.

'A bargain,' his father-in-law corrected him. 'The word "deal" is slang and should be avoided even when used in the sense of a piece of bargaining or give-and-take.'

'Fowler, I suppose?' Albert hoped he hit the right note of polite enquiry.

'For heaven's sake, Daddy,' said Elizabeth, 'Mr Fowler doesn't rule the world. People today make "deals" all the time. They don't "strike bargains".'

'Perhaps not in your world, dearest Lizzie, but they still do in my book.'

'Which edition do you use?' Albert asked.

'Thirty-seven. Revised, of course.'

'Of course.' And Albert added silently, into his brandy, 'Sweet bloody hell!' For it occurred to him then – though he tried to push it out of his mind – that he was sharing a house with an elderly foreign man who claimed to come from Harwich and lived his life according to Fowler's *Modern English Usage*, 1937 edition (revised).

CHAPTER THREE

A Spider in the Bath

When Elizabeth Turberville moved to Greyacres, she developed a passion for entertaining. She had never before thought of herself as a hostess. Now, for the first time in her life, she made use of her connections, and Albert's. She used her house and enjoyed her flair for assembling two dozen of the best and brightest under her roof.

In past years Lizzie Turberville had been to a few social soirées in the country and studied her hostesses with appalled admiration. They seemed all to own houses called Somewhere Easten or Easten Something and to enliven their living-room walls with Chinese papers of startling vacuity which their price did nothing to alleviate. The pale English sunlight fell on the yellow walls of the Forbidden City and one felt distinctly queasy. One watched the minglings of dainty jockeys and splay-footed three-day-eventing persons, ex-cabinet ministers with alarming amounts of hair and surprisingly tall, angular wives who said things like: 'For God's sake, Roddy – turn it up!' One was very surprised, not to say slightly bemused, to find the same sorts of guests turning up at Greyacres in absolute bevies in the months after Elizabeth and Albert made their home on the crest of Highgate Hill.

Elizabeth became suddenly so fashionable she turned up in the gossip columns, 'Politics and Prawn Crackers in Darkest Highgate' the papers said. She was quoted as saying: 'Not at all! I feed a few guests, from time to time. But I don't entertain them at all. Yes, we have some people from both sides of the

House. But they're just friends really, rather than politicians.'

Elizabeth's drink went round and round and she kept the lights low. Both skills appreciated by her guests. When, on one occasion, Max had come upstairs and gaped at the company, like a small boy in his dressing gown allowed to stay up for just a few extra minutes before being hustled away to bed, he thought Lizzie's friends, even the very young ones, all looked like frequently refurbished antiques. The moment the light hit their faces they showed all the tight effects of expensive glues and painful varnishes holding their heads together.

There were dons down from Cambridge with names like Moggridge who understood all about supply side economics, with spouses who said out loud: 'Fuck John Maynard Keynes, say I!' There were portrait painters who brought their white cats. There were young women called Lady Debbie who brought their literary agents. There were actresses who divided their time between London and LA, and arrived on the arms of well-known Pakistani cricketers, and left almost immediately for clubs called Poison Ivy, and Wankers.

Elizabeth did not have a Thai cook. She did not employ an Italian couple. She did not use caterers. She did as she liked and she did it herself. She had been known to order an entire dinner for thirty from the Green Dragon in Highgate Village and serve it straight from the brown bags with Chinese rice wine and prawn crackers. No less a figure than Lord Figgs, chief whip on the opposition benches, described it as 'bloody good nosh!'

Even Albert liked it. That was saying something. Albert said: 'Bravo, old girl!' and retreated to a corner to talk about attitudes towards the Argentine in the Ministry of Defence with the Duchess of Rutland. Lizzie tried to encourage her father to join in. She said: 'Daddy, Lord Gribble will stop by tonight. The mad federalist who wants to see us tied to Europe with a ball and chain. He's just back from seeing the German Chancellor, and you know how you hate the German Chancellor. Why not pop up and talk to Jimmy Gribble?'

But after his one visit to the world above when he had thought Lizzie's friends, even the young ones, showed their cracks and seams, and proved how imperfectly stitched together the rich were, how disappointingly plain so much of the time, Max refused: 'No, no, no, Lizzie! I won't impose on your life. You don't want an old man slowing proceedings. Quite right, too. If I were you I wouldn't invite someone like me to my parties. I'm happy down here in my quarters.'

It all began in the bathroom, in a simple, innocent, seemingly friendly way, as befits bathrooms: places of chastened porcelain, lovely enamel, steam, scent, suds, and, only occasionally, a spider crawling nimbly up the plughole and running frantically along the back of towering white cliffs, impossible to scale. The spider's Eiger. Ceramic alps of doom. Death in Switzerland. Poor creature smelling mortality in a place so clean.

In his snowy bathroom Max looked at the steep sides of his shining bath and mentioned after a month in the new house, in a gentle, casual way, that he might, just *might*, need a little help getting in and out of the bath.

'Oh, Daddy, you should have said!' Elizabeth was embarrassed. 'What have you been doing? How have you been managing if you can't use the bath?'

'The basin,' replied Max shortly. 'Why? Do I smell?'

'Of *course* not, silly. It's just that – oh – I wish you'd told me.'

Elizabeth bought him, moulded in white plastic, a cunning little platform which lowered and raised the invalid in the ivory bath, a machine called a bathability stool. Max looked at the contraption with deep suspicion. 'My God,' he barked, 'the bathyscope for the older man. What do you suppose Jacques Cousteau would say to that?'

'You never know till you try. Why don't I run you a nice big bath? And you hop in and try it out?'

Five minutes later an outraged bellow summoned her back to the bathroom. There he sat, balanced on top of the bathability stool, looking rather like an Indian fakir, wearing an ancient sky-blue pair of bathing trunks, suspended above water and steam, his knees hugged to his chest, his face set in an expression of wounded anger. 'Come in, come in! I'm decent! Damn thing won't work.'

'Just relax,' Elizabeth said soothingly. And as she spoke her father, still looking annoyed, began sinking smoothly beneath the water, giving the impression of some rather strange and eccentric burial at sea.

It never got any better in the following days. Either he wouldn't go down. Or when he went down, he could not arise. Instead, when the water grew cold he would begin shouting, 'I'm freezing to bloody death!' And back she'd go to the bathroom to find that now he had dispensed with the formality of the costume and seemed not to care about exposing his lank, stringy, bony body to her gaze. 'Just lift yourself slightly, Daddy, and the chair will do the rest.'

'Don't you think I've tried? Damn thing's stuck. Shoddy workmanship, if you ask me. No wonder the Japanese are beating us hands down. Can you imagine what it's like, sitting on some kind of portable camp stool that won't go down when it's supposed to go down and never comes up when you ask it to? What do you think would happen if the neighbours saw me now? What do you think would happen if I saw myself now? What do you think would happen if you look ahead into the years that will follow for you too, my darling, and see yourself sitting on a bathability stool in a steamy bathroom waiting to sink either into the water or into oblivion – whichever comes first?'

Elizabeth would reach into the tepid water and watch as with folded arms and water streaming from the wispy grey hairs on his chest, like the raising of some improbable shipwreck, her father would slowly rise to the surface, looking into her eyes and saying mournfully: 'I'm sorry if you find me a burden, Lizzie.'

It got worse. With every move she made to help and soothe and compensate for his failing strength, it simply got worse.

One morning he told her he was having trouble using the toilet. 'It's too low. Built for pygmies. I'm well over six foot four – if shrinking.' She bought a raised toilet seat so that he wouldn't have to bend. He discovered all the power points had been fitted in the skirting boards. 'I should have been born a dwarf,' said Max. She fitted power point raisers on all the electrical sockets so he wouldn't have to stoop. Then his back gave trouble and she found him still in bed at noon: 'I can't get up, Lizzie. I'm stuck.' She hung a rope ladder over his bed so he could pull himself upright when his back hurt. Max smiled grimly. 'The geriatric trapeze. Don't ever get old, Lizzie. The old are like budgies, always falling off their perches. Or hauling themselves aboard with trembling fingers.'

'Don't give in to it, Daddy,' she encouraged in the early days. 'Don't accept it.'

'My dear, I'm afraid it's already accepted me.'

Soon she was waging a war. She thought of 'ancillary machines for the aid of the elderly' – bought from the Age Concern catalogue – as tanks, pontoon bridges, artillery designed to fight the enemy of failing flesh. She even thought the machines might help her to win, until she encountered the enemy within. His incontinence grew worse. She'd hear him get out of bed cursing, and then stomping towards the lavatory. Always about the same time, four or four-thirty in the morning, there came the first call. By the time she reached the bedroom he had vanished and she'd find the bed awash. She took to setting an early morning alarm in the hopes of getting to Max before the deluge. 'OK, Daddy,' she murmured, slipping into the bedroom and touching his shoulder in the darkness, 'off we go!' When she did get to him before he woke, she hated herself for waking him. Grumbling, Max allowed himself to be hoisted from the bed. On those occasions when he had already wet the bed he went more easily at her bidding. When she felt the sheet was dry then she knew she could expect renewed complaint. It came once Max was seated on the toilet and he went supersonic, giving out a high-pitched whistle which faded only very slowly as the water came. In desperation and thinking that the situation might improve had he not to leave the bedroom at all and make his way to the lavatory, she bought him a wicker commode with elegant silver edging and a removable seat in flame retardant foam. It didn't help, the cry of the jet engine would ring out for what seemed like minutes. Albert groaned and pulled the pillow over his head. Then it would die to a murmur and Max, seated on his commode, Max the incontinent Boeing, pissed noisily into the plastic pot.

Sometimes he sat in the darkness and talked, in tongues she did not understand, about events which meant nothing to her while she scrubbed the mattress dry, pulled on a fresh sheet and plumped his pillows.

'*Pańskie jutro, a żydowskie zaraz.*'

'What's that, Daddy?'

The voice from the darkness sounded faint and far away. 'A Polish saying. It was collected near Cracow. There was a man who went round collecting such sayings from the Poles. The peasants had a very rich supply of them.'

'What does it mean?'

'The nobles tomorrow – the Jews immediately.'

'But why would they say such things?'

'Because they liked to. They were anti-Semites you see. They had lots of sayings like that, you could make entire collections of them. I seem to remember somebody did. In Cracow.'

'What were you doing in Cracow?'

'I've never been to Cracow.'

'You've wet your bed again, Daddy.'

'It has to be said Poland was a mess. A racial haystack. Full of ethnic splinters.'

'Needles.'

'What?'

'Come back to bed, Daddy. I think you mean needles, not splinters. It's needles that you get in haystacks.'

There were variations in both conversation and behaviour. For Max, only intermittently incontinent from the bladder, felt the need from time to time to ring the changes. Sometimes he'd jump from his bed or chair and head for the commode, moving at a swift pace, most especially considering that he'd already taken the precaution of dropping his trousers and so had to hobble, his elderly shanks scissoring inside the hoop of his trouser waistband which lay in an untidy circle about his ankles. It was an adept, an extraordinarily swift, shuffle. The trick seemed to be to get successfully to the commode and then urinate triumphantly, allowing his daughter – oh, so briefly – to share his liquid achievement. Which she did, she did!

It was about this time that Max, not otherwise discontented with his lot, began to grow rather concerned about Prince Philip.

Max did not ask the usual questions about the Royal Consort. Who were his parents? Where did he grow up? What was Earl Mountbatten to him in his younger life? These were the delectable mysteries that interested the readers of *Fealty* to which for years Max had been a devoted subscriber. But these were not things Max gave his attention to. He had come across a photograph of Prince Philip in a boat on a river. The photograph showed the Royal Consort looking as mad as a hornet despite his comfortable old blue jumper. He noted the furious downward turn of the ducal mouth, the fly rod held delicately as a conductor's baton in the right hand, the gull or curlew (or albatross? No, surely *not* an albatross) visible on the breast of the old blue jumper.

And to think, as it turned out, that at the end of the day it was not the Duke's car on the river bank after all. The offending vehicle illegally parked belonged to the very photographer whose picture of the Duke Max was studying in *Fealty*. No wonder Prince Philip looked hopping mad! Max hoped the overzealous policeman had been ticked off by his superiors – another of the Sergeant Pearce brigade. Forever arresting the wrong man.

Studying the lean irascible face of the royal angler who seemed to be on the point of saying something characteristically terse such as, 'Now look here, tosh!' or 'Get your finger out!', Max strove to detect the slightest sign of Greekness. Nary a one! Any Hellenistic tincture that might have once complicated the look or character of the consort, was long gone. Philip, Duke of Edinburgh, was as British as Max Montfalcon.

Max has written to the Prince to assure him on that point many times. The Prince's private secretary has replied thanking him for his concern and assuring him that His Royal Highness was proud of his British heritage.

As the weeks of Max's sojourn with his daughter passed into months in the big house on Highgate Hill which his money had bought her in exchange for – what was it now? – 'a room and board and a little attention now and then . . . ?' – Elizabeth snatched at any alleviation of her unending labour. Albert had left her to her own devices, he spent more and more time at the

House of Commons, returning now and then to say things like: 'Bloody hell! This place smells to high heaven. I've heard of dirty old men but *this* is ridiculous!'

The wrinkles Max devised were both cunning and cruel since they seemed to promise a little advance on what looked like an irresistible decline into dementia, only to disappoint so profoundly that sometimes Elizabeth thought she was going mad. He might, for instance, sometimes reach the commode without incident. Or, again, he might have left a pool of urine beside the bed before making his dash. He might, in fact he did on several occasions, leave a trail of small, round, shining stools like rabbit droppings behind him as he made his run. And as his daughter wearily cleared away the mess and fetched a flannel and vigorously soaped the rubbery ring of his anus (for if Max was to be believed he could now no longer clean himself) her father would refuse to see or admit any of the faecal damage he had committed. And since she could not allow him to return to bed in a soiled condition it no longer mattered whether she believed or disbelieved him, she had in a sense become his puppet and plaything. It felt as though he was controlling her. And Elizabeth began to close her eyes and grind her teeth and try not to hate him. He was her father. She did not hate her father.

Albert no longer woke when she arose at four-thirty on her pre-emptive toilet strike. He slept through it just as he had when she had got up years before to change Innocenta when she was a baby. And it was, indeed, rather like having another baby in the house except that Max was no infant – he was fractious, cunning, remorseless, the horribly leaky adult who had once been, for reasons now she simply could not quite remember, her tall, handsome, dashing, loving, adorable daddy. And so the feeling that grew inside her was one of angry, bitter patience.

Elizabeth did, for a while, stubbornly persist in giving very good parties in much the same way as Mr Kipling was said in the advertisement to bake very good cakes. But her parties decreased in number and dwindled to one a month. The strain was beginning to tell.

'I came very close to strangling my father this afternoon,' she told her friend Nancy Drummond during one of her celebrated take-away suppers as they delicately picked at slivers of beef in hot black bean sauce. 'It's like having a child in the house. A rather nasty, wicked child who is trying to drive me mad. Making me run down to him three times a night. Wetting his bed. Messing, messing . . . '

'We had something of the sort with Mummy,' said Nancy. 'In the end we had to put her in a place. Of course, we hated doing it. Promised Mummy, too. But what option do you have? If you like I'll give you the name and address. It's just around the corner. Take a look at it. You might do him some good, by taking him on a visit. Let it be known that this is what you're considering.'

'Threaten him? Behave – or this is where you'll end up?'

'Just warn him,' said Nancy carefully. 'You sometimes have to do that with them.'

'He has taken to speaking Polish,' Elizabeth said.

'Oh, Lizzie, you poor darling. I know just how you feel. Mummy claimed to be speaking Croatian towards the end. When she could still concentrate. She was already in this place I mentioned. Luckily they were very good about it. If she wants to speak Croatian then let her, said the little man who runs the place. They sent her off on Sundays to a church service in Croatian though Mummy never understood a single word.'

'I think Albert's having an affair.'

'Surely not?' Privately Nancy could not imagine that Albert would find the energy for an affair.

'I couldn't care less. I'm getting rather sick of Albert, too,' said Elizabeth. 'I wish he'd run off with her, whoever she is. He's no damn good around the house.'

'Shall I have a chat to him?'

'About his affair?'

'About your father.'

'Fine. If you don't mind conversations in words of one syllable. Don't be surprised if he pulls a pillow over his head. That's what he does when Daddy gets me up a third time in the night to change his sheets.'

*

43

To begin with Nancy got little reaction from Albert. 'You mean she might biff the old boy?'

'I think she might skewer you first,' said Nancy pleasantly. 'You're not her favourite man.'

Albert thought about this. He thought about the way in which Max's money reached Elizabeth. He took out his diary.

'What's the name of this place where your mother had such a happy time speaking Croatian?'

She soon came to realise that he knew just how to goad her. He seemed to have made it his special study – the steady pursuit of a dozen small but lethal ways in which to provoke and wound. To wind her up. To get her going. And so – at first to protect herself, or to save herself and then increasingly to assert herself and then even more so because she simply couldn't bear him any longer – she began in similar small ways to discipline him.

She left him in his flooded bed all night. He lay there until the sharp ammoniac smell of it had reached into every corner of the house and Albert said: 'For God's sake, the place reeks like a latrine! Do something, Lizzie!'

Max, in his sodden bed, pronounced bitterly on her ingratitude. 'That's what I get for giving you everything. I only hope you never go through what I'm going through. I hope you're never old and ill and at the mercy of a stone-hearted child.'

Her response was to reach over, seize the mattress and tip him on to the floor where he landed with a series of dry clicks and without another sound – it was like the fall of a sack of firewood.

He had bruises for days. They ran from his knees to his shoulders. His cheek was torn and a small, black and rather angry scab formed there which Max seemed to regard as a small badge of his victory, for he was forever tapping it and touching it. He was in fact quite cheerful for some days after the fall and talked again about Poland. 'You see we proved there had been Germanic settlements in the Vistula region since primeval times. Settlements, pottery and grave-goods proved it beyond doubt. Germans had been the predominant ethnic group in the east. The samples we analysed had the typical long-heads of the Nordic West European group and all we wanted, and I tell you

44

this truly, Lizzie, all I ever wanted was to establish the original facts in Poland.'

But Lizzie wasn't listening. She went to sleep and dreamt of Max on his bathability chair, poised above a very deep bath. She saw the chair descending and, with Max still talking, slipping beneath the water and she watched the bubbles rising, imagining each word he spoke floating to the surface in the way that they drew speech bubbles in comics until one by one the bubbles slowed and stopped altogether. Then when he came to sit up to meals Max developed a startling list to the left, or mostly to the left. He continued to insist on feeding himself though his eye–hand co-ordination, never very good at the best of times, grew suddenly very much worse. He sat there, with knife and fork or spoon poised, protesting: 'I'm perfectly competent, Lizzie. Old perhaps, but not yet enfeebled. I'll do it myself, thank you very much.' And even as he spoke he began feeding his chin, or his collar or his lapel, with egg and fish and meat.

'If you go on leaning like that, Daddy,' she warned him calmly, 'I shall rope you to the chair and feed you myself.'

Max responded by feeding his ear. The yolk of his soft-boiled egg ran down his ear-lobe and into his collar.

'Right, that's it!' She heard her voice, so cool, distant, that it did not seem to belong to her, so rational, so wonderfully calm. She found herself moving over to the kitchen drawer. Rope was actually out of the question – though she did think briefly of using the rope ladder that swung above his bed. Instead she took the roll of kitchen string, white and waxy to the touch, and began unpeeling it, listening with considerable satisfaction to its dry rattle. 'Right,' she said again, and she began winding the string, the thick white twine, around his arms and shoulders. 'I warned you. Don't say I didn't warn you!'

And that was how Albert found him when he returned in the evening. Trussed so tightly that he appeared to be wearing some kind of special bodice or jacket – almost a kind of strait-jacket. There was Max, sitting bolt upright before his ice-cold egg, the yolk he'd spilt earlier that day dried now to a golden crust on his ear and neck. Only the steady blinking of his blue eyes showed that he was conscious at all.

After that it was clear to Albert that other arrangements

would have to be made. Max's only comment as Albert unwound the string strait-jacket was startlingly lucid: 'I'm very concerned about Elizabeth. Do you think she's getting old?'

'She's at the end of her tether, Max.'

'A short tether.'

They put him in the back of Albert's silver Jag and Elizabeth gazed steadfastly through the windscreen trying to pretend that she was invisible, that Max wasn't there, that this wasn't happening.

'It's a bit like the old days,' he said, as they drew up outside the three-storey red-brick Victorian house on the corner of St Margaret Drive and Lord John Road, opposite the boys' school. Max was pretending to be engrossed in a copy of *Fealty*. In the back of the car, with a tartan rug pulled over his knees, and his red tie knotted thickly beneath his Adam's apple, he suddenly asked Albert: 'Do you believe in euthanasia?'

Albert glanced at his wife, who closed her eyes. No help from her. 'Yes. In certain circumstances. Intractable pain. Or a clear and rational desire on the part of the sufferer for release. Done with proper medical support. Competent but kindly supervision.'

'What is this place?'

'It's called an eventide refuge, Max. Serenity House.'

'Call it what you will.'

Max grinned in the rear view mirror. 'The trouble with it is, was, always will be – the moment you legalise it – someone has to do the business. Then the trouble starts. You set up units. Someone has to do the job. You? Me? Her?' And he jerked a thumb towards the back of the now frozen Elizabeth. 'Anyway, someone. Someone trained to heal people gets entrusted. Someone decides. Left, right. No, yes. Efficiently, yes. But finishing them. And that's where the problem lies. Of course it can be done. But for how long? The difficulty concerns those doing the killing. It's very hard, believe me. The problem's not with the dying. It's always with the living. Let's go home now.'

'Let's have a look first,' said Albert firmly.

'Do you think members of the Royal Family ever visit this place?'

'We can ask inside,' said Albert. He might have been address-ing a small child. Elizabeth half expected to hear him add: 'Only if you're very good!'

'The Princess of Wales might come by one day. She visited black babies born to drug-addicted mothers in New York. Surely she might call on her countrymen?'

'Perhaps. I am not privy to the Princess of Wales' engage-ments.' With relief Albert spotted a parking place.

'I have to use the lavatory.'

'We'll find one inside.'

'I don't need it then. Our primitive ancestors exposed their old and dying on the hillside. Some people call it cruel. But I tell you it was a bloody sight more humane than sticking them away in geriatric ghettos. Tell me – who does the selecting here?'

'Selecting?' Albert, concentrating on squeezing the Jag between two red Ford Escorts, found difficulty dealing with the question. 'What are you talking about, Max?'

'In all these institutions there's always somebody who does the selecting.'

'Selecting for what?'

'For who lives and who dies.'

'Let's go and take a look. Can't hurt to take a look.' Albert got out and opened Max's door. The old man sat there, illumi-nated by the car's interior light, quite silently. He opened his mouth, reached into it to remove his false teeth and sat with them on his lap. With the tip of a moistened forefinger he began stroking a molar. Hunched in her coat, listening to him, hearing a small cry of moist flesh on plastic, Elizabeth thought she was going to scream.

CHAPTER FOUR

The New Boy

Once Albert and Elizabeth had got Max out of the car, he surprised them by asking for his suitcase.

'But this is just a dry-run, Max,' said Albert, soothingly. 'No one's committing themselves yet.' Then he must have thought 'committing' was a bad word to use. He added quickly, 'The choice is yours. Anyway, you didn't bring a suitcase.'

'Yes, I did,' said Max. 'Would you mind, Lizzie? You'll find it in the boot. Next to it is a blue carpet bag – I will look after the carpet bag. The suitcase can be handed over to the authorities.'

The suitcase of dark red leather, chapped as an old cricket ball around the edges, stood in the hall of Serenity House. They all stared. Max had painted on the case in white letters: Max Montfalcon, b. 1909, Greyacres, Highgate, London N6.

'May I see my case placed in your luggage depository after I've unpacked?' Max asked Cledwyn Fox.

'Perhaps you don't have a depository?' Elizabeth asked, embarrassed by her father's assumption.

Mr Fox seemed surprised. 'But we do! It's essential.'

My God! thought Albert. A room chock full of the trunks and bags of the dearly departed.

Max seemed reassured. 'Knew you must have one. These places always do.'

Tea was later produced by a large-shouldered nurse whom Mr Fox introduced as Night Matron, a tall, rather boxy woman with a tiny smile shaped like a safety-pin. Lizzie noticed the big muscles in her forearms, coiled steel sheathed in skin. Even so she felt she had to offer to help with her father's suitcase.

'It's my pleasure, Mrs Turberville. The work of the Lord is light just as the love of the Lord is unending.'

'Unending or unbending?' Max asked.

Matron turned disconcertingly dark-green eyes towards Max who stood rigid in the corner, swallowing hard. 'You must be the new boy.' His Adam's apple moved like a heart beat above the knot of his tie.

'Sit, Mr Montfalcon,' Night Matron said firmly, and, case in one hand, she lifted a heavy green leather chair as if it were made of cardboard and deposited it gently at his side. 'The Lord bless you and keep you safe among us.' Max settled in the chair. Mr Fox covered his legs in a green tartan rug. Night Matron disappeared with his case. Max would not let her touch his carpet bag. He hugged it to his chest and rested his cheek on it, cradling it like a baby.

Mr Fox rubbed his hands. 'A Rhodesian lady full of fun and fire. Capable and energetic with a kind of inner resilience. A fine example of the old settler ethos. They live on a diet which is pretty much red meat from cradle to grave. And it shows! Believe you me. A saint and a carnivore is Night Matron.'

'Now, if I can give you what I call my Serenity House spiel. Very well, here we go! Serenity House caters to all tastes. Meat eaters and grain preferrers. We take them all. What we do not take are sides. We welcome smokers and drinkers, except in their rooms. People ought not to be punished for their habits. But we cater. We try to incorporate the latest discoveries into our everyday lives. Our chef is well aware of the latest restrictive diet programmes in America. Chef will give those who wish it a kilojoule-cutting diet. Up to forty per cent reduction without risks of malnutrition. A diet rich in minerals and vitamins. A regime low in free radicals.'

'Radicals?' Albert woke briefly from his gloomy semi-comatose state. He felt adrift in a sea of mixed emotions. Silent loathing for the bouncy Welshman and his tricksy manner yet thorough-going approval for the House. This would sort out Max. Serenity House was the solution.

'Cells containing a high count of reactive oxygen.'

'Excuse me for asking,' Albert murmured and Elizabeth gave him a sharp look.

'We fight the free radicals with beta-carotene and Vitamin E. Part and parcel of the modern world order in health. People believe in healthy life-styles the way they once believed in God. Yet Serenity House refuses any policing role in the matter of diet. We treat the health agnostics the same as we do the health believers. Are there people who want meat and gravy? Meat and gravy they shall have. Serenity House, it is fair to say, caters. What does your father like in the way of food?'

It was on the tip of Albert's tongue to say – 'Keep him away from eggs' – but a glance at Lizzie's face stopped him.

Night Matron returned. She wore, Elizabeth noticed, immensely strong brown shoes with thick crêpe soles. Boatlike though they were, she made no sound at all when she moved. 'I've unpacked Mr Montfalcon. I've switched on his electric blanket. His room is warm and waiting whenever he'd like to go up.'

'Bless you, Matron,' said Cledwyn Fox.

'Bless *you*, Mr Fox,' said Night Matron and withdrew as silently as she'd entered.

'Would you like a short tour of your new home, Mr Montfalcon?' said Cledwyn Fox, tucking in his apricot shirt with neat nimble gestures.

But Max had closed his eyes and appeared to have fallen asleep.

'Let him sleep. This way, Mr and Mrs Turberville.' Up sprang Mr Fox, so lithe, so agile, so brimming with energy it made you smile just to see him. With the light every so often glinting on his golden earring he danced ahead on a tour of inspection.

'Never more than twenty guests. Though that number is seldom stable, for – well, for evident reasons. As Night Matron would say – "we know not the day nor the hour . . . " Do you know who they are, Mr and Mrs Turberville? The guests of Serenity House? I shall tell you. They're *us*! That's who they are. If we're lucky. In a way I regard them as veterans from the wars of life. And sometimes as spacemen or deep-sea divers, out of their usual atmosphere. Out of their depth. Do you think

THE NEW BOY

they need our pity? God forbid. Do you know what they do
need? Equipment! Explorers venturing into another age, having
to cope in a totally new environment. Our elders are also inno-
vators, Mrs Turberville. That's what they are. When I look at
my guests, what do I feel for them? I'll tell you – gratitude.
That's what I feel. Where they lead today we will surely follow
tomorrow.'

It was like being led by a cricket, thought Elizabeth, a Welsh
cricket. For Mr Fox chirruped and skipped ahead of them from
kitchen to television room, to laundry, to toilets. 'Very, very
important, proper toileting arrangements!' A walking, talking
brochure.

Albert pointed to the television cameras poking their dark
sleek little heads from corners and cupboard tops. 'Do you run
those?'

'Eyes and ears, Mr Turberville.'

And so they went, with a hop, skip and jump, following merry
Mr Fox who waved his petite little behind in a manner which
made Albert flush and Elizabeth thought was really rather cute.

Nineteen 'clients' or 'guests' or 'elders' in Serenity House. 'At
the last count,' said Mr Fox. 'We're missing dear Mrs Greengross.
She went last night. Quite suddenly.' Three storeys. A garden
full of tall and rather gloomy beech trees. Cypresses lining
the fence. All mod cons, sensors in the bedclothes to switch
on the electric blanket. Bells to remind you to take your pills
from the built-in hoppers which sprang out of walls above the
special nursing beds. A selection of motorised wheelchairs,
the pride of the fleet being the Gazelle; then the slightly smaller
Antelope and even the homely little standard Terrapin. To each
according to his need. Closed circuit TV cameras on every
landing to monitor guests as they negotiated the stairs and
corners lest they slip and fall. All, in Mr Fox's words, 'Very
lovely. Very modern.'

Soon Elizabeth's head was spinning with names and ailments.
There was a very thin old lady in a blonde wig and pink silk
dressing-gown, called Lady Divina. One of the very first 'eco-
freaks', said Fox. Then there was old Maudie, who wept when
she saw Fox and tried to kiss his hand. He was very patient
with them and Elizabeth felt slightly ashamed of herself for

51

feeling so angry towards her father but then immediately cheered up when she decided that Cledwyn Fox would take care of Max far better than ever she could have done. They were intrigued by Imelda, the little nurse-aide from the Philippines. They met, but did not speak to, the Reverend Alistair, Margaret and Sandra because they all appeared to be asleep, sitting upright in their chairs before the TV. Mr Fox introduced them as if they were really awake, and encouraged Elizabeth and Albert to do the same. She felt silly taking the limp hands of the sleepers in hers. Albert managed rather better, bending over the sleepers and saying cheerfully, 'Albert Turberville, pleased to meet you.' Just as he did at election time, taking no notice of their response. 'They spend most of their days semi-comatose,' Mr Fox explained. They met two fat, rather untidy men, one of whom had his fly buttons open and Elizabeth could have sworn he'd had his hand inside his trousers and quickly drew it out when Mr Fox coughed upon entering their room. 'The Malherbe twins,' Mr Fox announced. 'Guests of long standing. Once very prominent in the Manchester wine trade.' From down one of the corridors came the sound of machine-gun fire and the crump of exploding bombs. 'Very realistic though clearly man-made. That's Major Bobbno', Mr Fox smiled gently, 'still fighting the war.'

'Most people find it hard to talk about incontinence,' Mr Fox said. 'We face it four-square. It may be stress-related. It may result from medication. We try various methods. Counselling. Exercise. Devices from the sheath to the catheter. *Plenty* of toilets, of course. One for two guests. That's a big step up on the recommended ratio of one to four. Commodes wherever requested. Exercises for the pelvic muscles. With our disturbed patients it is sometimes just a case of reminding them to go to the toilet regularly. This often prevents accidents without the need for special treatment.'

'Those TV cameras,' Albert said as they walked back to Fox's office. 'I suppose you know they're illegal?'

'I did not know.'

'Closed circuit cameras have been outlawed by the Department of Health. They constitute an invasion of privacy.'

'News to me.' Fox smiled thinly.

'My husband is an MP,' said Elizabeth.

'Ah, yes . . . ' Fox made it sound as if this explained some small but not very important mystery. 'Would you like to see a copy of the House Rules, Mr Turberville? Firm but fair I think you'll find them.'

Night Matron's brilliant torch played over the mountain of suitcases stored in the cellar of Serenity House, a room faintly lit by an overhead strip of speckled fluorescent tubing. A hill of leather bones, thought Max. A luggage ossuary. He said as much to Night Matron, broad and brooding by his side. But she said it was not a word she knew. Not a word they used in Rhodesia.

'Or if they did, not in my company. My father kept a bar, Mr Montfalcon. The words men used were shorter.'

'Bones,' said Max.

'It was the drink. Men and drink. Serenity House has rather careful rules about liquor.'

'Bones,' said Max again.

'Oh, bones!' Her torch stabbed the dimly lit cellar. The hill of leather gleamed softly. It seemed to breathe, exhaling the bouquet of decades: cowhide, pigskin, alligator and kid. The memorial mountain of dead skins. Each bag, case, valise, trunk, portmanteau carefully and clearly labelled.

'They take on the personality of their owners, past and present,' Matron explained. 'Like dogs do. I know a lot of them by heart. James Maclemman, born 1904; pigskin and silver, Prince of Wales Drive, Brighton; Dilys Jones, 1922, cream canvas and red buckles, The Crescent, Gwent. Mabel Greengross – dear Mrs Greengross. Just left us, Mr Montfalcon. She's the rather ghastly leatherette with the strap around it.'

Max shivered.

'We store them here,' said Night Matron, 'against the day our elders take their leave. The owners are given a receipt. We do try to persuade elders not to bring their best cases. But, as you see, they won't listen. Elders like to put their best feet forward. You'd think they were off on a world cruise. This is where they wait. In the dark. Ready for the big day.'

'I painted my own,' said Max.

'So I see.'

'It was the custom, back then.'

'Back when?'

'Back then.'

'The NKs never come to reclaim them. But they'd be down on us if we lost them. They'd be round in a flash asking for Mummy's Dior suitcase and Daddy's leather trunk.'

'NKs.' Max puzzled over this. 'Next of Kin?'

'Dead right. "Never Keeps", we call them. Never keep their promises – d'you see?'

'Ingratitude,' Max murmured. 'Sharper than a serpent's tooth.'

'You can say that again. Shall we sling your case? Here let me do it.'

'Might as well.' Max watched her practised heave and his leather suitcase sailed on to the leather hill.

'Good shot,' said Max.

'It's a knack. Must come from the shoulder. Rather like using a scythe.'

'What on earth do you do with them? The unclaimed baggage?'

Matron raked the leather hill with her finger of light. 'Sell them off from time to time – Serenity House luggage sale. Sad but there it is. We simply don't have the space. And if the NKs don't care, why should we? It's usually the more modern stuff that goes in the sales. The old-fashioned bags and trunks won't move.'

Max nodded. 'Space is always the problem in these places. Possessions take up more space than people.'

'Things,' said Night Matron with a touch of bitterness. 'There is nothing harder to get rid of. You want to add that carpet bag to the pile, Mr Montfalcon?'

Max shook his head and hugged his bag to his chest.

Night Matron had often seen this fierce possessive attachment to some treasured object. You got it in children. You got it in the elderly moving house. Whatever he kept in the bag was very special. He looked like he'd kill for it.

As they left the depository she asked: 'You from these parts?'

54

'Highgate, yes,' said Max. 'Briefly. Before that, Hampstead Garden Suburb and Harwich.'

'I'm ex-Rhodesia,' said Night Matron. 'You know – that place that doesn't exist any more. I was there, but they say it doesn't exist.'

'Oh, yes,' said Max. 'In my case they are prepared to believe that Harwich still exists. It is me they don't believe in. It rather irks one.'

'One can say that again,' said Night Matron.

Albert was studying the House Rules. 'Why do you refer to your patients as "she"? Here, for instance, " . . . she shall not be held responsible for damage in cases of certain mental infirmities, the definitions of which are given below . . . " '

'Statistics, Mr Turberville. If the male has his way in the morning and early afternoon of life, everything from teatime to the evening belongs to "her". Over the age of seventy-five, most of the elderly in Britain are women. Around two-thirds. Over eighty the news is even worse for boys like us. Three-quarters of the over-eighties are women. And at ninety! Well, ninety is almost entirely a feminine number. How old's your dad, then?' asked Mr Fox.

'Eighty-one,' said Elizabeth.

'Lucky,' said Mr Fox. 'If you're not too partial about the meaning of luck. Welcome aboard, Mr Montfalcon. Would that be a bit of a French name, there?'

'English!' said Max in his pebbly voice from his brand-new wheelchair.

Albert Turberville looked embarrassed and shuffled his shoes; he reached down and scratched the wrinkled knees of his trousers as he always did when asked a question for which, as an MP, he might have to answer one day in the House.

'Born and bred,' said Max. 'I went to Churtseigh,' he announced firmly, 'in Surrey, you know. A fine, traditional public school, which I believe,' he glared at his daughter, 'continues to this day. The Headmaster took Holy Orders. He was an Australian. I was victor ludorum – and the competition was damn stiff I can tell you. Everyone thought that Collingwood had it in the bag. But I took him in the shooting. Churtseigh always had a very strong shooting tradition. They had no less than three shooting masters. Three! In the Great War. I seem to remember it led to the expression very popular around Churtseigh, "the shooter shot"! A kind of variation on "the biter bit . . . "

'I was at Oxford in the mid thirties.' Max beamed. 'With Binkie Beaumont and that crowd. Julian Trefoil, the historian, Sir Julian as he later became. I'm sure you've heard of him. Ralphie Treehouse. And, of course, Matthew Babish. The only man as far as I know to take a double-first in Classics, make a splash in the Security Services and then, at the outbreak of war, absconded to Moscow, before anyone else. Admittedly Oxford never had Cambridge's record for breeding traitors. But what we did we did with style. And we did it first!'

Fox looked at the old man. Even at eighty plus he was a great big fellow. Well over six foot, very thin now with the bones smooth and clear beneath the skin. The assertive bone, the winning skeleton. Fox was reminded of the remains of unwrapped mummies in the British Museum, the skin lightly papering the bones. A kind of going to dust within, a saving dryness, a preserving desiccation, the desert inside that mimicked the likeness to life, though the life itself had long gone. He'd seen something like it in the remains of Bogmen, hauled from the peat looking curiously bony and yet so paradoxically supple. He noticed Max's eyes, a touch pale and moist yet wide and striking blue. A fine head of strong grey hair, and he wore a suit. Max Montfalcon was a man who came from a time when they always wore suits for making calls.

'That's the chair for you, Mr Montfalcon,' Fox said. 'We have them all here. We have most of the good walking frames. Height adjustable. I can recommend the rather beautiful little alpha frame. They fold flat – adjustable in height. Very good if you need just a teeny bit of help in getting about.'

'My father doesn't get about much,' said Lizzie.

'I'm a great walker,' said Max.

Fox noted that his shoes had been trodden into the ground. Max had walked on their heels and he had walked on their sides and they didn't so much as hold his feet now but gaped at his ankles, like two rather useless leather bandages.

'Mind you,' said Max, 'I'm not as quick as I used to be. I was a runner in my time. I do believe I could run again. If the prize was worth it. They taught us at Churtseigh that the prize was always to the players. The prize was only as good as the game. Often the game was better. So you played for the game. A very English virtue. And why not? I'm old enough to honour the name – Englishman.' Max looked defiantly at his daughter. 'None of this affected "British" business for me.'

'It's a pretty well-established term by now,' said Cledwyn Fox gently.

'Nor any of this Euro-nonsense either.' Max opened his lips and let loose a gleeful boyish chortle. 'A German racket – that's all it is!'

'I've always thought of the term "British" as a capacious umbrella which we could all shelter under,' Cledwyn Fox offered, with his attractive mixture of diffidence and clarity of utterance. 'We Welsh and we Scottish and we English.'

' "No Englishman ever called himself a Briton without a sneaking sense of the ludicrous." Not my words,' said Max, 'but those of the great Fowler. Look 'em up, if you don't believe me. And Fowler knew a thing or two about humbug, cant, affectation. Not to mention putting one over on your neighbour. Be proud of your Welshness. Trumpet it from the roof tops. Enough of this urge to merge. This desire to drown in a soupy unity. Euro-minestrone!'

Fox lifted appealing eyes to Elizabeth. 'Fowler?'

Albert answered for her. 'An old grammarian. Or language bod. Wrote a book about it decades ago and found in my father-in-law his most devoted fan.'

Max said nothing to this though he was clearly taking it in. When Albert had finished speaking, he began dribbling. Elizabeth groaned and reached for her handkerchief.

'When were you born?' Max demanded of Mr Fox, when his chin was dry.

The abrupt change of tack took Fox by surprise. He had to think for a moment. 'Nineteen forty-eight.'

'Really, Daddy,' Elizabeth implored. 'I'm sure that Mr Fox doesn't want a history lesson.'

But a lesson he was going to get. You had only to look at Max's bright, remorseless eyes as he echoed Fox's reply. 'Nineteen forty-eight! What a wonderful year. I remember it well. A great year for the country as we tried to pull ourselves up by our bootstraps after standing virtually alone against the Axis powers. A remarkable year. Remember the Berlin airlift. Who was it who broke the Soviet blockade of Berlin? Who saved the German bacon? We did! And what thanks did we have? No answer came the stern reply.'

'Daddy! Mr Fox wasn't responsible. He's not a German!'

But Max ignored his daughter's protest. 'There was a great fog in nineteen forty-eight, Mr Fox. It blotted out sun and moon for one hundred and forty-four consecutive hours. I sometimes think it must have been a cousin, in fog terms, of the mist that clouds good thinking today on the matter of European unity. Yes, quite a fog that was in nineteen forty-eight. The only other blot on the landscape was the arrival, on our shores, of the first coloured immigrants from Jamaica and such-like places. I understand the thinking behind it, but I thought then that it was a bad idea. They'd never really settle here. Never join. Never adapt. Never become truly English. Or Welsh.' This was a concession to Fox who was staring at Max in astonishment. But in his amazement there was a trace of admiration. Mad he might be, but the old boy did not mince his words.

'Praise to heaven there were other blessings in nineteen forty-eight! We saw the birth of the heir to the throne. Did you know that you were born in the same year as Prince Charles? The Prince of Wales.' (This was another sop to Fox.) 'For the moment. A baby destined to be the next King of England. Charles Philip Arthur George, known in the papers and announcements of the time as "His Royal Highness, the Baby." On the palace gates there appeared, for those of her loyal subjects gathered on that cold November night, but complaining not, Mr Fox, awaiting the good news, the announcement that Her Majesty was safely delivered of a Prince. Note the language. No mere "infant". And the time, I hear you ask? As far as I recall, correct me if I'm wrong – it was nine fourteen a.m. If my memory holds up.'

On the word 'memory' in came the boy, butter-yellow hair and neat white coat.

'Jack's just joined the team. He'll be one of our key helpers in a few months' time. All being well. We're very pleased with Jack. Quick as a tick. And American to boot. From Florida. Jack – meet Mr and Mrs Turberville. Jack meet Max Montfalcon. Mr Montfalcon's been telling us all about Prince Charles.'

Jack touched the tip of his finger to his nose. Like he sometimes did when he wanted to start thinking. Jump-start his brain. Hitting the mind-button, he called it. Something was needed here. Jack knew that. He hit his mind-button a couple more times and it came to him. 'Wow!' said Jack.

Lizzie watched the boy tapping his nose. It was as if he thought this word illumined and explained everything. His delight at getting it out was plain. The eyes stopped blinking furiously and reverted to their blank dangerous gleam. It was impossible, surely, that someone could have eyes of different colours? But the boy's eyes were very strange. Unless she was going mad. One jungle green and the other aquamarine, in some lights, perhaps. But now more blue than green. Square, chunky body. Jack's good looks did not mask another look, something, well, cretinous. Twenty perhaps? Shorter than her by at least a head. A shapely midget.

'Wow, indeed,' said Lizzie.

Jack took her hand and shook it. 'From Florida.'

'Florida?' Max looked hard at Jack. 'Where the sun shines?'

'Day and night.' Jack's grin was pure gold.

'I had a friend in Florida,' Max said.

'Everyone's got a friend in Florida. Pen-pal perhaps?'

'I don't remember.' Max's jaws clamped shut.

'My father's memory is not what it was,' Elizabeth said.

'Dear Mrs Turberville – show me the memory that is,' declared Mr Fox. 'The cells go, after forty. Take care to avoid too much alcohol and you can slow the process. But they slip away, all the same. Sad but true.'

'True but sad,' piped up Jack who looked delighted. Astonished. He'd done that without touching his nose. He felt real good. He was gonna help all he could. This poor old guy had lost a lot of cells, he could see that. He'd seen that all along, he guessed. Now Jack, helpful Jack, happy Jack, Jack who was really like, well, *caring* about Max – sprang forward. Beaming bellhop in Serenity House.

'Check your bag, sir?'

'No!' Max's refusal was hoarse, angry. He swung the bag away from Jack as if he held in his arms a threatened child.

CHAPTER FIVE

An Inspector Calls

Cledwyn Fox brought to his survey of Max Montfalcon the eye of an expert in the months that followed. Serenity House revealed the ways and faces of human decrepitude, the visible, sometimes beautiful, weatherings of flesh on frame, little scars and contusions, seams and ridges spreading across the human canvas. He recognised the colours and daubings by which, eventually, we come to be painted into place. But he also knew that what Max showed of himself was never the whole picture. The old man was shaky on his legs, yes. But there were times he straightened and walked almost freely. That Max Montfalcon suffered a touch of paranoia was clear. His complaints that he was being pursued. His constant references to 'my young friend'. Cledwyn Fox had thought at first that the 'friend' might be Jack who was remarkable in the devoted way he kept an eye on Max Montfalcon. But the old man certainly did not have Jack in mind as his mysterious missing young friend. His attitude to Jack, when he deigned to see him at all, was really rather scornful.

Soon after Max arrived in Serenity House he began getting calls on the payphone. Mr Fox had had payphones installed on each floor after Lady Divina's attempt to throttle Edgar the chiropodist with a telephone wire. Max pressed the phone to one ear, pushed a finger into the other, and shouted: 'You want to make me an offer? But you couldn't afford my price, my young friend!' Yet all the same he listened closely to the voice in his ear.

When Night Matron helped him to his room half an hour later he told her he'd been enjoying story-time from America. Night Matron said she thought Americans had given up stories and watched TV instead.

'They like stories as long as somebody is killed,' said Max.

'Fair enough,' said Night Matron. 'What's the story?'

'Once upon a time,' said Max, 'there was a merchant who met a boy selling stolen goods. Because the boy wouldn't sell all his stolen loot the merchant devised a cunning plan. He encouraged the boy to steal yet more. At the same time he warned the interested party of the boy's intention. That way, if the boy got away with his thievery, he might be willing to part with more goods. On the other hand, if the boy was caught in the act, the merchant would benefit from the goodwill felt by the injured party.'

'Sounds pretty grim,' said Matron.

'Lethal,' Max nodded. 'Because the boy proceeds on the assumption that people deserve to be robbed blind by young hoodlums. His culture teaches him this. In fact, this isn't always so. Among monkeys in the wild, violent young males are often despatched soon after puberty. By older members of the tribe.'

'Glad to hear it,' said Night Matron.

'One need have no more compunction than spearing a rat.'

'We have an infestation of rats', said Night Matron, 'from time to time. Serenity House is feeling its age.'

'I've seen the mildew.' Max smiled. 'A rich green mould. Climbing the walls like cheese.'

Indeed, Max had an eye for crumbling corners, cobwebs, rising damp, curtains that sagged on their rails. He would stop and stare at a patch of split carpet which had been tacked to the floor boards with two-inch nails.

'You ought to put a work party on to this.'

'Wear and tear,' Mr Fox had said apologetically. 'Serenity House carries quite a load.'

'It's always the same in collection camps.' Max began counting the nails in the carpet.

Now that, thought Mr Fox, was an odd way of referring to Serenity House.

But then the elders all had their distinctive little weaknesses.

Their neuroses, their small and great dementias; their problems with sadness and hygiene. They were like aliens or space explorers: the Manchester Brewing Twins, the Five Incontinents, even Lady Divina, now increasingly in a world of her own; even the 'sleepers', those like the Reverend Alistair and Margaret and snoring Sandra who sat all day long in their chairs staring into space and never said a word to anyone, just stared and dozed. They practised a form of strange ventriloquy, their bodies drifting, disabled spaceships in impossibly distant reaches of the universe. Like the remnants of infinitely far away stars, sending coded messages into the emptiness, on voyages so lengthy that by the time they were picked up on earth the worlds from which they had come had been dead for millennia. Body music. Max Montfalcon heard voices. The voices talked to him of the war.

So in time Max came to settle into Serenity House.

Albert and Elizabeth had arrived one evening with what Max called, 'a few sticks from my old quarters. They'll probably fumigate it and board it up now I've gone,' he told Lady Divina as they watched Albert struggling to lift a heavy oak cupboard he'd roped to the roofrack of the silver Jag. Night Matron sprang to his aid.

'A willing Sherpa,' Mr Fox told an embarrassed Albert as they watched Matron manhandle the cupboard upstairs to Max's room, aided in the final stages by Jack.

'I've been robbed,' Max said bitterly.

'Come on, Daddy,' Lizzie said. 'It's not as bad as all that.'

And Albert said: 'This was your decision, Max. Remember?'

'That man will never take responsibility. He just drives the trains.' Max pointed accusingly at Albert.

And they all stood looking at him helplessly.

'Trains? What trains?' demanded Albert.

'I'll change the locks,' said Max. 'They probably have keys to fit my cupboard.' This with a baleful glance at Lizzie.

'Matron will see to it,' Mr Fox murmured.

True to his word he got Matron to talk to the locksmith in Highgate Village and Matron asked Jack to take care of it and

Jack replied, 'Yes, ma'am!' He did not even have to think before answering.

Elizabeth was soon telling her friends that he had taken to it 'like a duck to water'. Mind you, it was a little distressing to visit him. Especially as he always insisted that she take him for a walk.

'But it's cold, Daddy. First put on your coat.'

'I won't.'

'Well, then, I can't possibly take you out. What do you think Mr Fox would say if I brought you back with pneumonia?'

'Blast Mr Fox,' said her father.

Or she would arrive to find him wearing his heavy winter coat of mustard gaberdine. 'Let's go, Lizzie. Take me home, please.' He stood there with a peppermint green scarf wrapped around his throat, climbing over his mouth to rest beneath his nose. 'I'm wearing my coat – see?'

It was Cledwyn Fox who came to her rescue. 'Look now, Mr Montfalcon. It's very dark to be taking a walk. Look at it out there. Black as a bat's wing at midnight.'

'Is it?' said Max in surprise. He walked to the window and tapped it with his finger-nail. 'So it is. Black as a witch's tit. Well, perhaps I'll go tomorrow.'

And so it was that, always getting ready to leave Serenity House, Max Montfalcon stayed and could be found attending Ballroom Dancing. Or chatting to Edgar the chiropodist about the Euromongering tendencies of the Government.

It might have continued like this had Albert Turberville not heard something disagreeable in the House of Commons' Tea Room one day and become obsessed with questions of number, and took to making sudden visits to Serenity House demanding to be told something called 'the truth'. At first no one else knew the purpose of these visits. Neither Cledwyn Fox, nor Elizabeth and, least of all, Max himself, who simply hadn't the faintest idea what his son-in-law was going on about. Didn't know. Couldn't care. Didn't remember. Albert's face turned red and his eyes bulged, and Max decamped for the relative peace and protection of the Stroke Club.

*

The lively meetings of the Stroke Club were a daily ritual, a special delight popular with the residents and open to all, whether or not they had suffered a stroke. There were tea parties and animated discussions of who had chosen what option (pain relief and/or mechanical resuscitation?) in filling out the forms for their Living Wills. And there were wonderful theatrical performances from Jack and the little nurse-aide, Imelda, in papier-mâché masks, disguised as two bright and winning mice. 'Mickey and Minnie Go To Market!' and the one that always made Major Bobbno weep: 'Mickey and Minnie Fall In Love'.

Everyone knew the Imelda behind the mask.

'A little chit of a person,' according to old Maudie.

'Just here to find a husband,' said George, the muscular lover of Angie whose children had disowned her when she announced she was a lesbian at the age of seventy-two.

But what of Jack, behind the other mask? 'Tell us the story of Jack, Brigadier,' Major Bobbno would order and Max would settle back and tell the tale of Jack, Florida Jack, the boy from Orlando, who grew up in a trailer park, lived with his poor old mother and one day set off to find fame and fortune in England.

'Read a book once, but it hurt his head!' said Major Bobbno.

'Lived on Chinese take-aways,' said Beryl the beard.

'The Angel of Death,' said Lady Divina.

Beside Divina sat the two Malherbe brothers, dressed in business suits which had last been fashionable in their native Manchester forty years earlier. It was quite impossible to tell the brothers apart. Extreme age – and both were now in their late eighties – had had the effect of withering them into an even closer identity than they had shared all their lives. And in any event, thought Max, the old begin to look alike. In the eyes of younger people they become some strange, wrinkled race. Old age was a kind of geriatric Asia full of natives all of whom seem to resemble each other. In the case of the Malherbe brothers the only way you could tell them apart was that the brother Joshua always had his fly open. He had his fly open and liked to stick his hand into it in a reflective manner, rather in a way that someone might massage the lobe of an ear or tug abstractedly at a lock of hair.

'Braggart,' Lady Divina liked to remark when Joshua's hand

disappeared into his trouser front. 'Live foxes never came out of dead holes.'

Lady Divina remained resolutely unimpressed. In the days before Alzheimer's had taken a grip on her mind she would give no quarter. 'Mr Malherbe, I had *bulls* with more charm than your fiddling brother.' And now and then, sometimes, the mists cleared in her head and she began worrying aloud about global warming or cried aloud for her daughter Doris who had deposited her one day at Serenity House some ten years before, in a furtive manner, and then crept away, rather as a frightened young mother might panic and leave her baby on the hospital steps. Lady Divina had been found in the back seat of an Austin Princess parked outside the front door, with a note propped on the dashboard written on rather good, deep green, bond paper which read: 'I can do no more for Mummy. I have been a carer for fifteen years and I am so tired! Please look after her. Financial arrangements have been made to cover her stay with you. God bless you.' The note had been signed 'Doris'.

Getting old, thought Max, very often meant being dumped. Your relatives drove you out into the countryside and, ignoring the notices which most specifically forbade dumping, they cast you away like an exhausted bedstead or an elderly car seat through which the springs would soon show in rusty ribs and the stuffing would spill out on to the grass and blow away in the wind.

It became difficult to keep track of the permanent residents since none of these were very permanent, except on paper, that is to say they were all in for the duration. Max took for his fixed and certain points such survivors as the Malherbe brothers in their antique but proper suits with their stiff collars and mustard ties who, when they sat in the television room of an evening, looked like a brace of performance artists, Josh and Ted, with Josh's hand absently and eternally stirring his unseen member. Patience without result; desire without efficacy; scandal without heat.

An unexpected series of diversions was provided by the visits of Chief Superintendent Trevor Slack, retired, who interviewed Max on several occasions. Mr Fox observed the visits with a feeling of mild alarm. Night Matron heard of them with distaste. It had been British policemen who had followed British MPs to Rhodesia in the old days, and they had meant trouble. Jack watched the arrival of the pale, polite, passionless policeman with mounting excitement and fear. It firmed up his own suspicions, but he did not want to be beaten to the draw.

Superintendent Slack asked Max a whole heap of strange questions to which Max was in the habit of replying: 'Don't know. Can't remember. Pardon?' Until one day Slack asked him about a young man called von F. What had been von F's feeling when he first set sail from Hamburg to Harwich? To which Max replied, unhesitatingly: 'Confusion.'

'What made him confused, Mr Montfalcon?'

'He got talking to these English passengers. Seeing he was German, they decided to have a little fun. Teach Freddie Foreigner a thing or two. They gave him some advice. Whenever terminating a conversation and wishing to be polite, end with the words – "Fuck off!" It's an old English custom, they told young von F.'

'Thought he was a stupid German, did they, sir? But he wasn't, was he? Spoke English as well as they did.'

'What confused him was English ignorance about their own history. Von F knew that the British Royal Family was absolutely riddled with foreigners. Germans, most of them. Look at Queen Victoria's husband, Albert. Before him, King William could only speak German. And today, as the consort of our own dear Queen, we have a Greek prince. And they're all as British as you or me.'

'And if they could do it, I suppose anyone can,' said Superintendent Slack with silky, ominous sympathy.

'Do what?' Max demanded.

'Pass for British.'

'That's going to be illegal soon,' said Max with a little angry laugh. 'Soon we'll all pass for Europeans and that will be that. Bloody Germans will run everything!'

'Don't like Germans, do we, sir?'

'They're all right – in their place. But that place isn't over here.'

*

Why were people always asking him questions? Max Montfalcon lay in bed and tried again to remember how many people he had killed. Or was supposed to have killed.

And down the corridor Lady Divina lay computing inside her sealed head, the numbers likely to perish when global warming set off climatic changes in the south of England.

'Give me none of your Upper Volta,' whispered Divina, 'or your Bangladesh. Think of Brighton.' Divina had lived once in Brighton. She could remember that.

Within a few decades south-east England would be too dry for cereal crops. What would they grow there then? Rice? People to whom she said these things imagined the paddy-fields above the sunken city of Brighton. She saw sturdy pink English calves reddening in the sharp sunshine, flat straw hats and aching backs, the slap of the palm on the fat flesh calf as another Anopheles mosquito bit deep into the English bloodstream. In her room, ceaselessly smoothing the roughened corner of her sheet, on which was stamped in purple capitals the letters D.H., Divina cried out in her pain and anguish, seeming to Max, as he began drifting slowly into sleep, to supply an answer to his question.

'Millions!' Divina cried.

CHAPTER SIX

From Tranquillity to Serenity

Let us tell tall stories about a barely literate young American, a key helper on the night shift at Serenity House, who has worked there ever since Max moved in. The fall of 1990. A couple of days before, to be precise, and Jack was there to greet him. A boy who has so much get up and go he left his underprivileged home in the Tranquil Pines Mobile Home Park on Orange Avenue, Orlando, Florida, USA, and flew to England. There he learnt a new trade and, to the delight of Cledwyn Fox, Night Matron and young Dr Tonks, became a dedicated member of staff in North London's Premier Eventide Refuge. Isn't that the American fairytale? Isn't that success?

Yes, but Jack *who*?

No one could say for sure. Equally, no one believed Mr Fox when he replied, 'Jack Robinson, of course!'

'Jack in the cellar.' This from Major Bobbno.

'Jack Frost,' said old Maudie, and shivered.

'Jack the Ripper,' Lady Divina asserted.

As for Jack himself, when he heard about the questions they were asking in Serenity House he laughed his big, broad-toothed laugh, put on his Mouse head, and asked them a riddle: 'I was a sweeper. Then a sperm. Then I grew a head. Who am I?'

No one really got close to the answer. It took Max, after some long serious thought, to say: 'According to one's researches conducted by letter and telephone over the past year since I was incarcerated, the story of Jack is as follows. Unexpected transformations are the norm in closed, artificial institutions.

Prisoners rise to positions of authority. His type is not uncommon in the camps.'

And then Max would settle back and recount once more, for the members of the Stroke Club, the history of Jack Robinson. Jack from Orlando. Jack the nimble. Jack the quick. Old Maudie would clap her hands and young Agnes would demand: 'Don't forget the Miracle of Conception Ride, Mr Montfalcon!'

Jack had a job, once. He was a sweeper in the Magic Kingdom, wearing black and white fatigues with a little veil hanging over the back of his neck, looking like a retired Foreign Legionnaire. He shuffled about collecting gum wrappers and cigarette butts from the paths and byways between the Swiss Family Robinson Tree House, ninety feet wide, 800,000 plastic leaves and the merry den of the Pirates of the Caribbean, engaged in their work of jolly arson and rapine. Oh yes, there sat that immensely drunk old greybeard with his scarlet breeches riding up to his crotch, drunk as a lord, a bottle in one hand and a squealing piglet in the other. Piglet? Sure. See for yourself, a merry old soul in a three-cornered hat and a piglet under his right arm.

The thing about the Magic Kingdom, Jack had discovered to his surprise, was that far from being very big (it covered forty-two square miles and welcomed hundreds of millions of visitors), it was actually rather smaller than life. The Crystal Palace was just a dwarfish echo of that lost Victorian marvel. The Tree House was domestic. Even the pirates' universe of cannon and carousing was cramped. Only the animals walking about had a little height – the mice, ducks, dogs and bears.

It might have gone on like this for ever.

'If only it had!' old Maudie would sigh, when Max described Jack's sole period of legitimate employment. And Major Bobbno would tell her to keep her chin up. This was the Magic Kingdom, where anything was possible.

Jack the sweeper caught the eye of the camp authorities, Max would relate, and he was sent to 'Spermatozoa' for kitting out in a brand-new outfit. The Kingdom rewards faithful employees. Jack was to be given a Ride.

'If only it had!' old Maudie would sigh again and Josh Malherbe told her to belt up.

A disabled soft-ware salesman from Tucson, on his first visit, was somehow spirited out of his wheelchair and put on the Miracle of Conception Ride, a simulated journey of the sperm cell into the vagina and up the Fallopian tube for a headlong confrontation with the female ovum, a ride which pregnant women, children and people with heart complaints are strictly enjoined to avoid. How the salesman got past the pushers, the guards whose job it is to police the rides, remains a mystery. But clearly their frequent warnings to 'Keep your hands, legs and clothing well inside the car at all times' were not of much use to the helpless salesman.

The novelty of the Miracle of Conception Ride is that the travellers in the fast-moving roller-coaster cars each feel themselves to represent a single sperm in its race to reach the egg. Alongside them, charging up the dimly lit, scarlet tunnel towards the distant ovum pulsing with the golden glow of a warm and welcoming sun, riding a kind of milky posse, are other hastening sperm, many with human faces and names like Butch and Freddy, and, yes, Jumpin' Jack! Built of fibreglass and moving at high speeds, looking for all the world like albino comets, the sperm Butch and Freddy smile and wink as they pull ahead of the car in which you're travelling and then drop back again. The salesman was struck by one or more of these passing sperm, perhaps Alec, who wore a baseball cap with the legend, 'Here I come', or Wayne, 'Small but fast'.

By which precisely it matters not. The mangled remains of the unfortunate victim lay spread across the blue plastic floor of the car when it arrived at the other end of the journey and entered into the Florida sunlight, where everyone began screaming.

At this point alarm bells, Max would say, had started ringing all over the Park. And old Maudie always wanted to add, 'And so they should have!' But a warning glance from Josh Malherbe silenced her.

*

Jack did in fact catch the eye of his CSC (Cleansing Station Controller) and Jack was, as they say in the Kingdom, to be given 'a head'. And indeed he was. He wore the fat white three-fingered gloves, the black olive nose perched between black oval eyes with their delicate Japanese eyebrows etched on the plastic face, the green bow-tie, the red trousers, white waistcoat and boat-like shoes. And he sweated a lot. For even though they do very careful fittings down in Capitation, those mice heads are hot and heavy and it is never easy to breathe through the smile. But as they say, to get ahead in the Kingdom, you need to 'sport your head'. And so Jack would have gone on quite happily sporting the head, because the heat is just there to be taken and breathing, as they say in the Capitation Unit, is something you do on your own time. And after all, this was the way ahead.

No, said Max, it could not go on for ever. Behind the Magic Waterfall, in the so-called Curtain of Mist, a young woman from Delaware was accosted. 'I turned round and there he was. I don't think he said anything. Not that I can remember, it all happened so fast. I bit one of his ears. But he was stronger than me. I remember he had this kind of, well, cheesy smell. And very hot breath. What could I do? I just lay there looking up at this insane smile!'

After the event charges were brought. But the cops had a problem because it wasn't technically rape and, anyway, how do you formulate a charge in which a rodent is supposed to have had sex with a human female? You may invoke the charge of sexual battery which, in the state of Florida, carries the same status as rape. But to make the charge stick when there is an entire school of identical mice running around the Park on any one day is a very difficult thing.

Jack, the fall-guy. Lost his head, expelled from the Kingdom. Sent home to sit in the trailer in Tranquil Pines, his old, adoptive mother ill and fading fast. Watching a variety of televisual delights from the Aardvark Video Emporium.

Yes, but Jack *who*?

'Jack the giant-killer,' said Max Montfalcon.

*

Mr Fox still preferred 'Jack Robinson'. Mr Fox's arrangements for paying Jack, cash on the nail, once a week, no questions asked, did not quite accord with the guidelines laid down by the Department of Employment in these matters and the thought of applying for a work-permit for Jack filled him with mixed emotions. Jack seemed a gift from the gods – you did not sully that divine help with paper-work.

Thus it was – for what were almost religious reasons – that Mr Fox did not like the anti-American note he heard in the stories told about Jack by the elders. Not all Americans were bad, surely? Not all Englishmen were gay. He could vouch for that. Despite what foreigners said and believed. Americans had been responsible for some very important advances in the field of Living Wills. They had passed legislation which required hospitals to have a jolly good natter to newly admitted patients on the ways in which they would like to die. A cup of tea and a chat about death. How did they wish to be treated when in the terminal condition? Death with Dignity. That was the issue, wasn't it? Medically assisted release. Med-assist, some American hospitals and, more importantly, eventide refuges in the States, were now calling it.

Dr August Tonks confessed to having learnt much from American standards. 'We're seeing the start of what I call patient militancy. They say – let the sick have access to the means of extinction. Why should termination always be doctor-driven? Six months to live and nothing but suffering? Hell, no, we want to go! Give us the tools, say patients to their doctors, and we'll finish the job! I like that. I like that a lot. You've got priests and ministers saying straight out: "We've reached critical mass." There are enough families upset by the time it takes their loved ones to die. Too long. And they're saying, damn it, that's not right! I respect that, Cledwyn.'

'And I respect that, August,' said Mr Fox. 'A lot.'

He felt so much respect he called a meeting of all the elders to hear about the new patient militancy. Night Matron was there and Imelda and Jack, licking his lips and grinning like a demon. He didn't look much like a giant killer, Beryl the Beard decided. That yellow hair, square jaw. More of a farm boy. Mr Fox promised to begin drafting Living Wills that everyone could use. Max Montfalcon, after listening to Dr Tonks, grunted.

73

'You think people should go willingly when they're past it?'

'Not past it. Up against it.'

'Somebody else will have to give them a nudge. Take the decision.'

'Someone has to decide now, Mr Montfalcon. Every time we take a patient off a kidney machine. Every time we decide not to resuscitate mechanically. Every time we remove feeding tubes. Every time a kindly family doctor overprescribes for his suffering patient and the family do the rest. Everyone who goes on a machine means we decide against that machine for someone whose need is arguably just as great. We're talking about merciful release versus merciless machines.'

'It will never work,' said Max. 'Believe me. It's been tried.'

'Not to my knowledge,' said Dr Tonks. 'Only the Americans are debating it. What are we going to do with ageing populations and limited resources in hospital and home?'

'Americans,' said Max. 'Poor devils. At least, once upon a time, killing each other was a young person's activity. Now the old will have it on demand. You reach a certain age. It's found you're ill. And why? You ate too much ice-cream. You didn't drink enough mineral water. They have you into hospital and you're doubly doomed. You have this disease. Failed once. You're old. Failed twice. So how do they solve this problem? You fill in a form. You make a neat death. Someone divided societies into those who chose the raw or the cooked. From now on it's the tidy and the untidy. What would happen if you sat down with a patient and asked him to sign a form ensuring a good life?'

'That', said Dr Tonks, 'would be an assault on personal freedom.' He appealed to Jack. 'What does our American think?'

Jack thought about it. He closed his eyes. He said: 'OK!' It was a start. But it wouldn't do. Un-fuckin'-real, thought Jack to himself. He put his finger in his ear and wriggled it. Then he said the word. He didn't like to use the word too often because it was the only one he always had in his head. Ready to fire.

'Video,' said Jack and pulled his finger out of his ear.

'Now that', said Dr Tonks in a quiet voice, 'is one of the most brilliant ideas I've ever heard! Don't get me wrong. I am not on the iron edge in this. You get some pit bulls among the geriatric profession who argue that life should never be extended beyond its productive capacities. I don't go that far. After all it's only a step away from that position to saying that life should be terminated as soon as it is not productive. And we all know where that led.' Dr Tonks gave his warm, brown laugh. 'Straight to the extermination camps.'

'Oh, right,' said Mr Fox, relieved that Dr Tonks did not have eventide refuges in mind.

'The camps began in the hospitals,' Max murmured. 'Then the hospitals moved to the camps.'

But Dr Tonks was in full flow. His eyes flashed, his affable smile came and went. He said: 'Don't follow you, Mr Montfalcon. Look – I'm not a pit bull. But neither am I a poodle in the med-assist matter, as our American cousins call it. I take more of a Dobermann line. If patient requests – well and good. Patient also to be advised on what lies ahead. Particularly in the EP–LTT frame.'

'What's that?' asked Cledwyn Fox.

'Excessive Pain, Low Time Threshold. Less than six months.'

Mr Fox heard how wonderfully August Tonks dealt with an EP plus LTT case when Serenity House admitted the Gooches: Elsie and her husband Norman. Dr Tonks made them a pot of tea and then chatted about last things. Norman Gooch was a bit testy at first.

'I don't want to die, Doctor.'

'None of us do, Mr Gooch. But may I respectfully remind you we do have a little cancer. And our cancer is in an advanced stage. Preterminal.'

'I want to live till I die,' said Norman Gooch, small and wan in his green checked coat and purple tie.

'That', said Dr Tonks, 'is not the nub, Mr Gooch. The nub is – do we want our dying to be prolonged?'

'The doctor's only trying to help,' Elsie Gooch told her husband. 'Norman is as stubborn as a mule, Doctor.'

Dr Tonks smiled warmly. He pressed Norman Gooch's hand. Norman recoiled. He had not had his hand pressed since he was a boy. 'The problem may be, Mr Gooch, unless you give instructions to the contrary, that when you would really prefer to be somewhere else, the medical staff won't be able to act. Fearful of the law. Maybe told by your relatives to keep you going, come what may, while deep inside yourself, Mr Gooch, but unable to utter a word, you are praying to—'

'Leave the room?'

'You've taken the words out of my mouth.'

Norman Gooch thought about this. 'My GP says six months. What do you say?'

'Without having examined you, Mr Gooch, Norman – may I call you Norman? – I wouldn't like to commit myself. But if you'll take a word of advice from a labourer in the vineyard, six months sometimes doesn't amount to six weeks.'

'Six weeks?' Mr Gooch unknotted his tie. 'Hardly seems worthwhile, does it? Why wait till it gets so bad I can't stand it? Is that what you're saying? Like taking a cold bath. Might as well jump in?'

'Norman hates cold baths,' said Elsie Gooch.

Dr Tonks looked Norman Gooch straight in the eyes, long and deep: 'That's up to your, sir. Absolutely. But if that's what you decide, I would respect your decision. I have a little form here, designed with people like you in mind.'

'Save a lot of bother, wouldn't it?' asked Norman Gooch, and now he was holding Dr Tonks's hand.

Dr Tonks was true to his word. A nod to Night Matron and it went like magic. Matron told Imelda and Imelda told Jack and just twenty-four hours later, the boys from Dove's were backing their collection vehicles up to the ramp in the back yard of Serenity House.

'There wasn't even time to leave his bag in the luggage depository,' Night Matron told Cledwyn Fox proudly and Mr Fox said, 'Bless you, Matron.'

'No, bless you, Mr Fox.'

And Jack said, 'Boy, oh boy, oh boy!'

'Where would we be without Americans?' asked Dr Tonks.

Elsie Gooch followed her husband a week later. It led to the first use of a phrase heard often in Serenity House on winter evenings, when the dovecall signalled lights out and the elders, by wheelchair and Zimmer frame and walking stick, on the arms of key-helpers, made their slow way to bed. The Gooches, it was agreed, had been 'tonked'.

Chapter Seven

Tales his Mother Told Him

Not so very long ago, in the Tranquil Pines Mobile Home Park out on Orange Avenue, south of Orlando, after he lost his job in the Kingdom and began lying about, Jack had trouble with his other mother, old Marta. She began dying. It was a time before he began taking it in. He had this selection of unusual videos from the Aardvark Video Emporium and they absorbed him. Except when he got hungry.

On the day they took old Marta away, Jack had been watching a fine piece of footage about wild-life in the desert. He liked it because it made him even hungrier.

Jack had listened for years now to old Marta telling him she was dying, and had simply not believed it. At eighty, she looked so solid still, with her thick grey hair and her clear blue eyes. She gripped his hand – boy, it hurt! – and said: 'I've seen enough of it. Shouldn't I know what is and is not dying?'

Jack had not been a very good boy. He still wasn't such a great boy. But he didn't try to kill people any more. He didn't keep going back to houses of correction, like about three times a year. Thirty-five offences by the time he was fifteen. Knives and chains. Stabbings and muggings. Mostly OK, so he'd tried to kill Miss Priam, his English teacher over at George Washington High. But that only because she tried to get him to read when she knew he struggled. Didn't he say 'Don't' when she pulled out her books and showed him pictures of turtles? She brought the turtles because she knew he looked at the tube a lot and turtles were on the tube. Didn't he say to her, 'Can't' when she pointed her finger at a turtle and said, 'Try, Jack.

Just try for Miss Priam'? And he'd said, sticking his finger in his ear and pulling the words from so deep in his head it hurt, 'Gimme zero. Just gimme zero! OK?' But she pushed him. So he popped her. Who wouldn't? The metal detector teams had not come round to George Washington High that day. So he had his piece snug beneath his arm. And she took a slug in the chest, did Miss Priam. And had they not staunched the wound with the fucking turtle pages, she would've stayed popped and Jack might have stayed in the iron box for ever and ever with even Marta not able to bail him. But the turtles saved Miss Priam and Marta got this lawyer who argued that Jack wasn't really bad. He just had this reading problem. And the way Miss Priam had pushed him, begged him, taunted him, had sent the poor young lad loco. Marta took him home. Marta hired him a bunch of piccies, his favourite piccies, from the Aardvark Video Special Adult Section. All Tastes Catered For . . . and sat him down on the rug and Jack had never looked back. Or up, much, either.

Marta had been looking after him since his mother 'went West'. Where Jack was when she 'went West', as Marta told him she had done, he had no idea. But in Jack's mind she'd always headed for cowboy country, to work in a saloon, or maybe a nice haberdashery store, selling buttons and bows, that sort of thing. In Jack's dreams his mother wore a cowboy hat, sometimes she carried a guitar, always she wore white boots. In his dreams nothing ever happened to his mother. Jack was not sure any more which came first – his videos or his dreams. She was the only person in Jack's dreams to whom nothing happened. She wasn't, like, shot in the face, the flesh peeling back to show the skull beneath, the teeth flecked with blood. Or disembowelled – one lunge and lift to the sword . . . No. And always when things got lively in Jack's dreams it was Jack who was doing the business. He'd fast-forward to action and do it. Then run the action replays. But nothing ever happened to Jack's mother in his dreams. Early, when he woke, she wasn't there. Again.

Instead he had Marta, his other mother, who had looked after him since he couldn't remember when. She was the one who tried to get him to go to school. She tried to get him to stay in school. Dealt with his probation officer. Kept him in pieces. Bailed him out when he got older and wilder and ran with Fat Mansy and that crowd for a time. Rented him his first videos – now that had really helped to calm him down. And she never minded what he watched. Nothing shocked Marta. She had travelled. Her stories were so good that he thought he must have seen the movie, until he asked for it, down at the Aardvark Emporium, and they said they'd never heard of stuff so good – and the Aardvark had every good thing. Their ads promised: 'If it's the goodest! The Aardvark's got it!'

'Once I worked with a man. He was so tall, Jack. And perfectly polite. He was a doctor and not a doctor. Not a medical doctor, I mean – like our Dr Castro. And he spoke English very well – not like Dr Castro. This man was a kind man. For instance, so you should know what I mean – he never did anything in the productions department in the place where we were. A thousand people in twenty-four hours was the production rate, at this time, Jack. You could see the two large smoke-stacks from the window of our institute – that's where I worked with the tall guy.

'I was a nurse, mind you, never a doctor. Not medical, anyway. We were both in the wrong place at the wrong time. What could we do but stick together? A surgical nurse who's got some years in the business knows more than some young doctors. Do you wonder how a nurse can be a nurse one day and almost a doctor the next? Then ask: how can you be a doctor one day and a killer the next? Such miracles! They were happening all the time.

'No, like I say, this man never did production in the place where we were. All he wanted to do was to measure. Heads, mostly. But me, little old me, I did production. Yes – when I had to. Because look – you get them coming in, the new ones. All are thin and sick – but some are dying. And so you say to yourself – if they come into the camp, then in a day or so they're dead. All Mussulmans. Those were the ones who were all bone and bowing down like they were praying to Mecca. Walking dead. Zombies. So you had to choose. And, anyway, you know you can't take more than another single soul in the hospital. So you choose. I chose. We were always having to choose in the place where we were. Some people think that they murdered us. Yes, they did. But we murdered us, too.

'But the giant, he had none of this. Heads, heads, heads! That's all it was with him. "Marta!" he would say. "My kingdom for a head!" That's a joke out of Shakespeare. This man knew a lot of English. Imagine that – in the place where we were. And he saved me once. I got typhoid. And they had me in the shower party. The trucks came – but then he came over and told them "Let her go – she's getting better. Can't you see?" And he said to me, close, hard in my ear, "Take my arm and walk. Walk or die!" And I walked. Another miracle. He was tall and strong and I walked on his arm.'

Especially, Jack enjoyed Marta's story about Morris the Mussulman.

'In my life, the life before this one, I had a friend called Morris. He was a pathologist.'

'Path-ol-o-gist!' Jack loved the round, brown taste of the word. He ate it up and licked his lips.

'In the place where we were, Morris died. That was before I met the giant. I made notes for Morris before he died. He was a doctor, Jack – with a fine sense of humour. He liked to observe his own progress.'

And what had been the progress of Morris the Mussulman?

Jack knew it by heart. Let Marta miss a single stage of Morris the Mussulman's progress and Jack would be on to her in a flash:

'Oedema . . . moderate emaciation . . . moderate oedema . . . intensive oedema with lowered plasma . . . '

'Death?' Jack would ask.

'Death,' Marta confirmed.

And that was the end of Morris the Mussulman.

But the giant lived on in Marta's stories, Marta's mind where she walked and talked with him. First, she remembered her home.

'In nineteen-forty-one I was in Cracow. Certain people were picked. Parcels. At first just small parcels were chosen. Then more and more. They were posted to the villages in the surrounding countryside. Or they were posted to the ghetto at Podgorze, on the other side of the Vistula. Small parcels.'

Jack would hold his thumb and forefinger to the light to show how small the parcels had been and Marta always said: 'A bit bigger, Jack.'

'Then bigger parcels. Then it was decided that everyone should be posted. Everyone in Kazimierz was expelled to Podgorze. Rehoused, they called it. *Wypchnąć zyda drzwiza on ci piecem wlezie.*'

'Is that Polish?'

'It means: "If you throw a Jew out of the door, he will creep back into the house through the stove". It's an old Polish proverb. Anyway, it explains why everyone was removed from Kazimierz. Sixty thousand altogether.'

Then there were 'the lice'. This was one of the giant's stories which he had told to Marta. The giant had known a certain Professor Huppe. This professor collected heads. Made plaster casts of them and sent them to the great skeleton collection in Strasbourg. But one day the professor picked lice off a corpse.

'Four,' said Jack.

'Typhoid fever,' said Marta.

'Dead in a week,' said Jack.

At other times, Marta told another story:

'First there was the selection on the ramp. Then the doctor rides the ambulance across to the showers. Then he decides how many pellets. Then he checks the result. That's when they put on the gas masks. And it was so funny – even if they looked like doctors first – because when they put on the masks they all looked like pigs. Afterwards forms to fill in. How many treated? How many teeth pulled? The dentists from hell got busy then. Some of the teeth always went missing. But with the people who'd owned them first gone missing too, how were they to be found? Two things were known about the place where we were. The doctor who wasn't a doctor was a good enough man. And he was rich.'

The best dreams Jack knew were those that kept you awake. One of the big downers about Marta dying was that she didn't tell him his favourite stories the way she used to. She just lay there on the big wooden bed with the angels in the painting between the bed-posts. Fat, pink, girlish angels playing fiddles that kind of sagged like they'd been put in the oven by mistake and melted. The picture was in a frame of black wood.

Dr Castro parked in the trucking depot, a stretch of wasteland behind the mobile home park. Slightly less chance of his beautiful Ferrari taking a walk, or being crippled, scarred or torched. No way would he drive into the park itself. Kids were so hyped-up in there it was like Beirut.

Dr Castro had treated Marta when she could still pay. She had not paid him now for months. But he went on seeing her. Immigrants should stick together. And the poor woman lived with the boy with a brick for a head; a tube where his heart should be. A slob, loafer, creep. Yes, immigrants should stick together and help to protect each other from natural Americans, like her crazy son Jack. Dr Castro double-locked his Ferrari, moved swiftly around the Burger King on the corner, and walked down the track between elderly Pontiacs and mobile homes with small chimneys in their roofs, and the rusted back-ends of air-conditioners, like wounds that would not heal, gaping moistly as he passed.

Marta's caravan was the last on the left, before you ran into a swampy patch of reeds and a dead, dark pond at the end of the track. Three-fifty a month. An elderly loquat tree leaned above the roof of Marta's home. A line of irritable crows carried on the kind of conversation he'd only heard from stockbrokers. Somewhere behind him the ceaseless traffic of Orange Avenue, north to Orlando, south past Lake Conway, on to Kissimee, roared like the ocean.

Yes, immigrants should stick together. Only that morning Dr Castro had learnt that his application for membership of the Clear Lake Country Club had been rejected. 'It's not that we have anything against Hispanics, or any other ethnic group,' the club secretary explained frankly, 'it's just that some of the members feel entitled to hear English spoken, now and then. They're American citizens; they don't like living in a foreign country.' When his own country was free again, and its dictator, his namesake, overthrown, then, Dr Castro prayed, it would become an island for the settlement of natural Americans: those who ate only pizza, dreamed of killing someone soon, believed all they saw in the movies and spoke only English. Like a country club reserved for their special use. Wouldn't that be good? 'You betcha!' Dr Castro told himself. He was learning English fast, though he travelled everywhere with a fat black Spanish–English dictionary.

Dr Castro knocked gently on the flimsy door of Marta's trailer and, stooping slowly, a dignified lowering of his shining dark head, he walked inside. Sprawled on the floor, in front of the TV, sat Jack wondering what it would be like to eat – a giraffe. He was watching pictures of the occupation of Kuwait, hungry Iraqi soldiers eating the animals in Kuwait Zoo. Now that was pretty neat. The cameras brought him close-ups of the carcass of a half-devoured giraffe. Its bones, barrel-like and bare, shone in the sun. Jack was reminded of Big Bennie's Rib Cage, 'Eat Till You're Beat!' said Big Bennie. And Jack said, 'Yo, boy,' to that. Jack ignored the doctor's presence and if he heard him enter Marta's bedroom he gave no sign of it. Nor did he look up twenty minutes later when Dr Castro left Marta's bedside and offered his diagnosis with the help of his Spanish–English dictionary.

Dr Castro looked around at the remains of dozens of Chinese meals in their Styrofoam boxes, piled one on the other. These were the walls in Jack's life, the Great Wall of China, made up of old Chinese meals. And then the video wall, box after box of nightly delights for the boy Jack. There was *Dwarf Killer 3* and *KIDS*. Yes, Dr Castro knew that one. That was about the Bolivian vet with an interest in particle physics who stalked and caught young children around Miami, ate their soft organs and, by a method known only to a remote tribe of Bolivian Indians, shrank their heads to a size convenient for their use as glove puppets with which he gave shows at kids' parties across the city. Very popular those puppets. The occasions, of course, were used by the Bolivian headshrinker to garner more kids for his larder. His greatest triumph came when a children's fund issued a series of Christmas cards featuring his puppets. The video had been one of the hot shots of the season and when busybodies tried to get it banned, civil liberties groups had picketed the town hall.

'Your – granny – is being taken. Her time is nigh. Are you listening what I tell – creep?'

Dr Castro closed his pigskin case, that sleek sausage packed with steel and glass. Jack heard the crisp snap and he thought, yes, that's Dr Castro closing his nice yellow case full of knives and rubber hoses. Nine neat syringes and a stethoscope. *Steth-o-scope!* Just to say the word made Jack salivate. Jack wanted to steal Dr Castro's case. He had wanted to steal it for ever so many years. The only trouble was that, in order to steal the case, he knew he'd have to kill Dr Castro first. He kept it chained to him, that costly pigskin case, 'because of the neighbourhood,' Dr Castro used to explain, peering out of the window into the soft, liquid, Florida light and shutting his case with its priceless click. 'Here I wouldn't wear a rosary. If a man walked round with a crown of thorns someone would mug him, believe me, Jesus.'

Dr Castro called the Abe Lincoln Memorial Hospital. He called the ambulance. He directed the guys when they arrived with the stretcher and Marta, eyes closed, was taken from her home – the ambulance men stepping over the reclining Jack who never said a thing.

He was watching a woman in chainmail castrating a stockbroker. You knew he was a stockbroker because this was taking place at night on the floor of the New York Stock Exchange and because the camera cut between the open mouths of the dealers bellowing like branded steers during the daytime's trading session on the crowded dealing floor and the O of horror made by the mouth of the man in the hands of the lady in chainmail who held a hunting knife in one hand and his erect penis in the other. Even at the door, Dr Castro checked himself and thought – a bit far-fetched that erection, allowing himself this little medical flourish in passing and pleased to be thinking again in native Spanish. I mean, some time to get a cock-stand! Oh, man! while watching her slice the stalwart member at its base in a mushroom of blood. Doctor though he was, he turned before she began on the testicles, while Jack licked his lips and watched the bloody globes dropping slowly into the sacrificial silver dish. 'Boing, boing!' Jack carolled happily. He'd seen *Chopper* several times and was entitled to the light, jesting demeanour of the film buff, not so much ribaldry, as affectionate recognition.

*

Reclining on the carpet in the main room of the box on wheels that it was his privilege to inhabit, Jack had run out of money for new videos. The distant portals of the Aardvark Video Emporium saw him no more. Instead, he was watching TV, propped by an elbow upon a pink leather pouffe.

Jack was hungry. No Marta. No money. No movies. No food. He had not eaten in two days. No more seaweed for Jack; no beef in black bean sauce, Mr Hung's speciality; no bean sprouts, no lemon chicken, no special fried rice, none of the delights of the Pleasure Garden wedged into a tiny space, on the broad and thundering grey macadam river that is Orange Avenue, red roof, lacquered shutters, between the Orlando Foot Clinic and the Syrian Lebanese American Club. No, not even so much as a prawn cracker.

Jack thought of the treasures Marta had hidden, of the times she would get out of bed and appear in the TV room, rather shaky, sure, but definitely Marta, swaying a bit and holding on to the back of the cane chair with the red cushion seat, wearing her old Chinese stole, the one with the dragons – 'Once, Jack, there were two Dragons, little and large, whose mother perished in a terrible fire . . . ' – her face so grey it looked almost blue in the flickering light of the screen. She held – what? Wrapped in pink tissue paper.

Now, Jack thought, he could go and take a look under Marta's bed.

If Marta had known about that she'd have killed him. How would she have killed him? Ah, well, she would probably have followed the method she'd told him about. It was one of his favourite stories: after forcing him to dig a trench in the ground she would make him kneel in front of it and then very quickly, but carefully (at least he had assumed it would have to be carefully, after all you couldn't be running up and down the line shouting oops! didn't do you properly, back in a moment), she would shoot him in the back of the head. One shot and he'd tumble into the ditch to join dozens of other Jacks. You could believe in it. Like you could believe in the story when Marta told it to him: 'Towards the end, when we began to get all these Hungarians, the place was too full. Maybe a few thousand each day had to be specially treated. All the facilities were full to overflowing so we went manual. To take care of the load. I remember a man called Breitkopf was one of those who did it. They made them dig first, a trench, in the early morning. Then they knelt along the side. Edge? Anyway, whatever. The border of the trench is what they knelt along. And then Breitkopf treated them and they fell into the trench one by one. Then the fire followed. However, and this is important, there was a shortage of fuel at this time. So what did they do? That's right – they *improvised*! They gathered the fat, yes? The fat that comes from our own bodies, they collected it. From earlier treatments. In pails. And with these pails the fires in the trenches were fed.'

'Snap!' Jack liked to shout at this point in the story. 'Crackle, pop!'

Jack drew Marta's treasures from the dark beneath Marta's big wooden bed, where she used to lie all day staring up at the pink angels playing their silent music until Jack wanted to scream and hit them so they would make a sound. He tore off the pink wrapping paper.

CHAPTER EIGHT

Jack Goes to Market

Nicely filling a brown bag from Mr Hung's Pleasure Garden, still with a hint of 'crab claws à la Chinoise', was a bundle of goodies scooped from beneath Marta's bed. Jack placed the bag carefully on the desk before Mr Kaufmann. Mr Kaufmann, having greeted him warmly in the Kissimee Flea Market, was standing elegantly before his table laden with antique 'sharps': hair clippers, nail cutters, scalpels, tweezers, cut-throat razors, pincers, moustache trimmers, ear-hair twiddlers, secateurs, nostril-hair shapers, flick knives, surgical probes, dental needles. 'Step this way, young man', Mr Kaufmann said, 'into my special office, my den. We will be less public, less pointed. The cutting edge of things without, the *anus mundi* within.' And Jack said, 'Gee, sir, anus – what?' and Mr Kaufmann smiled his gentle smile and said, 'Later, my boy, later. First let's see what you've brought me.'

Jack had made a sweep of the Flea Markets before finding Mr Kaufmann. They were dotted around from Kissimee to the far north of Orange County. Giant plastic oranges, as big as aircraft hangars, full of T-shirts and promises that they did not sell 'abused merchandise', offering instead Tex-Mex snacks, Disney souvenirs, Florida crafts, suitcases, clothes, cosmetics, toys and underwear and a thousand bad imitations of Swiss watches. Coral reef ripped untimely from the sad sea-bed and tortured into necklaces. Approximate imitations of 'big-name' perfumes.

Mr Kaufmann, thin and smiling, sported a cow's lick of

strong grey hair falling across his papery white forehead, shaped like a sickle, and little round steel-rimmed glasses that caught the light and threw it back in pinks and lavenders as if there was a party going on about an inch above his nose which Mr Kaufmann knew nothing about. He wore a grey suit. He looked like a businessman ought to look.

But his friends! Why, they looked just like butterflies, or tropical birds in vivid plumage perched around the sides of Mr Kaufmann's jet black executive desk. Mr Kaufmann went around the circle. Jack took in baggy pink and shimmering gold shot through with black thread. The Japanese-looking friend wore a pair of huge purple pants. Mr Kaufmann ticked off his friends, licking his finger each time as he pointed, as if he were turning the pages of a book, or, no – rather, as if he were counting off money from a big fat wad of greenbacks. Lick, flick . . . 'This is Agliotti, Giuseppi. And the gentleman here? He is Suares. That's Tony Suares to his friends. Right? And meet next Gary Soonono,' lick, flick. 'My partners and friends. Experts each in their fields. Madonnas of the Black Forest – Agliotti, who else? All of them of world renown, the only kind I'd have as my associates. Suares, Tony to you, handles sexual aids through the ages, belts, whips, inflatable rats for those of more Proustian tastes. You name it, Tony will date it, provenance it – float a figure for the catalogue. Soonono? Well, he's rock and pop ephemera through those same ages. Those ages get bigger, faster, as we move into modern times. Thus we can say that the leader of the Beach Boys is the Leonardo da Vinci of pop. And Tony Suares has his first surfboard, and Bill Haley's kiss curl, right down to the toilet seat said to be the very one upon which the late great King Presley expired in his bathroom. Though, in the case of this item, provenance is difficult to nail down. Am I right in saying that, Soonie?'

'Provenance a real bastard,' agreed Soonono.

Kaufmann patted the empty chair beside him. 'Sit, sit, boy, and show me what you've brought.'

Jack sat as he was told and handed over his paper bag.

'Mr Hung's Pleasure Garden?' said Mr Kaufmann raising wispy eyebrows like fragile feathers above his glasses. 'Crab claws à la Chinoise?'

Jack was so impressed he could only nod and smile, showing his strong white teeth. 'Live on 'em.'

'We all have to live on something – don't we Giuseppi?' asked Mr Kaufmann. 'It's only reasonable.'

Mr Kaufmann opened the bag and drew out three packages. Neat, wrapped in pink tissue paper, tied with waxy yellow twine. He placed them gently on his knees. With doctor's hands he lifted the first parcel on to the desk, undid the twine and began unwrapping it carefully.

What emerged looked like a pair of giant tweezers.

'Ice-tongs,' guessed Soonono.

'Fire-tongs?' Agliotti tried.

'Closer. Or at least warmer,' murmured Mr Kaufmann as he laid the tongs carefully in the centre of his big black desk. 'Callipers,' whispered Mr Kaufmann. 'Oh, Jack, what *have* you brought me?'

Then he took the next pink parcel and, so softly you could hear them all breathing, he unwrapped it. 'Well, gentlemen?'

'Easy this time,' said Agliotti.

'Too easy,' said Suares. 'Seen enough of those. Place is lousy with them. Whole damn country is lousy with them.'

'Shooting sticks,' Agliotti said.

'Pretty old and dirty but sharp and pointed. Needles. Definitely not to be passed around,' said Soonono.

'Syringes, two,' said Kaufmann. 'Circa nineteen forty-two or 'forty-three. Not used since then, I'll bet. All that time hidden in the darkness waiting for this day.'

'Under her bed,' Jack confirmed.

Mr Kaufmann held the syringes to the light. He looked up at their glass bodies high above his head and smiled a really happy smile. 'If you look carefully, you'll see a deposit adhering to the side of the glass. We'll leave it to the laboratory tests to prove it. But I'll lay a hundred to one we'll find phenol traces. It's rather yellow, you see? It would have once been a kind of pinky yellow. Directly into the heart, it was injected. They tried a lot of stuff first. Benzine, hydrogen peroxide, prussic acid. Even tried air. Yessir! Sometimes into the vein. But that took longer so they found a quicker method. A stubby syringe. Like this. And a good long needle. This wasn't for intravenous stuff.

89

This they pushed – just here,' and Mr Kaufmann tapped himself slowly on the chest. 'It went into the fifth rib space. Straight into the heart in fact. The numbers treated varied. "Sprayed" they called it. *Abgespritzt* in the jargon of the time. The going rate was about fifty treated in anything up to two hours. On a good day. If we can show that there is phenol in these syringes then the value quintuples. Oh, happy days!' And he wrapped up the syringes in their pink paper and placed them gently beside the callipers. 'It brings up the short hairs on the back of my neck.' Mr Kaufmann stroked the back of his neck and Jack did the same. It was true. He could feel his hairs rising. 'Very rare, these syringes. Very fragile and hardly any at all remain – except in very special collections. To have two, to have two survive, with traces! I say again, happy days!'

And now he was unwrapping the last of the three parcels carefully, gently, the fingers like wings, Jack thought, even though it was a very thin package. Because he hated silence and wanted to pass the time and was beginning so to like Mr Kaufmann, Jack made a little conversation. Mr Kaufmann had friends. So Jack told them about his friend Josh. The sound of his own voice broke the silence. Silence was like the grey cold hole when the screen went dead. Silence was like waking up in the deep of the night with nothing in your head and hurting from the emptiness.

'My friend Josh, he died,' Jack began. 'Ordered this real live gallows from Fat Mansy's catalogue. Silken rope, hangman's knot, mobile scaffold – the works. Black leather tunic and cutaway gloves. He spent hours trying it out in front of the mirror. Trying it out – right? Nothing serious. So what happens? One afternoon he slips, stumbles, falls – I don't know, anyhow, he *drop*! His girl, Miranda, she finds him. Swinging. What can she do? She gets over to Fat Mansy's place, Guns 'n' Gold, on Orange Avenue and says: What you gonna do about it, you fat dwork? And Mansy says: What d'you want – a refund? Did he read the instructions? Those traps can be dangerous, if you don't read the instructions. I'm pregnant, says Miranda. You are! says Fat Mansy. Well, you should've taken precautions!'

'What I'd like to know', Tony Suares chipped in, 'is do Americans like killing people? An inbuilt trait? OK we know they like reading about it. Love watching it. Videos – movies. In their heads. But is it natural? Part of the job definition? Like the French love garlic. And the British crazy about the weather.'

'Difficult one that, Tony,' said Soonono. 'In theory I guess you'd have to say they do. *In theory* yes, I'd say they like doing it. In art, they're streets ahead. Write a book about a man who kills nuns and slices off their breasts and you win prizes. So OK, why not? It's a free country. Tell the city fathers you want to take photographs of kids, while sodomising the little angels, and they'll give you a grant. Write a musical about a yuppy who kills tramps in New York and you'll pack 'em in.'

Mr Kaufmann had opened the package now. It held a large brown envelope. Jack's heart sank. Letters! Writing! He'd hoped for more *things*. Except Mr Kaufmann didn't seem the least disappointed. Out of the brown envelope he took a pile of letters written in dark ink in a crabbed hand. The paper on which they were written was white and it had shrivelled at the edges and gone a little yellow in places. These letters had a parchmenty feel and sound to them. They crackled in his fingers. Except for one which was written on blue airmail paper. Mr Kaufmann smoothed them out with his palm and smiled like he was very happy indeed.

'If you ask me, Tony, you put the question wrong.' Mr Kaufmann was reading silently while he talked. Jack was agog. Mr Kaufmann was reading something and saying another. At the same time! He had never seen anything like that before. 'The question is not: "Do Americans like killing people?" I think we've got a pretty much open and shut case on that. No, the question really is – and I'd say the jury is still out on this – "Do Americans like being killed?" And we'd have to say the answer to that question is "no", considering the fuss they make when one of their planes is bombed out of the sky. Or there is a war somewhere in the world which goes wrong. Or some crazy guy drives a truck of dynamite into a barracks full of soldiers. They yell so loud you can hear them in Timbuktu. Now what d'you call that, Gary? Tony?'

'Unreasonable?'

Mr Kaufmann applauded. 'Got it in one, Tony.' He picked up a letter and hit it against his open palm. 'Now, you take the

Germans, they're different. At least there was a time when they were different. I've got a German letter here, Ed. Listen to this.' And Mr Kaufmann began reading from the letter, translating as he went along, which he had just been beating against his palm.

Today, I really got into my work. I am processing the forms at a great rate. After which I take measurements. I am managing to process at least forty forms in a morning but I hope with practice this will increase soon. From a scientific point of view the work is fascinating and will bear much fruit in the future . . .

Mr Kaufmann leaned back from his desk and smiled a smile as big as the moon. 'Forms,' he said. 'Processing!'

Soonono and Suares and Agliotti looked puzzled but respectful. They loomed around Mr Kaufmann in their gorgeous clothes and their reflections glimmered in the polished surface of his black desk.

Mr Kaufmann touched the tips of his fingers together. 'These are *some* letters! You note the punctiliousness of utterance, Gary – Tony – Giuseppi – Jack? Behind "the forms" here talked about we may detect doomed people. Men and women destined for death. Indeed many of them may already have been dead. By injection. Yes, Ed, you guessed it, the syringes. Each form was a human being – to be put down like strays in a dogs' home. The place from which these letters come has been blanked out. The censor, I expect. But they are dated, all of them, 1941. That's also interesting. Listen, here's another:

Well, at long last Berlin has responded to my request for help. Measurements are often difficult and accuracy is of the first importance. I have today taken delivery of a new assistant, one Behrens. He is not very well qualified but he shows willing . . .

'This is an approximate translation,' Mr Kaufmann explained. 'A more elegant version will be available later.'

'I guess the date is important,' said Soonono.

'Oh, yes. I think this referred to the early stages of a project which was secret at the time. They code-named it 14f13. It grew out of what was called T4. And that, in turn, was something we might call enthanasia for civilian purposes. 14f13 built on that early work. It was the militarisation of the killing programme across a very wide front: gypsies, gays, Jews, Jehovah's Witnesses, the screwy, the ill, masons, Communists, Catholics. But, here, let me hit you again.'

April '41

My little rabbit,

Work progresses very favourably. The theoretical point at issue, which as you know interests me greatly, is how to provide scientific anthropological, or at least archaeological, evidence, from prehistoric times which will help to support the present investigations of our scientists into the various identities of races in the eastern Raum. Unfortunately much miscegenation had taken place and so you get, as you would expect from funerary evidence, much resemblance between peoples. You get chunkier heads, flatter faces, you get a high incidence of prominent cheekbones, you get broad noses and thick hair. In other words we have to get beneath the skin, right down to what I might call the bone of the matter in order to make distinctions. The early German settlers in these eastern lands were, as we know, overwhelmed by the Slav hordes.

The urgency of this work cannot be underestimated. There is evidence that the very material upon which we work grows every day scarcer. Tracing the unfolding of ethnic complexities is a painstaking business. There are blood groups to be taken, fingerprints, studies of the eyes, particularly the iris. Quite apart from my own interest in skull formation.

I am sorry to say that Behrens, my new assistant, is not proving very worthwhile. He is clumsy and seems quite unable to understand that material must be treated with restraint, even after the event. And Berlin – oh, Berlin! – it asks for more and more. I am now processing anything up to two hundred and fifty forms per day. That is a considerable rate, even with Behrens hindering more than he helps. And yet the pressures on those responsible for this processing increase. Berlin asks for more and more irrespective of whether I have completed my measurements.

Luckily, I have had a stroke of good fortune. I now have assistance from the reservoir. Marta is her name. Trained as a nurse, without fundamental anthropological experience, she is none the less neat and careful in the measurements. That is all I ask.

Think of me, my darling rabbit. Your tall fir tree makes plans for dropping in on a visit soon.

Loving kisses,

M

'Fascinating reading.' Mr Kaufmann shuffled the letters on the table as if reconstituting a deck of cards. 'Think of it all: the troublesome Behrens, interfering Berlin, M – the measurer. Marta the helper . . . What a happy family. Good. Now, Jack, let's talk business.'

You might have thought to look at him that Jack, poor Jack, did not know much. You would have thought, such being the tough circumstances of the business world, that Mr Kaufmann saw him coming. But Jack, though a mere boy without family or fortune or employment, lazy, feckless, dreaming only of crab claws and exceptionally violent videos, was no sucker. He knew an offer was coming and when it did he limited his sales to the three 1941 letters only.

'At a thousand bucks a throw.' And was amazed when they agreed.

The airmail, longer letter, also in German he asked Mr Kaufmann to translate for him, and listened entranced while he did so and clapped at the end, marvelling that man could think in German and speak in English. It seemed to Jack that if this were a cache of material of such value that Mr Kaufmann would part with big bucks for little bits of it, then there must be more where that came from.

Mr Kaufmann agreed with an elegant inclination of the head. The airmail letter contained an address.

'In London, England,' said Soonono.

'Across the sea,' said Suares.

'Ever thought of travelling?' Mr Kaufmann enquired.

94

For the three 1941 letters, Agliotti paid Jack in new, bright notes. 'Could be a bushel where that came from,' said Agliotti. 'If you bottom out your collection.'

'A unique collection.' Mr Kaufmann's glasses began to hold their airborne party again. 'Material of the first importance. Items for which some mighty fine people I know would give their right arms, my dear Jack.'

Off at the shoulder or the elbow? Jack wondered, but all he said was, 'You're kidding!'

'Most everything is collectable these days. If very special tastes are involved. Gary, copy Mr Jack's long letter and I will give him a translation. Unique!' said Mr Kaufmann again.

'No copies!' Jack smiled. He put the letters into the back pocket of his jeans and sat on them. No copies they said in his videos, too. It stopped the pirates. Mr Kaufmann did not look like a pirate. Certainly not like the 'yo ho ho and a bottle of rum' pirate, or a pirate with piglet like they had over at the Magic Kingdom. But Jack was not taking any chances.

'You talk it in English,' he said to Mr Kaufmann. He pointed at Agliotti. 'And you write it for me. In big letters. No joined-up writing.'

'Smart kid.' Mr Kaufmann smiled his party smile. 'OK, Giuseppi, got your pen? Got your paper? Here we go.'

'Boy, oh boy, oh boy!' said Jack. Marta would get better. He'd buy her doctors and nurses. Now they would have private rooms and prawn crackers and at least six new videos. He wanted to tell them but he didn't. He felt it wouldn't be polite and, say what you like about Jack, he could be polite when he wanted. Instead he asked: 'And what's your special thing, Mr Kaufmann?'

Mr Kaufmann had the blue letter in his hands and the lights in his glasses were dancing like this was some kind of victory parade. He talked and Agliotti wrote it all down, and the eyes he turned on Jack when he laid down the letter had in them a considerable kindness.

'Fire', Mr Kaufmann said quietly, 'and fury. My special thing is the world aflame and burnt to a cinder.'

'Yes,' Jack asked, still polite, 'but what do you – like – collect?'

'Ashes,' Mr Kaufmann replied. 'Ashes from the *anus mundi*.'

'The arsehole of the world, is what that is,' Agliotti explained.

'Giuseppi is our Latin *fundi*,' said Mr Kaufmann. 'In the first place being Italian, it helps. Related languages, you see. And then he needs Latin for his Black Forest Madonnas.'

'Useful tongue, if you're into madonnas,' Soonono said and they all laughed, though even Jack could tell it was an old joke.

Mr Kaufmann liked it, you could see how the skin around the corners of his eyes crinkled nicely and the lenses of his thick glasses glittered. And Jack felt happier all the time, what with madonnas and arseholes and three thousand bucks – what more could a guy ask?

'Who knows what else he may have stashed away, this letter-writing man?' said Agliotti. 'Because my nose tells me that this is one audacious, irrepressible, valuable guy with one helluva lot to give. Bring home the bacon, Jackie boy.'

Jack put his finger in his ear. Fishing for words. He could feel them coming. He wanted to tell them he'd never been out of Orange County. Didn't know where to begin. 'Where?' said Jack.

'Air?' cried Soonono. 'Sure you go by air.'

'No, *where*?' Jack tried again.

'Not nowhere,' Agliotti smiled. 'Tell him, boss.'

'Jack, I believe we know where to search.' Mr Kaufmann held up the blue airletter. 'Observe.' Mr Kaufmann lifted a finger at a time and Jack rolled his eyes. 'One, this letter is recent. Two, it gives an address. See here – Jack, this is the address. In London, England. Three, someone takes a little stroll Englandwards and asks around. Who knows what he might turn up?'

Jack stopped him there. Jack had heard enough. Jack was *way* ahead of Mr Kaufmann now. He jumped to his feet, his yellow hair flew in all directions and then settled again on his square forehead. 'And then you'll buy 'em, won't you? All of 'em? Because if there's some already, there must be others. Out there in London, England. Waiting to be found and brought home to be put in your *anus* . . . ' Now he did falter—

'*Mundi*,' said Agliotti, the Latinist.

*

When Jack got home to Tranquil Pines, Dr Castro's red Ferrari was parked in the lot. Jack made for the pink pouffe, but Dr Castro was already sitting on it, reading his book. He thought of the scalpels in Dr Castro's bag. He'd have a glitter of scalpels in there, behind the brass tongue and costly teeth. Thoughts fluttered in Jack's head. Like a flock of birds that had flown through an open window into a closed room and now couldn't find their way out. He put his finger in his ear and wriggled it, clearing a passage. No good. He opened his mouth, perhaps they might escape that way? He didn't like these thoughts, feathery things, brushing against the top of his skull. Why didn't they go? Why this pain? It took a while to know what the reason was but he worked it out in the end. You couldn't fool Jack for long.

'Turned off the fucking TV!'

'Bastard.' Dr Castro turned the pages of his dictionary. 'Poltroon. Rapscallion. What you need around here is caring, cleanliness, comfort. What do you have in your cranium to leave a lady in this *merde*, mire, misery?'

Jack wasn't one to give up easily. He knew what was what, did Jack. He'd worked it out. He knew what was hurting him. The screen was grey and cold like old fridge water or the winter fogs you saw in horror movies. It made him shiver. It made him mad. 'Turn on the fucking TV,' said Jack, not moving, his hands in the pockets of his jeans showing his yellow socks, the colour of uranium cake.

Dr Castro looked at him with undisguised distaste. Those yellow socks. He shivered. He has fat ankles, thought Dr Castro, with an unusual shock of pleasure. His head is square, a brick head with blond hair. Dr Castro adjusted his signet ring, which wore on its onyx face a golden eagle seizing a snake in its left talon. He checked the knot of his Hermès tie. He looked at the time on his Audemar Picquet watch and he made for the door. 'Come, creep. She's on her way. You come to the hospital. Jesus, this place, it's fourth world, let me tell you.'

Dr Castro took him driving, in his red Ferrari. Over to the Thomas Jefferson Memorial Hospital. Jack had only ever been driving with Dr Castro in his dreams. When he had planned to kill him with curare. Wet and twitching dreams. A scratch, a little sleep. A stop-over in the lot at the Park. Happy's lot, or

97

Dopey's. Dr Castro sleeping nicely in the trunk. Snug as a bug in a rug. Jack got a warm feeling when he thought of these things. Like he did when he played with himself.

Marta lay in her bed, wired up. Head, arms, Marta was wired to more machines than Frankenstein. And Jack, he really felt concerned. Did she want some shark's fin soup? Did she want some lemon chicken? Anything, Marta!

From his pocket he took out an envelope and waved it like a flag. From the envelope he took an airline ticket. 'I'm going to London, England. I fly tonight.' Something about this really impressed Jack. Like it was a line from a movie or something. Like, say, 'I plunge this knife into your heart.' Or, 'I'm gonna rip your head off, punk!' He said it over and over to himself. 'I fly tonight!' And all the time he said it he kept waving the air ticket in front of Marta's eyes.

And what did old Marta do? Did she jump out of bed and hug him? Did she burst into tears and tell him he was the cleverest boy in the whole wide world? The hell she did. Old Marta struggled to sit up. She pulled the drip out of her arm. Her apricot hospital gown slipped to show a freckled shoulder. She opened her mouth, revealing strong teeth. 'Schmuck, moron, nincompoop – you been under Marta's bed?'

'No, Marta.'

'Don't lie to me, Jack. Where did you get the money? You been under Marta's bed! You sold off all we had. And you bring me air tickets!'

And before he could stop her she snatched his ticket and threw it out of the window. Then the nurses rushed in and Dr Castro hustled him out.

It was the last he saw of Marta. His ticket he found easily enough, crumpled into a ball by Marta's strong, angry hand. Usable still. And so it was that Jack, the boy from Tranquil Pines Mobile Trailer Park, who got lucky one day at the Kissimee Flea Market, climbed 35,000 feet into the sky on a Northwest Airlines flight from Orlando, Florida, bound for Gatwick, England, in search of fame and fortune.

Meanwhile, back at the Kissimee Flea Market, Mr Kaufmann was making plans of his own. 'Name and address and phone number,' he told Agliotti. 'Then he gets to hear my story. About

Jack who comes to call. The guy with the loot gets a good offer: he can deal with Black Jack, or he can deal with the dealer. Who would you deal with?'

'No contest,' said Agliotti. 'And Jackieboy, he finds him for us?'

Mr Kaufmann nodded graciously. 'Jack finds – we phone.'

CHAPTER NINE

Jack Goes to London

The flight from Orlando had been full. Red-faced men wore Mouse hats. Round black ears waving above their heads gave them the look of blunted stags. Women touched their blonde hairstyles and said: 'Shan't be bloody sorry to be back in Basildon, I can tell you. Tracy was sick three times on the Space Mountain roller-coaster.'

The movie had been bad. He knew it inside about a minute and a half. One of those about husbands and wives. They kiss each other, shout and cry, and the rooms are *full* of things, pictures and lamplight. People living together in furry warmth, made him think of bears in caves, also made him shiver.

He shut his eyes and ran his own movie: *Dwarfstruck*. The one about a midget rapist who preyed on large black women in downtown Chicago, roped and trussed them and rode them like steers. And all the dickheads ranted about the close-ups, complained especially about the branding scene, so realistic you could almost smell the burning flesh. It said so on the video case. Well, the bleeding hearts were told to go and stuff their hands because this was really a fine attack on the way the warped white-power machine exploited the blood and guts of black people.

The searingly sweet aroma of scorched human thigh was in his nostrils as rubber kissed the Gatwick runway and the captain told them that it was raining in London and thank you for flying Northwest.

An elderly woman in a Duck hat, a curving surfboard of a beak below thickly lashed round blue eyes, wearing pink

Bermuda shorts with an olive green anorak and a fur collar, didn't wait for him to get out. No, she simply upped and clambered over him heading for the doorway, kicking him sharply on the right knee-cap in passing. Jack opened one green eye. 'You want a beak up your snatch, lady?'

'I beg your pardon?'

'You're welcome,' said Jack, and showed her his other eye.

Jack emerged from the underground somewhere in downtown London, nose twitching. He saw a man in a funny hat stuck right up there on his column. Like he'd jumped up there to get away from an attack by killer rats! Didn't help – the pigeons got him anyway – flying rats! He chose a road at random, a road with an overhead arch, and found himself on a highway, coloured red, grass on either side – a lake, ducks. The highway ended suddenly in high black iron railings and a fountain thing with gold statues sitting right up there, all shining, and loads of foreign people standing around chattering just as excitedly as the pigeons had done in the square, where the man in the hat stood.

From the railings Jack took a good look. At first he thought it must be an hotel. Standing outside, in neat little houses like skinny dog-kennels, were these guys in red blouses and funny black hairy hats. He figured it was maybe some kind of hokey British theme park. Small scale. About as high as the Howard Johnson's in Kissimee, Jack reckoned, but a lot wider and a hellavu lot older. And the same colour as Aldo's Pasta Palace over Apopka way. The guys in red blouses could hardly have been doormen because they were carrying rifles and every once in a while they'd step out of these neat little wooden kennels and stomp up and down. He turned to a little Japanese who was clicking away with his camera.

'Say, you know what this is?'

The photographer lowered his camera and stared. 'This is a palace.'

'Go on,' said Jack, 'pull the other one.'

Even the Pasta Palace, out in Orlando West, was a darn sight bigger. Fountains out front and great creamy columns. Four courses, plus antipasti, including your entrée. All ten dollars fifty. Now that was a palace!

'Buckingham Palace. Where the Queen lives.'

Jack nodded amiably. Little Japanese fucker, thinks he can take me for a ride. First they buy the Rockefeller Center and half of fucking Hollywood and then they take the piss out of a guy who's new to London!

Jack got off in the mote-laden air of the station and faced a very steep escalator that wasn't working. 'We apologise for the inactivity of the escalator' a handwritten notice attached to its black handrail explained. 'Those unable to manage the stairs are advised to continue to the following station and disembark there.'

'Disembark,' Jack said. Man, that wasn't a word, it was a fucking book! Jack had read a book once. It was called *Elvis: The Truth*. Never again. Bad head for days. He ran up the wooden stairs two at a time: 'Dis-em-fuckin'-bark!' said Jack. 'Un-fucking-real!'

Greyacres. An old house on Highgate Hill. Everything was so old! Strawberry bricks and the grey slate roof which gave it its name. The branches of a weeping willow hung like the finest tracery across a great picture window.

Jack opened the gate. He walked slowly down the path. He took from his pocket the long letter which had caused Mr Kaufmann such excitement. He pressed his eye to the glass spyhole in the front door.

Nothing to see. He went around the corner of the house, his brown cowboy boots sinking into the lawn, adjusting his red neckerchief across his mouth till he looked like – a highwayman, stick-up man, bank robber, (all of 'em!).

Sitting at a table in the apartment downstairs before a single egg in a wooden cup, was an old man with thick white hair. A blonde woman carried a ball of white string. Round and round the old man she walked. It looked, through the window, like spaghetti. She was breathing hard. He saw her breast moving. She went on walking until the old man was trussed so tightly he could have turned to stone. He seemed to have something in his ear, running down the side of his face. Pure gold!

And so Jack got to coming back regularly to the garden of the house in Highgate where the old boy had been tied to the chair. He felt pretty happy about that. He took a room at the Avalon Hotel, small, dark and cheap. Just around the corner: 'Holy Jeezles,' chirruped Jack to himself when he saw the damp hotel lounge that smelt of soup even though meals had last been served there many years before, 'happy hour at the morgue.' Just a five-minute walk to the house.

All through the final troubled days of the Grand Bargain Jack watched and waited. He took note of Lizzie's struggle with her father. If he crouched beneath the living-room window sill he could hear everything. The blonde with the string had a husband. She used to tell him loudly: 'I'm at the end of my tether. It's like having a child in the house. No, it's worse than that. A child, a sick child, a difficult child, might at least get better, grow up. But he's only going to get worse.'

She called him Albert. He called her Lizzie. Albert and Lizzie kept Jack occupied many a night. Jack heard how much Lizzie loved Daddy but real professional help was required; Albert let him know Daddy's name and Jack was very pleased. 'Mmmmm for Mmmmmax,' Jack would whisper to himself as he crouched in the darkness.

Albert told Jack about a place called Serenity House.

'The sooner you get him in there, the better,' said Albert. 'Before you do him some permanent injury. You were jolly lucky he didn't pop off in that chair.'

Jack also felt jolly lucky. He found Serenity House easily. He rang the bell, did Jack. And Mr Fox welcomed him with open arms. Answer to a proprietor's prayer.

And Jack watched Max. Lizzie said she couldn't face him any more. Albert came down to bath him now, red-faced from the steam, towel in hand, while Max chatted shrilly to him about something called a comma, the Queen and the Common Market. Max walked tall, like he was some sort of space-commander, and the large pink man called Albert, with the dark blue bath towel, was a slave. But when the Albert man went back upstairs, Max would sit on his bed and put his face in his hands.

One night Jack watched him get into bed. But he didn't go to sleep. As soon as Albert and Lizzie had hit the sack, Max got up, turned on his bedside lamp and took from the big brown cupboard beside his bed an old leather suitcase. He packed the case and then he fetched himself a pot of paint and brush and, while Jack watched, he painted his name in big white letters on the side of his case. So big Jack could read them easily from twenty feet: Max Montfalcon, b. 1909, Greyacres, Highgate, London N6.

So it was that, in late November, when Serenity House opened its doors to admit a new guest, the day Max asked Albert about mercy killing, and Lizzie thought she'd scream if she heard the sound of her father's finger rubbing his gum for another second -- Jack was ready and waiting.

Jack waited. When the Turbervilles thought they were safe, he made his move. Lizzie opened the door to the young man from Serenity House with the yellow hair and the square head.

'Yes? What can I do for you?'

Jack took out the letter, a bold hand on big white pages, and waved it like a handkerchief. He had to wave it three times before she reached for it.

She held the letter with the very tips of her fingers. She shook her head in astonishment. With her nose, only her nose, she pointed to the address. *Her* address.

'Who do you want?'

'Mmmmm-Max!'

'As you know, father doesn't live here any more. Is this his letter? Where did you find it?'

'I didn't mean to hurt him,' said Jack in a passable imitation of Lizzie's own words about her father. Jack circled his head with his finger – tying himself up with string. He only stopped when she invited him in.

She led him into the pink and gold sitting room. Watching her leading him Jack decided that this was a real lady in her olive green floral skirt and cream silk blouse, with her careful but delicate step and her hips swaying gracefully as she walked. Yes, sir. One of those real English ladies.

'Mr Albert be home soon?'

'My husband? Yes. Who *are* you?'

'Jack,' said Jack.

She seated him on the leather chesterfield beside the fire. She did not offer him tea. She did not pour him a drink. She looked at this boy with his intensely yellow hair and his red neckerchief and his oddly coloured eyes. He was without doubt a strange-looking creature, one of the strangest she had ever seen. His head was the most curious shape; his hair, full and thick, was somehow unhealthy in its aggressive sheen and texture. He didn't say anything. Just nodded in a friendly way when she asked if she could keep the letter. And when she reminded him her father now lived in Serenity House, the boy simply nodded again and stuck his finger in his ear.

'Well, now,' said Lizzie, 'is there something I can do for you?'

Jack got the word out: 'Mmmmoney!'

She looked at the letter. She looked at Jack. 'I really don't understand. Perhaps I will call my husband.'

'Yes, please,' said Jack. 'Call him.' He stood up when she left the room. He could be polite, could Jack.

But when Lizzie came back into the room he was gone.

As if it were not enough for a man who had had a hard day in the House of Commons with a vindictive former mistress who shows him police reports over lunch, he has to arrive home to find his wife in tears.

'Steady on, old thing,' said Albert Turberville. 'Tell me again. I hadn't a clue what you meant on the phone. Where is this boy?'

'Don't you bloody patronise me,' said his wife.

She told him how she'd opened the door to find 'that boy' on the step. 'Albert, he gave me this.' And she handed him a letter.

Albert drew the curtains. He poured himself a large whisky. He sat down with the letter.

Marta, my dear friend. I am writing to ask you for help. In the final days, back then, in our old work place, when things were so mad and bad, and you were so brave, as the Russians swept ever closer and the normal regularities of life in the Facility, which we had struggled so hard to maintain in our time together (a time I must say I recall with great affection and admiration) were fatally and finally interrupted, it seems that certain belongings of mine were discovered behind the fireplace of my old house.

Marta, you can imagine my shock when I was told of this discovery. I was by then myself a prisoner of the Russians having been captured on the Eastern front where I was serving as a regular soldier. You remember how I left the Facility. You remember the curses of the Commandant, and in particular Dr von Hehn, which were heaped on my head. Even while he, Dr von Hehn, enjoyed the comforts of Berlin at least once a month, I sat in three feet of snow and broken boots outside Minsk. Be that as it may – what does it matter now? I have forgotten about it. Yet I must confess that scholars, archivists and researchers all gave of their best in the Russian campaign and what a toll it took of our best men. Poor Dr Lück killed fighting the Maquis near Périgueux. Stelzebind lost in the U-boats in the Arctic. The medievalist Professor Vanille, who did such great work in establishing the varied intermixtures of races in Eastern Lands in '41, killed fighting partisans in Warsaw. Dr Max Dollinger who died when his niece's apartment block in Spandau was destroyed in the Allied bombing of Berlin. Even, poor, useless Behrens, by then I believe in charge of an *Einsatzkommando* in Lvov, and, so I am told, by then carrying the rank of SS-*Untersturmführer* (will wonders never cease?) killed by a booby-trapped case of wine. Did Behrens ever learn to think before he handled something? It seems not. But you and I know that. We have only to recall the damage he did, almost without trying, to our materials in the Facility. If anyone could be said, single-handed, to have held back the advances of ethnic research, Behrens was that man.

But I wander – as an old man will. My favour which I have to ask of you, let me come to that. The pieces hidden behind the fireplace (a precaution induced by the war) were a few samples of my work, tools of the trade, I suppose you might call them, as well as a few letters written to my wife Irmgard, in Cologne, in 1941. Poor Irmgard was a victim of allied bombing but my letters to her survived. The fortunes of war! Perfectly innocent,

indeed dull, if occasionally sentimental, these letters mean
nothing to anyone except me. If it is the case that you have been
holding these few mementoes for me all these years I cannot tell
you how thankful I am to you for your faithful custodianship. If
you would now give a last token of your loyalty to our old
friendship and return them to me at the address above you will
have exceeded even my fondest and most cherished memories of
your good heart.

Naturally, I would undertake to defray any and all expenses
required to return my property to me as quickly and as safely
as possible. Let this run into a few pounds (dollars to you) or
into thousands, I would not hesitate, dear Marta. In fact I would
be honoured to cover such expenses, twice or even threefold.

I know I can depend on you now, just as I did in the past.
Let me hear from you soon.

With greetings and profound respect,

M

'What does it mean, Albert? It has our address on it. I suppose
it must have come from Daddy. But what would he be doing
writing to someone in Florida?'

Albert Turberville did not reply. He drained the last drops
of whisky. He said: 'Lizzie, I don't know how to say this.'

Then he said it anyway.

'Not Daddy!' said Lizzie when he'd finished. 'A police report?
All these years. Here. Without anyone knowing about it.'

'Harwich.' said Albert bitterly. 'Some kind of Teutonic joke.
Your father appears to have been fooling us for years.'

'I simply can't believe it.' She took the letter, folded it and
laid it on the table as if it had nothing to do with her. 'He's the
writer of this? Daddy is this M? Then who is Marta. What does
he want back from her?'

'Where is the boy now? The American?'

'Falkenberg?' Elizabeth frowned her disbelief.

'Montfalcon. He simply anglicised it. Neat.' Albert poured
himself another whisky. 'The boy – did he say anything else?
Where did he get the letter from?'

'Why did no one know? Surely there were checks after the

war? Even if it's true. Just because they say it's true, it doesn't mean they're right. I'm sure I read somewhere that people coming from those countries were checked.'

'The American,' Albert persisted, 'where did he get the letter from?'

'God knows. But I'd say he's sure to come back.'

'Of that', said Albert Turberville, 'we can be sure. For God's sake, buck up, Lizzie. If it's any consolation, we've got time to think things over. He doesn't seem to be in any hurry, this boy.'

But nothing, Albert knew, would ever console him for the way he had heard the news earlier that day.

CHAPTER TEN

How Albert Got the News

Albert Turberville was lunching off steamed cod and brown rice in the Members' Dining Room when Erica Snafus sat down beside him, stared accusingly at his hands, and said, 'Well, Albie. What have you been up to?'

Erica was on the MCC, the Members' Cuisine Committee, which had been instrumental in changing the eating habits of MPs. White rice had gone the way of cigarettes. Although not able to remove all fried foods from the daily menus she had campaigned for months for a separate seating area for those who wished to indulge fatal appetites for French fries or bacon or doughnuts. The MCC was also known to younger, more profane Members in the bars of the House of Commons as the Mad Cow Council, a slighting reference to Erica's campaign to right what she saw as a monstrously dangerous wrong: the decision to slaughter, and then bury, all cows found to be carrying mad cow disease. All such animals should be exhumed and incinerated, Erica argued, since spongiform encephalitis was a virus which could last for years in the soil and threatened to enter the food chain. It was a time bomb ticking away, threatening the health of the nation. When the Government balked at the huge expense of this scheme, Erica had advocated building walls, or at least tall fences, around the grave sites of these deceased and lunatic animals, and marking the places with some appropriate warning symbol, a green cross, for instance.

Ms Snafus, if she has her way, would turn parts of Britain into something akin to the battlefields of the Somme . . .

commented one newspaper with that peculiar mixture of exasperation at the endless silliness of political life, mixed with undergraduate glee at having found something clever to say about it. Albert hated the smart editorials in the quality press.

... Will she also support some sort of War Graves Commission for these departed lunatic ruminants?

the editorial concluded with a neat flourish in which was to be heard the brassy trumpet note of chest-hugging self-satisfaction. Two hundred years of crusading journalism and all it does is end up as a chortle, Albert thought bitterly.

Erica Snafus was also part of the unofficial team that had dedicated themselves to watching – or indeed encouraging, or even forcing? – the passage of the War Crimes Bill through the House of Commons. A Labour MP of many years' standing, a woman of distinct discernment, Erica was one of the people (and their numbers were on the increase) dedicated to getting things done. Together with Gavin Pertwee and Herbie Long, Erica had been indefatigable in reviving the flagging attentions of fellow MPs in the matter of suspected Nazi war criminals living in Britain, during those long months when the War Crimes Bill was off and on the boil.

On the day that Erica sat beside him in the dining room and looked so hard at his hands, Albert put down his knife and fork. He hid his hands in his pockets. Erica wore a grey suit that matched her eyes. Her expensively dyed blonde hair was cut square across her forehead. Even at fifty-two she looked trim, packed. The pink Hermès scarf at her neck depicted interlocking chains of some marine kind, golden and grappling. She reminded Albert of a missile, a weapon, a kind of human mortar loaded, primed and ready to fire.

'Surprised to see you weren't in the House yesterday, Albie.'

He flinched. Her own pet name for him. He'd never liked it. It made him sound like some sort of foreign little mannikin.

Albert clenched his hands in his pockets. 'I was busy.'

'We're all busy. You know that. It's really a pity you weren't there.'

'Why?'

'Well, as I'm sure you know by now, we won. The War Crimes Bill went through, with a big majority.'

'It's been through before. The Lords will stall it.'

'Maybe. But the worst is behind us now. The Government will use the parliament act, if necessary. If the Lords make trouble, so can we.'

'You'll force it through?'

Erica nodded. The light danced on her hair. Albert's cod cooled. His hands in his pockets were sweating. Erica smiled. She reached over and took a long sip from his glass of Soave. 'Cheers!'

The trouble with love, thought Albert bitterly, was that it always had a way of hitting back at you. When he and Erica had been lovers, it had all seemed fine, in her little flat in Majuba Crescent, on the first floor of a Victorian house in Islington. A black and white kitchen. Views of the old bakery which had become an Indian vegetarian restaurant called Tickety Boo. And 'Tickety boo!' was what Albert said, frequently, as he took a cab from the Commons and picked up the key under the concrete Egyptian cat with the agate eyes which guarded the front door, and mixed himself a Campari and orange, at around three of an afternoon. Even better when Erica arrived and kicked off her shoes. Best of all when they took to the big mahogany bed with the pink duvet, Albert always insisting on keeping his socks on until the last moment.

It might have gone on like that for ever. Well, for some time, anyway. The ride to Islington, the key under the cat, the big bed and the pink duvet and him keeping his socks on until the last moment. Tickety boo! And nobody, but nobody, suspecting it for a moment.

'Sentimentalist!' Erica liked to say, unhooking her bra, stepping out of her pants and lying down beside him as the Islington afternoon sun painted her body beige and silver. All London seemed to be waiting under a low, leaning sky, as if something were about to happen. As it always did, at around about that time of day in Majuba Crescent.

Why sentimentalist? 'Because you cling to the last to

something small. Personal. A talisman. You hope it might protect you on your journey into the unknown. It's quite touching.
Even boyish. But it looks pretty damn silly, all the same. A very
large man wearing nothing but a pair of tiny blue socks! Get
them off, Albie, get them all off!'

She would invariably mount him. Erica was a top sort of
person. She had the very muscular thighs and the straight back
of the born equestrian, though, as she drily acknowledged, there
had never been much call for horses or riders in the little village
in the shadow of the steel mill where she grew up. In another,
former life, said Erica, she must have been a man. Certainly, in
her next life, she would be a man.

That their lovemaking took on the rhythms of parliamentary
debate was perhaps not surprising after nearly forty years of
shared experience in the House. An unexpected coalition. Backbenchers from opposite sides of the House. What a wonderful
cover it made! Sir Horace Epstein, whose seat in Deeping
Wallop Albert had inherited, had once advised him on sexual
mores for budding politicians: 'Never sleep with your secretary.
She really wants to marry you and is too po-faced to tell you.
But she'll tell your wife, if she has to.' And he also said: 'On
no account sleep with a constituent. Secretly each and every
voter suspects that Members of Parliament couldn't give a fuck!
Never give them cause to form the opposite impression. They
will not forgive you.'

Albert had followed Sir Horace's advice. He wondered if he
would have approved of the relationship he had with Erica?
What would he have thought of a liaison with someone from
the party opposite, from the ranks of the enemy? To Albert's
way of thinking it had considerable merits. Not only were Erica
and he from opposing sides of the House, they came from different ends of the country, from ideologies so formally at odds
with one another that they were left with absolutely nothing in
common, citizens indeed of two nations, and the very idea of
the pair of them spending afternoons in bed was preposterous.
Albert with his gleaming, aerodynamic, black Italian shoes and
his damp, cunningly indecisive Conservatism. His head of fine
full hair he liked to smooth back at moments of rhetorical
excitement. And she with her Hermès scarves, her irritable,

clever, pragmatic socialism. Her black silk underwear bought on her numerous trips abroad, always at the airport, economical naughty French lace but English proportions. His ridiculous small socks, his damp hair and large pink cheeks. No, their affair was so improbable as to be not even above suspicion. That was precisely it. The Islington afternoons of Albert and Erica were below suspicion.

Did she rise above him in a series of leaping movements, higher and higher, so that it seemed she must unseat herself? Well, what was that, seen through half-closed eyes, but something very like the curious bobbing motion that goes on when members leap to their feet in the attempt, usually vain, to catch the eye of the Speaker. And why did she lift herself to these heights, why did she jump up so often? Well, because she was allowing, by varying degrees, her vagina to ascend higher and higher up Albert's small but broad, thick indeed, uncomplaining member. And their very coming together, what was that – in its increasingly incoherent, ecstatic murmurings, as she moved faster and faster on him and he rose to meet her descending, streaming mass of pubic hair – but, yes, a way of saying, 'I beg to move the motion.'? For this was indeed a fleshly version of their many parliamentary encounters with all its own secret phrases: 'Indicators indicate', and 'Figures for car sales shown'; its own goads and spurs and doubts – 'What do you say of these saving ratios for the fourth quarter?' And in its vigorous, flourishing climax, after which Erica came slowly to rest, dripping wet, her hair soaked, her face pink, was there not exactly the downward movement of the head he had seen so often in the House as she concluded a vigorous attack, in a drum roll of damning statistics which had the members opposite baying like wolves. 'Order! Order!' cried the Speaker. And well might he cry, as Erica and Albert lay beside one another with pounding hearts in the fading early evening light.

Where was Albert in all of this? Well, the odd thing was that even though he had no clothes on, though he had expended himself with about as much force as his damp, decent Conservatism permitted, he remained to the last a backbencher, on those afternoons in Islington when he was so slow to take off his socks. Flat on his back lay the disconsolate Tory.

In fact it had lasted for only half a parliamentary session because of a discovery Albert had made on leaving the Islington flat one evening at about six. The moon was just beginning to rise over the vegetarian restaurant which, that evening, was offering as the specials of the day marrow *au gratin* and artichoke pie followed by mousse of lychee and cloudberry sauce. The moon had a yellow, lugubrious, rather threadbare look that reminded Albert of the old days when ponderous and sad officials from the Iron Curtain countries visited the House for fraternal exchanges of greetings. Their eyes were liquid and melancholy. The moon could have been made in Albania.

Erica had left the flat early for a committee meeting. Her colour was high, her very fetching green costume with gold epaulettes looking somehow rather martial but very trim all the same. A regular cannon of a woman, Albert had thought. Stacked, solid, muscular, with a kind of brassy gleam that reminded him of a big artillery shell. Their session that afternoon on the pink duvet had seemed a bit off. He couldn't quite put his finger on it, but it was the sense that Erica had not been her bucking, rollicking self. True she had still laughed at his socks. She had swung into the saddle with practised ease. But he missed the wild thudding drive, the sense of something given and got. And when he reached up, as he knew she liked him to, and seized her breasts, instead of throwing back her head and galloping even more wildly, she had seized his wrists and held them off, until she came in a series of grunts and interjections and calls to order.

What was all that about? It occurred to him that Erica's somewhat inhibited performance possibly had to do with the introduction of television into the House. The cumulative effects had been dire. Members were not only better dressed these days, they were better behaved. They seldom slept openly after lunch. They hardly ever put their thumbs in their ears and waggled their fingers at members opposite who mixed up their savings ratios with their figures for car sales. They no longer shrieked at each other, because the cameras did not like it and there was always the chance of the viewer glimpsing flying spittle. Television influenced even the quality of the insults. Nowadays they called each other Kermit or Noddy or JR –

more evidence of the power of television. Vilified the party opposite by calling them names you knew the viewing public would recognise when they saw *you* on television, because they had seen the originals, on television. Really, it was too bad. He had voted against it, of course. But they brought the bloody cameras in anyway. Most of his back-bench friends had voted against. But Johnny Public had got his way. And Johnny Public regarded backbenchers as the lowest form of life.

On that fateful Islington evening Albert had stooped to place the key beneath the cat. Its unwinking agate eye, its right to Albert's left, took on, in that cheap Albanian moonlight, a faintly mocking gleam. 'Bloody cat!' Albert declared, straightening up and then gave the base of the cat a sharp kick. That's how it was. He might have missed her if he'd straightened a moment later. If he hadn't paused to kick the cat he might never have known. If Erica had not had to get back to the House so early. If any one of a thousand things had happened, he would have missed her. As it was they almost collided.

'Innocenta!'

'Hello, Daddy,' said his daughter, or someone who was certainly the spitting image of her. 'What are you doing here?'

Such questions around evening in Islington take on a formidable force, and Albert was obliged, not for the first time in his life, to take refuge in that most useful of evasive tactics, surprised indignation. 'What on earth are you wearing, girl?'

Innocenta really didn't want to say. The sight of her father exasperated and depressed her. She had not seen him since she walked out on Max's Grand Bargain.

She said: 'How's Grandpa? Hating it, I'll bet.'

'Your grandfather decided he'd be happier in a more structured environment,' said Albert.

'What do you mean?' asked Innocenta suspiciously. 'Where is he?'

'He's moved to one of these residential care centres. For senior people. Elders, is the preferred term. Place called Serenity House?'

'Old age home, you mean?'

'Eventide refuge. North London's best.'

Innocenta laughed bitterly. 'Poor Grandpa. He's looking a bit like King Lear after all. You've shipped him off.'

'His choice,' said Albert, 'entirely.'

'You broke the bargain. But you kept the house. That's pretty good even for someone who is bound into the power structures of the Other World.'

'What "Other World"?'

'Any world that has not joined the Aquarian Conspiracy. The world that's left behind. Your world. The world that's lost touch with itself.'

Albert stared at his daughter. She had on her Doc Martens. Over her white robes she wore a heavy tweed sport coat. It gave her a vaguely Arabic look. Innocenta was wearing white because that's what the Master had ordered. The Master, in far-away Poona, clearly had no idea how difficult it was to keep to his firm dress code if he kept changing his mind about colours. At first, everything had had to be orange. Then he said it should be maroon for meditating. But white when sitting in Buddha Hall. Around her neck she wore a necklace of wooden beads.

Innocenta had been around. She'd tried truancy as a school-girl. She'd tried grass. She had tried to live in a squat in Camden High Street. She had tried loving her father and hating her mother. She'd had a phantom pregnancy at fifteen and a real one at sixteen. She'd had an abortion on her seventeenth birth-day. She'd tried aromatherapy and the flotation tank. She even tried good works and served as a meals on wheels driver for the Haringey Council, for about a week, until they discovered that most of her meals on wheels ended up in a squat in Camden High Street. Prone as she was to emotional enthusiasms, Innocenta had also practised abstinence for higher religious reasons, particularly Karezza, an Indian technique in which orgasm is deliberately suppressed during sexual intercourse in order to raise mystical awareness. She had developed a bad nose after three weeks on coke. She had shown signs of wishing to become a nun and indeed had been accepted by the Sisters of the Sacred Heart as the right material. But she ran away to the Poona Ashram instead. At that time the Bhagwan changed his name to Osho. Disenchanted, Innocenta returned to London and the squat and an offshoot of the Bhagwan's movement –

run by a dissenting ex-accountant, once named Trevor and now known always and only as 'The Master'. The trouble with Trevor, as Innocenta told herself in her lighter moments, was that he had no idea of the cost of things. The response from various church members to this piece of blasphemy was to accuse Innocenta of being 'a church of one'.

She stood on the top step of an Islington house in Majuba Gardens and contemplated her father who appeared to be rather pink in the face and panting slightly, as if he had been taking exercise. She touched her necklace.

'This is my *mala*. One hundred and eight sandalwood beads. With a picture of the Master.'

'And may one know where you're going, togged out like that?'

'I'm not going anywhere, Daddy. I'm here.' Innocenta pointed down the stairs to the basement flat. 'This is my church.'

Albert felt suddenly very uncomfortable. 'You go to church down there?'

'Have done for weeks now. The International Church of Meditation. ICM. Islington Branch. We believe ICM is to the New Age what IBM is to the Other World.'

'What do you do, down there?' Albert jerked his chin. Not liking even to acknowledge the church in the basement, the cult beneath his love-nest.

'Energy balancing. Bodywork. Orgasmic undoing. Intuitive massage. Rebirthing and regression.'

Albert held up a hand. 'Heard it before. Five hundred quid a month, plus VAT.'

'Six hundred,' said Innocenta, 'and if you're wondering how I can afford it, I've been getting large cheques from Jeb Touser. He says they arise out of recalculation of the Grand Bargain. Sounded daft to me. Now I see what he means. Grandpa's been recalculated into an old age home. You and Mummy are left with the loot. I suppose Grandpa's clawed back my share. The share that he was going to give to Mummy.'

Albert thought of the pink duvet above and Innocenta, and the International Church of Meditation, below. What on earth was Orgasmic Undoing? He could imagine what the papers would say if they ever got hold of it.

Turning his head away from the flight of steps that led down into a small well where a little blond light glimmered above a green painted door (inauspicious entrance to Innocenta's place of worship) Albert noticed again the Egyptian cat. Its agate eye held a look that seemed both dismissive and superior.

Still, he could not give way without scoring a point. The parliamentarian was strong in him. 'There is not an Other world, Innocenta.'

She looked at him closely. 'If there wasn't another world, lots of other worlds, how come you've exiled Grandpa to one of them? If there weren't lots of other worlds what are you doing here? Anyway, what's Grandpa's address? I want to go and see him.'

Naturally it couldn't go on. Albert knew that. He never returned to the little house in Islington with the pink duvet and the black and white kitchen.

Now Erica sat next to him wrapped in marine chains, and drank his Soave. She downed the last inch of his wine, and then she told him, while he kept his hands in his pockets and his cod and rice cooled into rocklike ridges and plateaux, like the smooth and serrated lava from some very tiny volcanic eruption.

'All that remains in the way of a full investigation of the Nazis we know are living in Britain is the passage of the bill through the other place. It's only a matter of time now before the hunt starts. Of course not everyone suspected will be looked at. We know there are well over seventy cases still alive. That's according to the report of the War Crimes Inquiry team. But it's only suggested that perhaps a handful will be looked into. Three. Maybe four. The killings these men are responsible for took place in countries like Estonia, Latvia, the Ukraine. Soviet territory. At least in name. But one is different. He was busy in Poland and he was a German. His work in the camps was what they call scientific. Which meant working on people who'd been killed. Or having people killed so as to work on them. Anyway, I felt you should know. For the sake of kindness, Albie. Never let it be said that I was someone to harbour a grudge. Here, take a look at this.'

'This' was a small piece of paper, about six by four, on which the following information appeared in single spaced type:

Falkenberg, von, Maximilian, b. Potsdam, 1909. m. Irmgard Kassel 1939 Berlin. d. 1941. Churtseigh, England, 1924–7 Univ. Munich, Leipzig, Göttingen, etc. Rhodes Scholar, Nonce College, Oxford, 1936–8; interests: anthropology, ethnic studies, racial science (*sic*), various establishments Germany and Poland 1940–42. Service on Eastern Front, Minsk, 1943. Contact lost thereafter. But more 'racial studies' suspected. Entry into Britain, 1947–8? No trace. One daughter, Elizabeth Augusta. m. Albert Turberville MP.

'This is a libel!' Albert said.

Erica Snafus stood up and smiled. 'No, Albie, I'm doing you a favour.'

CHAPTER ELEVEN

Jack Gets a Job

They entered Serenity House, let history record, in a bleak November, Jack just forty-eight hours before Max. Mr Fox will testify. Dr Tonks will back him up. That Jack should appear nowhere in the records of the House is easily explained.

When Cledwyn Fox opened the front door of Serenity House one morning and looked at the boy on the doorstep he was under the impression, sharp, though misconceived as it turned out, that he was some kind of religious freak. Strange how powerfully sure this impression was, certain in that curious way of first impressions, however false they may prove later. Ever afterwards when Cledwyn Fox thought of Jack, something of the aura of a religious salesman, proselytizer, doorstep Bible-puncher, coloured his memory of the boy – the feeling of something spuriously if convincingly holy, the way light through a stained-glass window seems sacred.

Imagine, if you will, the external scene. The mist coming off the path and rising into the beech trees, stroking the cypresses like smoke. And across the road at the private school the boys arriving in twos and threes, their pink faces under their grey caps taking on shades of that same grey. All this seen through the eyes of a man who has had little sleep. And there on his doorstep stands a boy of colours, red, blond and blue, who says: 'If you can use another pair of hands around here, then I'm your man.'

An American in Highgate at eight in the morning. Clean, strong and cheerful. Mr Fox has had a hard night. Two of his overnight staff, to wit, Dale and Sally, have not shown up. Dale had called in but only to resign, in his querulous New Zealand accent. 'I'm off, Mr Fox, true as true. It's back to the sheep for old Dales.' Never trust a New Zealander, Mr Fox reflected bitterly. Only in matters of rugby and mutton are they sound.

Mr Fox asked about a work permit.

Jack said: 'What's that?'

Mr Fox was pleased. Would Jack be happy to be paid in cash?

'What else is there?' said happy Jack.

Government regulations insist that there should be one trained nurse on duty for every four patients during the day. The ratio of patients to a nurse rises to eight to one by night. In other words, you can get away with more after dark. By then the patients are supposed to be asleep. Trouble is that in private establishments (and there was none more private than Serenity House) you get no overlap as you do in the state homes when the day shift clocks off and the night shift clocks on, a little human leeway, a little extra nursing cover. The day staff clock off. If the night shift don't show up then there's nothing for it but to call the nursing agencies and that can be very expensive. That's if you can get nurses at such short notice. Otherwise, if two of your carers simply don't turn up, then all you can do is to roll up your sleeves. No wonder so many people running small Homes suffer from what they call in the trade 'proprietor burn-out'.

Well, Cledwyn Fox was too tough to burn out but he'd been very badly scorched by long hours and late nights when staff did a vanishing trick. Last night had been very long indeed. The very least he could get away with was a single nurse on duty, Night Matron plus a helper. And even then he thought that the nurses sometimes passed around the sedatives rather too freely. That was the trouble. When the staff were run off their feet they tended to use any method possible of subduing a patient. It was much the same in prisons. The only place you didn't have trouble with an overly large intake and too few staff by night was the morgue.

Daytimes he managed the staff rotas not too badly. There were Crispin, Audrey, Cissie, Bert, the nurse-aide Imelda and four or five auxiliaries under the firm command of Mrs Trump and by golly did they not make a solid team? His domestic cleaners, two women who came from the school where they worked across the road, were happy enough to do the honours because he paid them an incontinence allowance, which doubled their average hourly rates.

But nights, oh, God, the nights! They were the real killers. So when an American boy with a wide smile offered his services, 'Morning, noon and night – I really don't scare easy, boss,' Mr Fox uttered a silent prayer of gratitude to the patron saint of nursing home proprietors and never hesitated.

'You mean you'll do nights?'

'Day and night – and day.'

'There's a six-week induction course. During that time you will be taken around by one of the other carers. Learn the ropes.'

'Ropes?'

'It's an expression. It means getting to know your way around.'

'I like it!' Jack said, repeating the word, 'Ropes! Weird. You've got a whole lot of old people. You've got these ropes. My friend Josh, he had a rope. He went swinging. Do they go swinging? Skinny old Tarzans, yelling all over the place.'

Mr Fox looked stern. 'We never use that word here.'

'Swinging?'

Mr Fox dropped his voice to a whisper. 'Old. I don't care what sort of language is used for the rest. Be as rude as you like. In fact you've got to have a pretty tough skin to work in an eventide refuge. Elders, you see, are supposed to be another race. They live in a world we don't believe in. The grey archipelago. Oldies, wrinklies, they're nothing of the sort, Jack. They're just young people who've lived for a long time. Survivors. Now we're going to go on a little tour of Serenity House, Jack. And at the end of the tour I'm going to ask you one question. So I want you to look very hard at the people here and think about what you see. Then afterwards you answer a simple straight-forward question I'm going to ask you.'

*

Jack's first hours in Serenity House were an absolute treat. He loved it from the start and when snoring Sandra woke unexpectedly during lunch and attempted to stab Lady Divina with her fish-knife and Lady Divina expertly disabled her with a sharp blow to the knee-cap, and it took at least two carers to separate the women, Jack could not have been happier. He met the nurses, he met the carers, he met the auxiliaries, he met the elders, and he did all he could to still his impatience till Max arrived.

As day turned to evening in Serenity House, he met Matron Two, who was sitting in her little office – the only private room in the house was reserved for Matrons One and Two. Night Matron was reading a copy of *Immortality Now*, a newsletter issued by the Female Friends of God, one of the new religious movements. Night Matron had belonged to FFOG for some ten years now and, although Mr Fox would have preferred her to have given Jack an introduction to the cares and joys of the everyday life of an employee of Serenity House, she preferred to talk about God. It was Jack's American connection that did it. It was the fact that without America there would have been no Female Friends of God. And one sometimes had the feeling that without America there would have been no God. Anyway, as somebody had told somebody else – had it been Saddam Hussein? – anyway whoever said whatever it was to whoever he said it to, what he had said was that this was the 'American century'. And there seemed no arguing with that.

'Our magazine's produced in Wyoming,' said Matron Two proudly, as if Wyoming was an especially superior brand name of something. 'That's probably down your way.'

'Give or take a couple of thousand miles,' smiled Jack, who, in truth, had no idea where Wyoming was. But then it didn't sound familiar so he knew it couldn't be in Orange County.

'The Female Friends of God is one of the most modern and the most enlightened movements in the world,' she assured him. 'It's based on a close reading of the New Testament and the words of Jesus which very clearly show that we can expect life everlasting, not later, but now. Everyone's capable of immortality.' Night Matron was on her feet now. 'It's a matter of getting in touch with the immortality quotient within your own cell structure. FFOG believes that death is a physical limitation that cannot be accepted any longer. Death results from the collusion of bad cellular forces within the body. Stop the conspiracy and find immortality.'

'I wish you a whole heap of luck,' said Jack.

'Thank you, dear. And God bless you.'

'You're welcome,' said Jack.

And who can be surprised that they didn't all take to him? Or almost all of them. That incongruous American accent, the odd, mismatched eyes. Two tone. The lively happiness of the boy at all he was shown and heard was infectious.

There was Bert who was to help him in his first six weeks. Bert pointed out to Jack the Five Incontinents, sending a five-fold stream into five large chamber pots placed beneath the high chairs into which they had been strapped. Strapped? Certainly not! said Bert. Strapped would not be the word in Serenity House. 'Don't look glum, boy. We don't go in for restraining procedures here. That's the American way.' No, the 'leather rigging', as he called it (and gave Jack goose flesh) was simply there to support and comfort the individual elder. Bert was full of the most remarkably useful advice. What to do when under attack. 'Call the Manager,' said Bert. 'Look now – here's Major Bobbno,' he continued. 'He fits the profile of our elders pretty closely. Remember, what you'll find is that they either go in the legs or in the head. That's the common run of things. The Major is partially sighted and suffers slightly from osteo-arthritis. He's also inclined to be a bit skittish. Even in a wheelchair. Come over here with me and meet him. Careful how you approach him. A hand on the shoulder if you approach him from behind will warn him that someone is here.'

Bert pushed Jack forward into the ambit of Major Bobbno who sat in hs wheelchair sucking his moustache and working out how to take a particular hill where the enemy was well dug in and protected by enfilading machine-gun fire. Military fashion, beneath his arm he carried a long plastic claw.

'Morning, Major.' Bert touched the Major's shoulder lightly. 'I'd like you to meet a new man on the staff. This is Jack.'

'Spratt, Frost or Robinson?' the Major demanded.

'Jack Robinson,' said Jack unhesitatingly, liking this game.

'Look, his shoelaces are undone. Kneel down and tie them up for him,' Bert whispered. 'He'll like that.'

Jack knelt and began to tie the Major's shoelaces. He felt a sharp blow on his shoulder. Major Bobbno grinned and replaced the plastic claw beneath his arm. It hurt. 'What was that for?'

'He's just having a bit of fun with his hand-reacher. Go on, do his laces for him. I'll keep an eye on him,' said Bert. 'Now, now, Major – that was naughty of us.'

'Arise, Sir Jack,' chirruped Major Bobbno.

'He likes you,' whispered Bert, 'and that's good. He can be a real old devil. Yet you know, love 'em or loathe 'em, you'll find out, Jack, as time goes by, that it's very hard when they die. No matter how many times you've seen it. And I've seen it often. The new ones come in and they've been married a lifetime and suddenly they find they're sleeping in a single bed and you hear them crying at night. Not much you can do. Maybe they'll hold your hand and tell you they're lonely and want to go home. Or they're scared you're going to treat them like a child or a cabbage. I can tell you, young Jack, that some don't survive the shock of transplant. They leave the house they know and come to Serenity. But the shock's that great they're gone within a few weeks. The CV, that's the collection vehicle, is backing up to the ramp at the back door and off they go. You'll hear the elders sometimes talk of the ramp. "Oh, she went down the ramp," they'll say. I know it sounds callous, but it isn't really.'

Jack wasn't really listening to that. Jack was watching Major Bobbno leaving his wheelchair. The Major stood up, took a step forward and fell on his face. 'Goodbye, sucker!' said Jack who'd knotted the Major's laces together. 'Nobody fucks with Jack. Nobody!'

Jack met old Maudie who kept putting on her coat and asking if it was time to go home, and when Bert pointed out to her that there was trifle for lunch she took off her coat and said she might as well stay for lunch.

'She'll stay for supper too. And breakfast tomorrow. And lunch. In other words – she'll stay. But she won't stop putting on her coat and getting ready to go. That's the way it is,' said Bert.

He met Beryl the Beard and Bert taught him 'standard waking procedure'. 'She's a confused person. Right? Don't just barge in and shout, "Wakey, wakey," in the morning. Come in quietly and say to her: "Good morning, my name is Jack and your name is Beryl. It's time for your breakfast, Beryl." And don't be surprised if ten minutes later she can't remember your name. Introduce yourself again.'

He saw the great circle of chairs facing the TV. 'Try as you might,' Bert explained, 'that's where most of them usually end up. Give 'em painting classes, give 'em flower arranging. Or senior karate for strengthening the muscles. But the bloody box still wins hands down.'

Two days later Mr Fox brought Jack to see Max.

He sat reading in his room. A copy of *Fealty*. Princess of Wales's exercise regime. Readers Special Offer of a replica of the Royal Leotard. Max smelt him before he entered the room. Nose sharp, he sniffed. What was the boy enveloped in? Salt? Soy?

'You two new boys should get to know each other', said Mr Fox.

The new boys eyed each other.

Jack stuck out his hand. 'Friend of yours, she said – "Say hi to the giant." '

Say hi? Max pondered this. Chinese, perhaps? He had it now. Monosodium glutamate. The boy reeked of Chinese food.

'Friend in common?' Mr Fox enquired kindly. 'Jack's all the way from Florida, Mr Montfalcon. He partook in the entertainment business. In one of their famous theme parks. You go on stage, don't you, Jack, when you go to work? You don't wear a uniform, it's a costume.'

'Not work. Entertainment!' Jack added.

'Imagine that, Mr Montfalcon. You have to hand it to the Americans when it comes to making work fun. Of course we're pretty small beer compared with Jack's previous experience of dealing with the public.'

'Fifteen to twenty million a year,' said Jack.

'Their chef cooked his way through fifty thousand meals a day. Five million pounds of meat from Monday to Friday. And

Jack knows a friend of yours. Isn't it a small world, Mr Montfalcon?'

'I have no friends,' said Max.

'Everyone,' said Mr Fox cheerily, 'has a friend.'

'They're all dead. My friends are history.'

Jack beamed. 'Doesn't stop 'em being your friends. Just because they're dead.'

When Max's cupboard arrived a few days later, roped to the roof of the silver Jag, it was Jack who helped Night Matron shift it into position in Max's room. Ran his hand affectionately over its polished oaken face. Max, who watched the gesture, immediately arranged to fit a new lock.

'Well, now.' Mr Fox's golden earring swung from his lobe, a musical pendulum, beginning the countdown. 'You've met our elders. Now for that question I promised you: who would you say they are?'

Videos made flesh? Better than anything the Aardvark Emporium had to offer? Pure happiness? Fame and fortune? Jack did not say a word.

Mr Fox's musical pendulum counted him out. 'You and me, that's who they are, Jack. They're us!'

CHAPTER TWELVE

Max and The Broad Pelvis

The trouble, Max decided, was that people knew little history.

Consider young von F, that bright German who had come to Oxford in the thirties, direct from Göttingen. A Rhodes Scholar. The sort of chap one regarded as a 'thinking German'. And a patriot. How strange and distant that boy seemed now. Today people looked at the fall of the Berlin Wall and said that the unification of Germany was a good thing. Well, even back in the thirties, young von F had had his doubts about displaced Germans and their lonely remoteness in the Sudetenland.

'I tell you, Montfalcon, this chap Hitler is quite something. I mean he has energy like billyo. I watched him in Munich, back in 'twenty-seven. Marched his men through the English Garden and into Kaulbachstrasse and held an impromptu meeting. There were boots, belts, masses of brown. The odd moustache or two. I can't tell you what that brown colour did to some of us. It was so ugly, so vulgar! One felt ill. Even though one knew that one's reaction was – how shall I say? – somewhat patrician. But there was no doubting the sheer verve of the man. And his picture of the lost Sudentenlanders, that struck a chord. Unity! It was a hunger among Germans. Now I don't claim that I saw any of this as particularly historical, that afternoon in the rather gracious surroundings of Kaulbachstrasse. I didn't. It never occurred to me that I was witnessing the beginning of the end.'

And here Max had gently corrected his young German friend on the use of the word 'historical'.

'I think what you want to say is "historic", meaning memorable – certain to take its place in history. That's what you saw, something historic. I'm following the great master of modern English usage H. W. Fowler. Now "historical" means something more ordinary. Something occurring within that unfolding sequence of events which we call history. To fail to distinguish between an historic moment – which is to say the sight of the German dictator addressing members of his party in a Munich street – and the mere passage of moments in the past is the sort of sloppiness which Fowler deplores. He calls it "backsliding".'

How long ago all that was. And what had happened to his young friend, von F? They had been to the same school. Von F loved to recall his happy school days in England.

'School Road from Churtseigh to Guildford. A fabulous entrance gate. The pillars were crowned with griffins and there was a long curved drive, a stretch of forest and a hundred rooms. It was a real noble mansion, an estate. The chapel doubled as a laundry and was originally used as a boiler room. It was carefully dilapidated. You looked out over the lawns and in the distance there was a lake. Slightly muddy, but it didn't matter. The woods dotted around included a few lovely cedars. There were sheep in the far distance keeping the grass down, a formal flower garden to the right of the house. We were taught how to hold a teacup. How to sit down without spilling the tea. We wore grey flannels and blue blazers with a lion on the pocket. The headmaster's wife's sitting-room was covered in chintz, there were comfortable chairs, the windows were often open. I was a prefect once. We toasted muffins in front of the fire. There were no fags. I failed my exam.

'My Berlin school was built pre-First World War. It comprised six villas in the grounds of a large house. Many of the boarders came from Pomerania. They were the sons of landed gentry. There were some nobility. The name of the place was the Dahlem "Arndt Gymnasium". Our classes numbered thirty boys and they were all unruly. Punishment meant that you had to make a cat's paw of your fist and you got hit on it with a ruler. There was nothing free and easy about it. It was run in Prussian style. "*Guten Morgen, Herr Lehrer!*" I didn't do well. I hated it. I was bloody glad to get away. It was a Sunday because father was at home for a change. Sunday late spring and my father said, "There are only two possibilities now, either we shall be Communists or we shall accept Hitler." We were in town somewhere, my father was with me and a woman came up to us and said, "They are going to start shooting at any moment now." I heard a shot from across the square. It was in the twenties sometime and it went on for four or five years. I remember horses and carriages, I remember the Marschstall riding school which was later converted into two indoor tennis courts. At our school we had to learn to play tennis and to swim. We also had to learn good manners. All such things were part of the gentleman's education. The money in Germany was being continually devalued. The prices were incredible. A million marks for one egg. Once a week the driver came in the car with a basketful of money, a laundry basket, and my mother shot off and bought whatever she could get.

'Our house was opposite a cornfield where there was a battle between Communists and others and everyone moved into the cellar. But the battle wasn't much of an event. Just a few shots. In wintertime we had the new rich, the *nouveaux riches*, giving a picture of gaiety in Berlin amongst starving ex-soldiers and beggars. There were twenty suicides a night, and yet it was Charleston time. A man came and said suddenly, "We must forget the Treaty of Versailles. I can give you bread, work." On the other side there was the Spartacists, the Communists, fighting and shooting. He had the most fantastic powers of persuasion, and everyone said, "This is it!"

'No one really took the anti-Semitic business seriously. That was party politics. We didn't believe it till it happened and then we still didn't believe it.

'I heard Goebbels and left absolutely screaming with enthusiasm. He was a wonderful speaker. But you must remember always that Germany is a military country. It was drilled into people ever since Frederick the Great. Under the various Kaisers the officer class was everything. To give you an example of the sort of way it was I can tell you that if my mother and father wanted some dancing partners for my sisters they would call up and send for eight young officers. Five minutes before seven they were outside the door. At three minutes to seven they rang the bell. At one minute to seven they left their hats in the hall. At seven o'clock precisely they were greeting my parents.

'This hatred against the Jews is as old as the hills. There were pogroms against the Jews in Russia. In Austria. And in Germany later. And I have to say that to a certain extent they were justified. Because what happened in Germany was a reaction against the Eastern Galician Jews. Amongst themselves they were fine but towards the non-Jew, towards the Goyim, anything was allowed. I can remember when Hitler came to power and we were invited to the Avalon Hotel to watch the big and highly impressive march through the Brandenburg Gate with torches, Unter den Linden. It must have been 'thirty-two or 'thirty-three. You were drawn into it and you went with it.

'The first of May nineteen thirty-three that was when the world fell in on us. My father was not allowed to go into the office. I decide, said Hitler, who is a German and who is a Jew. And yet my father felt himself to be a Prussian German officer. He died in nineteen thirty-five in Switzerland. That was a turn-up for the books, by golly!

'We spoke English at home. When I was five we had a French *mademoiselle* and a year later an English miss. Her name was Miss Natalie, she was heavily built and an excellent short-distance sprinter. I could jump like a flea. I went in for swimming, skating, skiing. But I was no good with a round ball.

'So when I went to England I was in trouble. I started in the scrum and then played three-quarter. In the summer there was rowing. Either I rowed stroke or number seven. There was absolutely no feeling of foreignness.

'My father, you see, though a German, was an anglophile – and we were educated like Prussian princes. He spoke English a great deal in the house. My father coming back from London, I remember, with a carving set from Aspreys. My father's evening shirts were washed and starched in London. This was not out of the ordinary. So what I learnt was a cross between English and Prussian manners. One side relaxed and the other very strict, very formal.

'I took to the life in England like a duck to water. Everyone was friendly and polite. It was a pleasant, peaceful country and we drank cider in the local pubs. No one was interested in one's background. That was private. I was never struck by the feeling: "You don't belong here – bloody foreigner, get out!" We were simply human beings. I remember for our set books we had *Gulliver's Travels* and Chaucer's *Nun's Priest's Tale*. "He fethered Pertelote twenty tyme/And trad hire eke as ofte" – What does it mean, Sir? I played Julius Caesar though I was only one of the soldiers who ran upstairs and shouted, "Caesar is dead!" Contrary to the German school, I simply blossomed like a primrose after the rain in the English school. I learnt to do double somersaults of self-confidence and assurance. But I never knew what was what. I remember catching a train from sooty Paddington. I read the *Daily Mirror*. Why? Because I liked "The Adventures of Jane".'

Von F had been something of a sleuth. He was interested in the disguises of the past. Some might take pleasure in detecting ancient Saxon place names hidden beneath modern variants or corruptions. Just so young von F was keenly interested in the roots of Saxon settlement, particularly amongst the Lusatian Sorbs, or Wende. Place names, and in particular the presence of Slavic place names in German territory, were a source of huge concern to scholars in the thirties. Young von F was original in this as in so much else. He was not much taken with the secrets of place names beyond the river Elbe. He left that to others. He took his *Abitur* in the spring of 1927 and had it marked 'good'. Having matriculated he decided on pursuing his interests in the interpretations of peoples. In anthropology and ethnology. But surpisingly then the only place for him to begin his studies in earnest was at Leipzig, where the chair had just been occupied by the greatest German authority of his day, fresh from Vienna, Professor Otto Reche.

Although von F began his studies in Munich, where he learnt to fence and loved to bicycle along the Isar, which busily bisects the city, it was in Leipzig where he found his scientific desires most closely met in the lectures of Professor Reche. He did not stay there all the time. German universities allow their students considerable freedom after they have completed one semester. Young von F was to spend seven semesters at no fewer than four universities before completing his doctorate.

The life of the German student of those times is difficult to convey. Young von F would astonish his Oxford friends by recounting a typical day: 'After a cup of coffee, to the gym for an hour's fencing. Then to the range for some shooting. Smallbore usually. Then classes for an hour. Philosophy. And that meant Hegel. Poetry and that meant Hölderlin. Before lunch, from about eleven to twelve, a ride. Lunch to follow and then the ins and outs of fencing, a theoretical class. Usually, in the evenings, we went to the theatre. Oh, yes, I had a lot of fun.

'What are these scars? Do you mean here? Ah, those are duelling scars, I'm afraid. An affectation of German youth. In the old corps mine were won. In Göttingen. In the *Mensur*. A duel, that's right. Yes, precisely. The scars were not obligatory. Well, not exactly. But they came, eventually, if one behaved correctly. They show one to be what we used to call *satisfaktionsfähig*. How would you translate that? Capable of giving satisfaction, perhaps? And these here on my cheek, beside my mouth, date from an encounter with a certain Pfeister. He drew blood once. I did so twice. Its mate, the one you see running parallel to it, I got on a different occasion. About a year later, when, on a return visit to Munich, I was challenged by a certain Brackmann. We'd fallen out. Oh, yes, you guessed it. A young lady, of course. Perdita she was. A tiny vaporous blonde with ice-blue eyes. I don't suppose she was worth it. But that's besides the point. It was a question of honour. The *Mensur* was banned, as you probably know, by the Weimar government in the twenties. But students of the corps had been doing it for hundreds of years and no government decree was going to stop them. May as well have banned the devil drink. And we were often drunk, my lord, yes. Drunken is what we were.'

Young von F spoke beautiful supple English when he came to Oxford, with only tiny lapses. Such a likeable boy! Very tall, six foot four in his black silken socks, a huge shining forehead under a mass of blond curls, large liquefying sea-blue eyes which, when they softened in reflection, were gentle and almost feminine. Of course his English was good. His father an officer, a gentleman, a manufacturer of sanitary ware. And, most unexpectedly, a Jew. This had came as a tremendous surprise since von F's family had absolutely no knowledge of it until the Nazis sprung it upon them. Even the Nazis seemed less than sure, since after his father's suicide in Switzerland in 1935, they appeared to have forgotten all about it. They had never objected when von F returned to Germany, had they?

His mother had been half American. An heiress, one Daisy Milteagan from Savannah, Georgia, whose fortune had been made in what young von F called 'perishables'. In fact, slaves. It irked Max to detect this embarrassment in the young German when he described where his family had made money. Retrospective moral judgements in historical matters were vulgar. One did what one did at the time.

Young von F arrived in England in March 1936. He had graduated *summa cum laude* at Leipzig and his doctoral thesis was commended by the examining board. It read *The Broad Pelvis: A Saxon Bequest*. Though the work of a very young man, there were further accolades for this thesis from the great Professor Reche himself, who applied to it the term 'elegant' and, if that were not enough, Professor Reche helped to secure von F's future as an anthropologist and ethnographer, by going even further and calling it 'incisive'.

That these encomiums were not misplaced is shown by the degree of quite brilliant anticipation revealed in the work of the young von F. He had a gift undoubtedly. And this was to be proved again later in his life, a gift for being wise before the event.

In ethnographic circles in the thirties in Germany a storm was blowing up. Studies of Saxon remains showed a high incidence of dislocated hip joints. This phenomenon is not unusual in people who possess broad pelvises. But what electrified debate in Germany in the thirties was the suggestion that in those territories east of the Elbe river and, worse still, even in parts of Germany itself, Slavic settlements in ancient times preceded the arrival of Saxon settlers and they were responsible for clouding the gene pool, issuing in the dominant trait of the wide pelvis. Though this discussion was not openly aired at the time, it worried the best scientific minds, most of which were firmly committed to the idea of widespread Saxon settlement east and west of the Elbe from the very earliest periods. Von F's 'elegant' suggestion was that Saxon settlement had been so extensive and went back so far into the past that the very notion of 'Slav' dissolved under scrutiny. In his words, 'Saxon fact prevailed over Slavic perhaps'.

It was young von F's pioneering work in this field which later allowed eminences such as Professor Otto Reche to show conclusively that the dislocated hip joint was not a genetic ailment inherited from earlier, impure Slavic forebears and to go on to suggest convincingly that the reason for it was that Germans had lived east of the Elbe for so long that to speak of Slavs at all as a specifically 'racial' category, was unscientific. It's true that young von F never went so far as his former mentor in asserting that the settled German territories to the east of the Elbe – here he used a cunning English pun to make his point – were 'enSlav'd' by barbarian riffraff. No. Von F was always temperate in his science as in his politics. He wished only to follow the truth. Let others draw conclusions from basic and good scientific research. That was the scientist's job.

Von F took up residence in Nonce Hall, Oxford, in the summer term of 1936. Nonce, though founded in the mid-sixteenth century, came to be represented in the twentieth by a rather gloomy collection of smoky Victorian buildings in the centre of town. The college possessed no view of the river. Its quad was dark and damp, even in May. It had a reputation for philosophical astringency, logic and epistemology. This was tempered by a political radicalism, especially among numbers of the younger men. And although the thirties was a lifetime away from the gaudy excesses which swept through the university in the years after the Great War, there hung about Nonce an air of sexual intrigue, particularly bisexual adventure, which had scandalised and heated the town from time to time. Not for nothing was the 'new' School of Philosophy, Politics and Economics seized upon by the students of Nonce with enthusiasm. For well above the usual pursuits of college life – rowing, sex and snobbery – the men of Nonce were determined to be modern.

Young von F flung himself into Oxford life. He went punting on the river and managed to pick it up pretty quickly, which is saying something in a man of his height. It was a well-known fact that men over six feet four often experienced difficulty with the poling technique. To punting he added hunting, at Blenheim no less, with Tubby Semple, an amiable loafer who was never known to do a stroke of work and widely respected for it. And it was perhaps von F's depiction of poor Tubby as 'a being of low but amiable mind' that, even at this early stage of his Oxford romance, set him apart from his English counterparts in ways which were to tell deeply over the years he spent at Oxford.

Unlike several of his colleagues he also slept with a number of women, and with some of them repeatedly. Take Cynthia Pargeter whom he met through his membership of the Socialist Club. It was to Cynthia that young von F confessed feeling a mite suspicious about the British capacity for having 'a good time'. Later Cynthia was to tell Max that young von F had in fact often remarked: 'They possess a measure of seriousness but not high seriousness.' What she did not tell Max was that they had both been naked at the time and that young von F had been lightly scoring her body with a succession of kisses beginning with each of her ears and then descending via her chin in a straight line which bisected her breasts, allowing as he did so his cheeks to brush her nipples at the same time, ending in the fur of her groin. Nor did she tell him that she lay back and took a very firm hold of his very rampant penis while he did this which meant that von F was forced to arch his back above her till he looked, thought Cynthia, like a giant white naked caterpillar.

After this manoeuvre, which von F liked to refer to as the 'decline of kissing', he generally entered her at her urgent insistence. The lovemaking of von F and young Cynthia Pargeter was noisy and unabashed. She called his name, getting louder with every answering stroke from him. He whispered in her ear in German and generally, at the moment of climax, he would intone, somewhere between a sob and a prayer, a fragment of some poem, with beautiful diction, softly in her ear. Only later did she find out it was Hölderlin, his favourite.

All she said of this to Max some time later – 'I've never known anyone so divided. Wherever his body was you could be sure his mind was somewhere else.'

Oxford, then, was lovely. But Germany was serious. And it was Ralphie Treehouse, a friend from the Socialist Club, later a high flyer in the Foreign Office, and two years von F's senior, a man who had himself spent several years in Germany, who drew attention to the irremediable nature of von F's Germanness.

'Teutonic from T to C,' Treehouse remarked at the time. His later comments were to be much harsher. 'Show him the moonlight and he thinks of Beethoven. Talk to him of Germany and you get Goethe. Well, who could talk of Germany and tell me where it is? *Deutschland? Aber wo liegt es?* Exactly. Where is it? I wouldn't let his lovely English fool you for a bloody moment. The man's pure Hun.'

Even so they all liked him. Ralphie Treehouse especially.

At about this time young von F retreated into the music of Haydn and Beethoven. He slept just as often with Cynthia but he no longer practised the decline of kissing. He rounded fiercely on Tubby Semple for making jokes about 'that jolly silly little bugger, Hitler' and he told Ralphie Treehouse, already then beginning his dizzying ascent in the Foreign Office, that he grieved for his country though he thanked God for science which was pure, impersonal and might still be turned to the good of man.

Treehouse remembered him years later. 'He held up the tools of his trade to me – a pair of callipers and a micrometer – which he carried always in a brown leather bag. I think the case came from Argentina. I seem to remember, in his thorough way, that he insisted on telling me about the system of measuring by which you could say, work out somehow, a person's sex and race with very great accuracy. You could tell simply by checking on the measurements. And you could do it, he insisted, long after a person was dead and buried. By the measurement of the bones or even of scraps of bones, even splinters or charred remains, you could go on to tell whether the person in life had been caucasoid, negroid or mongoloid. I believe it was a system developed in the nineteenth century in France by some-body called Bertillon. It all sounded pretty rum to me. But that was von F. And when he got going, there was no stopping him.'

Von F became a fellow of Nonce College and might have stayed there for ever. Indeed he'd often announce his intention of doing so. But Hitler had other ideas. And from one day to the next, without telling anybody, and without warning, young von F decided to return to Germany. He sailed from Southampton in the late months of 1938. His friends were appalled. Only Cynthia was there to see him off. They paused in London though, the route was circuitous, and went to a *thé dansant* at the Palais de Danse in Tottenham Court Road. Afterwards they shared a blissfully deserted carriage and by the light of the reading lamp which showed first green and then grey as the train swayed through the night, they made love for one last time. It was done without their usual finesse, a greedy tearing at each other, much constricted by their despairing sense of time running out, as well as the ludicrously small confines of the compartment. She took him in her mouth. He upended her, literally stood her on her head, and, with her thighs pressed tightly against his ears, closing off the hateful hurrying wheels of the train, forced his tongue deep into her vagina. 'England pendant,' he called it. Then, when they found that making love in any conventional position was out of the question in that awkward space, he lay on the floor and stuck his long bare legs out of the window. Carefully she mounted him and while he lay back and closed his eyes, she brought herself very slowly and carefully to a climax, checking every inch of his penis, in much the same way as he had once moved down her body in the decline of kissing.

When afterwards she asked him what he had been thinking about, he said simply: 'Von Papen. Hindenburg has made a great mistake appointing him. He's as bad as Hitler. Worse, because he's weak. Not that I expect Hitler to prevail in the long term. Big forces are against him.'

Cynthia had laughed in the darkness. 'I think I preferred it when you whispered a bit of Hölderlin to me. I hoped you were thinking about love.'

Von F drew in his feet from the open window and showed her the blackened marks where flying smuts from the engine had landed. 'It felt like a form of firewalking. As to love, I was thinking about it. First we had England pendant. Then Germany subdued. Delicious symmetry, my darling, on a train bound for Southampton.'

Cynthia looked down at the long lean line of him and said with mock severity: 'Really! You know, Ralphie Treehouse has a point about you. You are incorrigibly German!'

In the early dawn on Southampton dock when Max unexpectedly joined them to wave goodbye, von F was still trying to explain to her that, yes, he was indeed incorrigibly German, but not in the nationalist sense. Simply in the ordinary committed sense that she was hopelessly English. 'Make her understand.' Max recalled him saying. 'I'm simply a patriot who must go home and fight for his country. What would Fowler say to that?'

'He'd say that you use a soft A in your pronunciation. Fowler reserved that for the adjective "patriotic". But he doesn't really mind. Patriot whichever way you look at it is what you are. Whether hard A, or soft A.'

Yes, Max remembered it well. He saw the ship pulling out and he saw Cynthia on the dock. She was waving. And he remembered something about the way that Cynthia had looked at him as if she had a question for him. He knew what the question was but he could not now remember if he had been asked for an answer on that rainy August morning, with the mournful gulls and the ship's bells. What was he doing there? Max looked back down the narrowing tunnel of time to those tiny figures on the dock in Southampton and tried desperately to remember. Why had he been there?

Now, lying in the darkness of Serenity House, and hearing Major Bobbno leading an attack over the top against the German lines, he could not answer the question. But he remembered Fowler on Patriot/Patriotism. 'The false quantity', says Fowler in his magisterial, liberal fashion, 'is of no importance.' Of no importance, certainly, to young von F who had been dead now many a year.

CHAPTER THIRTEEN

Innocenta to the Rescue

Once again Max came home on the arm of Sergeant Pearce. A little discussion of the problems of the fused particle. And about the love-life of William IV.

'Is it true he had a whole bunch of kids on the wrong side of the blanket?' Sergeant Pearce piloted Max Montfalcon into St Margaret Drive and the boys leaving school stared at the policeman and the tall thin old man with the blood red tie, the revolving arms and broken shoes, even though the sergeant and his companion were a familiar sight to the boys across the road who never tired of whispering to each other, 'It's a fair cop, guv!' They relished the sight as much as they did the appearance of Beryl the Beard at an upstairs window of Serenity House. They called Sergeant Pearce and his companion 'the cop and the skeleton'.

'King William had two by his legal wife, only two, unfortunately,' Max explained. 'She was German.'

'Now who would have thought it! You amaze me, sir. Pukka German?'

'Through and through,' Max assured him. 'Both royal children died in infancy. But he went on to have ten more by his mistress, a comedy actress called Dorothy Jordan.'

'Bastards, sir.'

'True. But good *English* bastards, Sergeant.'

Mr Fox met them at the door of Serenity House. 'I'll take delivery of the prisoner, Sergeant. Thank you for your help, as always. What are we going to do about our wanderings, Mr

Montfalcon? We really can't have you disappearing into the blue yonder like this. I have a very awkward time with enquiries from your family.'

'It's a free country,' said Max.

'They don't seem to see it that way, Mr Montfalcon. I think I'm going to have to offer you a paging facility. Clip a little box to your belt, and bleep you when family come to call. Then wherever you were you could pop into a phone box and have a word. It's becoming rather difficult with your son-in-law. He doesn't seem to think you should be out walking on your own.'

'In these islands, Mr Fox,' Max said proudly, 'we have learnt to fight for our freedom.'

'In Serenity House', Mr Fox countered smoothly, 'we have our freedom without fighting for it. Now, let's go upstairs. We have a visitor.'

She sat at Max's table wearing an apricot robe and a purple headdress beaded with small pieces of coloured glass that gave her the look of an Egyptian Pharaoh except that she carried a bulky black plastic handbag.

'Hello, Grandpa.'

'Innocenta, go home.'

'Not until you tell me what's been going on. Not to put too fine a point on it, you've stirred up a great big black cloud, Grandpa. Mummy and Daddy keep talking about Germany. It's Germany, Germany, Germany! When I think of Germany all I've ever thought of up till now is that they're good at tennis and everybody's frightened of their money. Are you German, Grandpa? As far as Daddy is concerned you're about as bad a German as you can get. Second only to Adolf Eichmann. Where do you come from?'

'Harwich,' said Max.

'Yes, I've heard about the Harwich claims. Thing is, Grandpa, between you and me, I don't think Harwich is going to cover it any longer. Did you know that there's talk of police going to trample round Poland looking for clues to your past?'

'Poland was a racial haystack. One had to sift through the straw to identify the different ethnic splinters.'

'Yes. Mummy says you must have been in Poland. She says that when you stayed with her she heard you speaking Polish.'

'Lizzie's wrong. I've never been in Poland. That was young von F. He did a tour of duty in Poland. He was a young German I knew years ago. Before the war. He served in one of their establishments. I don't need to go into detail. Suffice to say he never supported their programmes. He resisted the trends.'

'He was a good German?' Innocenta asked.

Max hesitated. 'He was not a *bad* German.'

'Let's have a drink, Grandpa.'

'Go home, Innocenta. And stay away from me. This is a fight to the death.'

'Look, I'm really the one who owes you a lot. Without you I might have ended up marrying Nigel. A fate several million times worse than death. You don't seem to have any glasses. Never mind, we'll use teacups.'

Lovely, lissome Innocenta, pulling a bottle of whisky from her black bag; lifting her chalk white face anxiously to Max, showing the dark red rouge on her cheekbones, and masses of purple eyeshadow. What a sight for sore eyes. How well she filled the screen, thought Jack in the observation room, down the corridor. Even on the small screen Innocenta dazzled – flaming hair, green eyes. Curved yet taut, Innocenta seemed to the watching Jack to be something he wished to touch. The way Max stroked her shoulder, and Innocenta's silver lips parted when she spoke: no, there was something in those parted lips which told him she did not so much speak – as sing!

'If what Daddy says about them coming to get you is true, Grandpa – ' she stroked his hand as it lay on her shoulder, – 'you may have to get on your bike. And for that you'll need some help.'

'I was a fast mover', said her grandfather, 'in my prime.'

As a boy he had been a fine sprinter over the hundred-yard dash. No one at Churtseigh held a candle to him. Even the Bishop of London told him that. He'd approached the Bishop on Palm Sunday and asked a question which had been troubling him: 'Your Grace, as this is an Anglican school and I am a

Lutheran, is it permitted for me to receive Holy Communion?'
'What's the difference?' The Bishop had asked in his cheery
way. 'Of course you may. The boys say you don't play rugby.'

'I think you have to have been born to use the oval ball, Your
Grace.'

'Nonsense. See me after lunch on the rugger pitch.'

And on the rugby field after lunch, tucking his skirt into his
belts, the Bishop took the rugby ball and punted it high into
the sky.

'Well done, Your Grace!' he had cried and the Bishop had
wiped his forehead on a large white handkerchief before
replying.

'If I can do it, anyone can do it. Keep up the sprinting. The
boys tell me you are very fleet of foot.'

Max should have listened to the Bishop of London and kept it
up. It was definitely the sprint at which he had excelled. Not
the spurt. Although Fowler allowed that nowadays the two
terms were almost interchangable, pointing out that the word
'sprint' in modern usage increasingly applies to a race run at
high speed. While 'spurt' is increasingly confined to a spasm of
mental or bodily effort.

He forced his mind to move now in mental spurts. He gave
up his mind to getting ahead of the game.

'There is something you might do, perhaps, Innocenta.'

'Tell me.'

'First, a story. About a poor boy who went to market.'

'Let me guess – to sell his mother's cow?'

'Not quite. But close. He didn't sell his mother's cow. He
traded it for something he thought better.'

'Jack and the Beanstalk! That's what it is, isn't it, Grandpa?'
Innocenta refilled their cups. 'Tell me the story.'

The point about all such stories, said Max, is that the boy
gets the better of the giant. Steals his gold, robs him blind,
kills his friends, slaughters the goose that lays the golden eggs,
deceives his wife and disrupts his nights. And ends up murdering
him. The point about all such stories is that the boy gets away
with it. The point about the story, Max told Innocenta, was

143

that, this time, it would be different. Max pointed to the sleek black snouts of the eavesdropping cameras. 'Who watches the watcher? The thief in the night?' He stroked her cheek from time to time and said: 'Thing is to stay close to him, my dear.' And when Innocenta asked 'How close?' Max smiled, 'As close as you can get.'

And Innocenta saw it as a matter of life and death. Of salvation. Could Max be saved? Her parents, the queen and her reckless consort, had expelled the old man from his home. And she, Innocenta was not going to allow it. 'Over my dead body,' muttered Innocenta, and her grandfather said: 'I don't think we'll have to go that far.'

Did he mean it? Did he not think that she would be the bait to his trap? Max asked himself the question coldly. He had watched the way the watcher watched Innocenta. Max loved Innocenta. But he told himself that this was war. 'You'll be,' said Max, 'my cuckoo in the nest. My eyes and ears.'

And Innocenta thought, yes, after all, she'd been many things, from a vegan to a follower of Sri Chinmoy and taken part in a peace run from Glasgow to Dover. She had been a Raelian and waited night after night on draughty Clapham Common for the arrival of 'our fathers from space', and worn the six-pointed star with the swastika in the centre. She had been a friend of the whale. She'd never knowingly abused the ozone. Now, she was a somewhat discontented member of the International Church of Meditation, and she felt further than ever from salvation. Max needed to be saved and she, Innocenta, was jolly well going to do it.

But what would it take to save him? When Max told her she swallowed her surprise and said firmly, 'If eating Chinese will do it, then eating Chinese it will be, Grandpa.'

Innocenta sighed and stood up.

'We're not allowed to drink in here,' said Max.

'In that case, I'll leave you the rest. Here's something else.' From her black bag she pulled out a small dark green bottle. 'This is a protection potion I made for you. It's got things like salt and myrrh and a pinch of wolf's hair and a speck or two of graveyard dust, some spring water and a sprinkling of iron shavings. Whenever you feel threatened dab some on your wrists and on your forehead. Just use a dab now and then. A little goes a long way.' She placed it on the table beside the whisky bottle. 'I'll be back, Grandpa. Leave it to me.'

For about half an hour after she had left Max sat at the table with his head in his hands. Then he groaned and stretched and got to his feet. He walked to his cupboard and unlocked it. The picture on Jack's screen was clear, the old man's gestures slow but decisive. From the cupboard he took a box, it looked like an old cigar box tied in red ribbon. The camera looked down through the skylight, looked down on the top of Max's grey head. It could swivel, Jack knew that. But swivel he preferred not to do just in case the old man should look up, in case he wised up. But zoom he could and zoom he did, dropping like an eagle on to Max's wrist, checking over the cigar box, coming in close and clear. Max poured himself another slug of whisky, sat down at his table and very slowly undid the ribbons around the box. What he took from the box the boy at first thought were buttons, or dice, or some kind of candy. But they were heavy, he could see that, he could see it from the way the old man rolled them in his hand, rolled them in the way you did dice, weighted dice, rolled them on the table beneath his forefinger.

Why, tonight, Jack boy, what you see in your camera is a box of very heavy teeth. And what is heavy enough to make teeth roll like that, like dice? Why, only one thing, Jack boy, one thing. Gold! The old man was counting his teeth. He counted them once, he counted them twice. He must have counted them a dozen times, rolling them across the table into neat piles. There were around thirty or perhaps forty, Jack guessed. Little and large, all of them heavy. Though on each count the level of the whisky bottle dropped another inch and Max's head got lower and lower and his whole body took on the lines of his grief, the agony was in the angle of the head, the way the right hand was thrown across the table, the fingers touching the box, the left arm, like a human dyke, held within its wall showing the red ribbon like a warning – go back! advance no further! – a pile of white and golden trinkets.

145

As Max had predicted, Jack was in the observation room, glued to the bank of monitors. He was quite unaware of Innocenta's presence until she said, close by his ear, 'You must be Jack. My grandfather told me to look out for you.'

And boy, did he jump! He'd seen her leaving Max, and here she was. Magic! She moved quietly as a silent movie, a TV with sound down. All he said was, 'Yes, ma'am', and studied her out of the corner of his eye. Red hair, weird robes and funny headgear.

To stay cool he flicked through an assortment of elders. Lady Divina, corners of her sheets knotted in her anxious fingers, watching behind closed lids the inexorable drowning of the Maldive Islands. Major Bobbno reaching for his gas mask as incoming gas shells burst about the trenches. Max asleep, his trinkets cradled in his arms. Just to show her he did this all the time. 'Serenity House night service,' said Jack. 'Lights-out countdown. Sleep tight, don't let the bugs bite. Hey, love your hat.'

Innocenta savoured the compliment. 'It focuses the rays of the universe.'

'No shit?' Jack blinked admiringly.

'I belong to the International Church of Meditation.'

'Me,' said Jack, 'to the Aardvark Video Club.'

From there it was an easy step to the Green Dragon, Highgate Village, two evenings later, Jack's night off. Bird's nest soup followed by lemon chicken, carp with chestnuts. Beef in black bean sauce, plenty of tea, prawn crackers with everything. Toffee apples to finish. Jack in his new white carer's drill uniform. Innocenta in jet black.

'Two squares looking for a chessboard,' said Innocenta and, boy, did Jack laugh. She rather liked his laugh. She stared in fascination at his mismatched eyes. His head reminded her of one of those cheesy rubber erasers. She hoped it was OK to like his laugh. All Max had said when she told him she was eating Chinese was: 'Play his kind of music, my dear. Stay close.'

He told her about Josh his friend who had hanged himself with the mail-order gallows.

She told him about Shree Trevor.

Jack said Shree Trevor was 'a big fake'.

146

Innocenta said fakes were sometimes better than boring originals. She helped him to read the menu, watching in fascination
at the effort the boy made to read the items, his tongue between
his teeth, finger stumbling from syllable to syllable.

'Trevor's a fake, sure as hell,' said Jack again. 'If Trevor isn't
a fake I'll lick his arse in downtown Orlando on a Sunday.'

'I don't think he's likely to be visiting Orlando,' said Innocenta sweetly, 'on Sunday or any other day of the week.'

'Everybody should visit Orlando.' Jack turned sullen. 'I got
a place in Orlando. 'Cross the road from Fat Mansy's "Guns
'n' Gold".'

He was a real patriot, Innocenta realised. When they reached
the toffee apple stage she asked if he would be going home.

Sure he would. Just as soon as he'd finished his business in
London. Back home to his place in Tranquil Pines. He'd draw
her a map. On a paper napkin. 'If you're ever down that way,
be sure and stop by, you hear?'

And of course she promised she would. She slipped the map
into her bag, didn't she? But, better and better, Innocenta had
had an idea. She did not know what Max would think of it. But
he had said to get close to Jack – hadn't he?

After Max left Greyacres in such distressing circumstances his
daughter Elizabeth had struggled to come to terms with herself.
Her remorse had been huge. Then came the rage. Since Albert's
revelations about her father, she found herself increasingly wishing she might have acted on her impulse to push him under the
water on those nights when he gave trouble on his bathability
stool. No longer occasions for guilt, those bathroom memories
now seemed more like lost opportunities. It would have been as
natural as drowning a spider.

She still gave rather good parties and worried aloud about
seating plans. 'The trouble', she told another newspaper, 'is
when you find people deep in conversation before dinner and
you know you've placed them at your table cheek by jowl.' But
her conversations showed signs of a new sharpness. She told
Tony Hyslop, chair of the Commons Select Committee looking
into the adoption of a common Euro-currency, that he had

better bloody well watch the Germans. 'Give them an inch and they'll be everywhere,' she said.

She feared especially the knock upon the door that she knew must come. It might be that dreadful American boy who left the strange letter to Marta and whom she'd seen at Serenity House. It might be the police making enquiries about 'your father's entry into Britain after the war, and his movements prior to that'. It might, indeed, be her father. He said, when she visited him, that she had sent him away to the 'camp'. He said there was no escape. He told her there were dogs. Electrified fences. She told him not to be silly. He could leave Serenity House any time he liked. But this was not something she liked to imagine.

She had lasted nine months of the Grand Bargain with her father, until Max finally wore her down. Not that they wanted to send him away, but what was the alternative? And he seemed quite happy these days in Serenity House. Certainly there were times he demanded to come home, indeed there had been occasions when he did come home, unexpected and uninvited. Once she found him making himself tea in the kitchen. On another occasion she found him asleep in his bed wearing a bright red, conical, knitted cap. He always went back to Serenity House, but it was awful. He became quite rigid with resistance and she was reminded of how badly her cat Marmaduke had behaved whenever they went on holiday. At the sight of the cat basket prepared for the trip to the kennels he spat and scratched and howled, did Marmaduke. Max simply went very stiff, he turned into a kind of clothes horse and she'd have to propel him down the path towards the waiting car.

Her whole life seemed to be measured in terms of 'before'. Before they'd moved to the big house in Highgate, her husband Albert had seemed more solid somehow. Now he seemed increasingly, well, pneumatic was the only word she could think of. He wasn't where he was. Slothful, sly but solid Albert, substantial, sweet if somewhat vague at home, serious in bed, when, beneath the ceiling covered with patterned wallpaper, gold fleur-de-lis on a navy ground (his choice) inset with a large oval mirror (her inspiration) they made slow, somewhat sweaty, but satisfactory love around once a week, usually on a Friday night, as if having completed his business in the House of Commons, Albert was free to turn his attentions elsewhere.

Albert's love-making, like Albert himself, was methodical and unstoppable. In the early days of their marriage, he had suffered from premature ejaculation. Seconds before his cock slid into her vagina, Albert would be convulsed by a violent orgasm.

It had been three years from the beginning of their marriage before Lizzie had achieved her own climax. It came quite suddenly, one Friday night, after Albert had expired quietly on her breasts and lay there, a little perspiration dripping slowly from his eyebrows on to her neck. She moved. Just a little. And suddenly a deep and distant fluttering like the beginnings of a sneeze or a giggle began somewhere down there and grew, mushroomed hugely as if someone had turned up the volume, like a violent thunderstorm with stereo effects, so loud that, as she lay there, she had covered her ears and so did not hear Albert's surprised and slightly aggrieved question: 'What on earth's happening, Lizzie?' Oblivious, she did not hear him, nor did she hear her own shrill papery cry as the sound and the wetness overwhelmed her.

Albert's ejaculations grew less premature. She learned to take, steal, would be a better word, her pleasure from the straining, heaving bulk of her husband's body. In his brief ascendancy, some years earlier, as a parliamentary private secretary to the Minister of the Environment, Albert had entered a new phase in his sexual relations. He took to asking Lizzie to straddle him and might lie that way motionless for up to ten minutes, and his climax was barely a ripple, as if his responsibilities were such that he could no longer spare the energy in bed. At the same time his demeanour suggested that, rather like taking a drive in a dull but dependable old jalopy, if she wished to take him for a spin now and then, he would not object, always providing she did not expect much by way of acceleration or excitement.

After a time this ceased to worry Lizzie who became adept at taking her pleasure in semi-private, managing sometimes as many as three orgasms whilst straddling the white and pink bulk of her immobile husband. She did not care to work out how her husband could keep erect for so long his short but powerful penis, angry aubergine at the tip, thick and yellow where it arose from his pubic hairs like the stem or stalk of some slightly dubious forest mushroom. But what the hell! Riding the carousel or taking the inflatable were just some of the phrases that she used to herself when referring to this weekly exercise.

Innocenta had been such a sweet baby, and had given no sign of her horrifying future. That had soon changed. Even as a child she had not been easy. Her early stories had been about Tibetan lamas with third eyes. When other children had been reading about rabbits, she frightened Lizzie with accounts of rebirthing techniques. Always a forthright girl, she thought nothing of demonstrating the correct foetal position by lying down in Selfridges. The neighbours would complain about her Primal Scream.

Now, said Albert, she had become a religious zealot and was attending a church in a basement somewhere in Islington. Lizzie had asked him where precisely in Islington. Albert had become very exasperated and said he had no idea. He did not know Islington and was unlikely ever to do so.

Albert's temper grew worse. He visited Serenity House twice a week now, trying to get Max to tell him 'the truth'. When Elizabeth said it would be better if her father were dead, Albert replied that, even dead, someone would have to get to the bottom of things.

'Poor Lizzie,' Albert gave his committee smile. 'What would happen if the spider didn't drown after all, and come back one morning? Back up the bloody plug hole? Spiders do that, you know.'

When the knock on the door finally came Elizabeth ran into her bedroom and locked the door. She waited there for about five minutes, shaking and pulling the pillows over her head. Albert was at the House. She was quite alone. But the knocking did not stop and, in the end, she had to go and peer through the spyhole, shivering and pulling her pink cardigan around her throat. When she saw Innocenta, her relief was so great that her mood shifted from terror to delight.

'Darling!'

'Hello, Mummy.' Innocenta carried a small wand about the thickness of a bicycle pump, a gift from a friend who'd belonged to a Wicca group, for she had the unmistakable feeling that she was going to need all the protection she could get. 'I'm coming home.'

'Are you, darling? How lovely.'

Her mother was using what Innocenta thought of as her 'we are now addressing the brain-damaged' voice.

'Have you become a witch, Innocenta?' Lizzie wished Albert had been more specific about Innocenta's new religion. She eyed the wand. 'That must be very interesting.'

'I've got my things in the car,' said Innocenta.

At that moment, thank heaven, Albert arrived, leaping from the silver Jag and shouting at the top of his voice: 'For God's sake, Lizzie, this is the last straw! Heard today that the police are promising to hit the ground running in the matter of you know who. And here am I, the befuddled foolish son-in-law. I'll get the truth if I have to wring it out of him. Can you imagine what the papers would make of this?'

He stopped short when he saw Innocenta. He rubbed his eyes. He said: 'It's the Queen of the Fairies. Except for the club she carries. Are you offering witchcraft or violence, Innocenta?'

'She's coming home, Albert,' said Elizabeth. But Albert was looking at something else. There he was, walking up the garden path behind Innocenta.

'Well, well,' said Albert, 'it's the American boy.'

'I told you I had my things in the car,' said Innocenta. 'Daddy and Mummy, this is Jack.'

'How do you do,' said Jack carefully. It had taken Innocenta ages to teach him. It must have been rather the way Professor Higgins felt when he trained Eliza Doolittle.

'We've met,' said Elizabeth. 'We've still got your letter. What are we to do with it?' Albert looked angrily at Jack.

'Lots of time for that,' Innocenta smiled, sweet and slow, 'when we're living here.'

'Over my dead body,' said her father.

'That flat belongs to Grandpa, even if you drove him away.' Innocenta pointed out. 'We had a good talk. Now he wants me to have it.'

'If Innocenta wants to come home, then that's what she'll do. With her new – friend.' Elizabeth led the way indoors.

Jack smiled to see the house looked as good as ever. In a picture over the fireplace a horse with skinny legs leapt over a hedge with its rider inches out of the saddle. Two blue porcelain cats sat on either side of the fire. Behind them spread upward, rich and red, in their leather covers, shelf upon shelf of books. An entire fucking wall of books!

'Jack will take the spare room. I'll have Grandpa's. Don't look so fierce, Daddy. You'll hardly know we're here. You're as quiet as a mouse – aren't you, Jack?'

'What do you want?' Albert put his hands on his hips and leaned over Jack. 'With your letter and your threats? We have laws in England. I should warn you. My father-in-law is now a police matter.'

'Old Max, he's down the road in Serenity House.' Jack smiled. 'Ain't saying nothing to nobody – yet. Old Max and me.'

Albert said heavily, 'All bloody roads seem to lead to Serenity House.'

'That's right, Daddy.'

Jack thought the English were screwy. Everyone knew that all roads lead to the Magic Kingdom.

CHAPTER FOURTEEN

Albert Puts his Foot in It

'Give us a shout if we need anything, Mr Montfalcon.' Mr Fox leaned over Max and adjusted his blue Kumfee wheelchair cover with its extra warm Thermalux lining, before he slipped away to deal with Lady Divina, who was once again having trouble with her pill-hopper. Albert, making another of his increasingly angry visits, sat grimly, making a megaphone of his hands, pressing them to the old man's ear: 'We're going to sort this out!'

The thought that Innocenta and the American boy were living in his house added to Albert's sense of helpless grievance. He shook Max roughly.

Max opened his blue eyes and stared blankly. 'Who are you?'

To the problems facing him, that is to say the difficulties of memory and the question of number, Max Montfalcon brought a novel approach. To remember something, one needs, in a sense, an occasion for doing so, some sort of reason. Without some reason, recalling an event, or remembering anything at all, becomes, literally, pointless. One did not remember because one wished to be accurate – at least he did not – but precisely because one did not wish to forget. The buried reason for not wishing to forget, though it may be lovely, fraudulent, dishonest, heartfelt or false, is the place where the spring of memory resides. There is a kind of policy for allowing this fact rather than that to resurface. Just as there is a motive, whether you acknowledge it or not, for forbidding its resurrection. Memory, after all, was not history, but more of a system of values. Sometimes it was a form of rebirth. Often it was a matter of will, even of power. How else could you explain the anger of his son-in-law who for reasons Max did not understand now sat beside him, hands to his mouth, demanding in a monotonous voice, over and over again: 'Tell me what you can remember.'

'I began in Harwich.'

'Harwich! Now, Max, you know as well as I do that that is not true.'

'Harwich, gateway to the continent.' Max was firm. He could see it all now. Dear old Harwich, a splendid town with a colourful history facing the estuaries of the rivers Stour and Orwell.

Albert, it seemed, was not really interested in Harwich, although Max could have told him a good many fascinating things about his old home town. He could have spoken about the old Electric Palace, the very first cinema in Britain. In the light of Albert's job, the news that Samuel Pepys had been MP for Harwich might have found an answering echo. But no, Albert just glared. And Albert, for his part, had a word of his own with which to challenge Harwich. And he bared his teeth when he said the second syllable, his lips peeling back: 'Poland!' said Albert Turberville. And after that he would ask, again: 'How many?'

Mr Fox danced lightly into the room carrying a copy of *Homage* opened at a painting by Winterhalter of Queen Victoria's consort in a splendid crimson tunic and blue and gold sash. 'Something rather troubling about the eyes, don't you feel, Mr M?'

Max studied the painting fiercely. 'Look at him. Teutonic arrogance. Imagine what would have happened if Victoria had died and Albert lived!'

'We're having a private conversation,' Albert growled.

'Your father-in-law rang.' Fox leaned forward and opened Max's jacket to show the bleeper clipped to his trouser waist. 'He's wired up, is Mr Montfalcon. On account of the little walks he likes to take. So I wired him with the bleeper so he could call home if he was in trouble. He's never used it, until today. I think he's learning.' He leaned over the old man. 'I'm proud of you. Well done, Mr Montfalcon. Next time maybe you'll use your bleeper when you go on one of your walks. Now I think we're a bit fatigued, Mr Turberville.'

'I haven't finished.'

'Look at him. You'll get no more out of him.'

The old man sat motionless in his chair, his tie up around his ear, until one of the carers bustled in and took him away. 'Lord, oh, Lord, Mr Max. You look just like a schoolboy with your tie under your ear.'

'What's he keeping in that cupboard?' Albert demanded.

Mr Fox inclined his head. 'Precious possessions. But none of my business.' He explained with a solemnity which Albert found infuriating, that Serenity House encouraged guests to bring with them a few things they prized most dearly. Such mementoes sometimes helped to ease the pain of transplant. The pain of leaving a beloved house. Moving to a single bed after a lifetime of sharing a double bed with a partner. The loss and dispersal of books, pets, kettles, pictures – these things can be so strong that elders have been known to die from shock within weeks of moving into a refuge. Transplant failure.

The next day Albert was back. Back with his question: 'How many, Max?' Back with his own answer to his question: 'A lot!' Regarding his son-in-law through half-closed eyes, Max decided he was the sort of man who never let one get a word in edgeways.

Or was this noisy, shaggy intruder who interrogated Max perhaps a clone of his son-in-law? The identical blue suit, the same shoes, the elephant's knee wrinkle to the trousers. 'Clone' was the new word. Back in the University in Cracow, in the old days, someone – had it been Hippius? – (Max really couldn't remember) had called it 'the human building material'. One cell, in theory, was enough, old Hippius had said, and you might one day re-create identical copies of the original. Imagine it, a Poland full of beautiful Germans, all with long heads. Such ideas had been ahead of their time. They'd come to nothing, to ashes. Why was that? Max couldn't remember exactly. 'Ash on a young man's sleeve.' Wasn't that T. S. Eliot's line? Eliot, he felt, would have been a poet to understand something of the difficulties of those times. At any rate, now we had clones, we could work directly on the human building material. And so there rapidly approached the possibility of making unlimited copies of Albert Turberville MP who stood before his wheelchair shouting 'How many did you murder?' and then answered his own question by shouting, even louder, 'A lot!'

The vagueness of it irritated him. How many was 'a lot'? It was so imprecise a manner of speaking. The English were sadly slipshod about questions of number. Did it mean 'a few'? 'a large amount'? or even 'one or two'? Such phrases, as always in English, never meant exactly, or even inexactly, what they said.

Albert groaned. His eyes were watering slightly and the mottled flush in his plump cheeks glowed and paled, seemed to be pulsing. A clock-face of flesh, and deep within it hid something coiled to strike. Max sat tall and upright in his wheelchair. Though he still liked to walk, particularly out of doors, he preferred to sit in the wheelchair in his room. Mr Fox had chosen for him the Gazelle. A cushion, deep and soft, a comfortable perch.

As Max stared mistily at Albert's pulsing face he began, in a delicate and vague way, to do his pelvic exercises, tightening the sphincter muscles, promising himself to keep it up, planning one day, he liked to tell himself, to build a pelvic floor like cast bloody iron! His incontinence, never more than partial, had definitely improved since he had started the exercises. He settled back, counting to four with each contraction, letting go slowly. Then he looked at Albert's shoes, and had an idea.

'On questions of number Fowler says that "*a few*, *a great many* and *a good many*, are idiomatic, but *a good few* is facetious or illiterate; *a very few* is permissible—".'

'Max!' Albert's outraged bellow rang in his ears. 'We are talking of crimes! Hideous, horrible crimes!'

'—whereas *very few* means not-at-all-many-though-some.' Max thought his son-in-law looked like a mastodon, a shaggy mammoth with the head of a traffic light. His clothes seemed to go off in all directions. He was rough, springy, hairy and muscular all at once.

There followed what seemed to be a lot of noise, perhaps a sudden storm or low-flying aircraft or those dreadful boys from the school over the road. The ones who teased Beryl who grew hairs on her chin. 'Show us your beard, Beryl!' they shouted. Beryl had wept. 'I know I should have them off – but, see, Mr

Montfalcon, they're all I have!' And she'd touch the nest of white hairs warming her chin. Max had to put up the shutters in his ears, retreated into strategic deafness, because the noise which appeared to be coming from Albert really was unbearable.

That's how Cledwyn Fox found them, with Albert declaring, 'We're talking about death!'

'Please, Mr Turberville,' said Fox quietly, 'my other guests . . . You can be heard as far away as D wing.'

'I don't care if I can be heard in kingdom come!'

He had what Fox thought of as a House of Commons bray, the sort of voice accustomed to being raised, a weapon to bludgeon the jeering opposition. The phrase 'kingdom come' hung in the air and suddenly Albert felt rather embarrassed. He seldom used that phrase, except when he was praying 'Thy Kingdom come' and 'For Thine is the Kingdom, the power and the glory.'

Now in Albert's heart there warred two conflicting emotions, both deeply embarrassing. He didn't know which was worse – being ignored by his stubborn, obtuse, infuriating father-in-law or being thought of as religious by the poncey little Welshman with the golden earring.

From down the corridor came the shrill cries of Lady Divina. The widening hole in the ozone layer was disturbing her particularly that day. Now not one hole – 'But two! But two!' Dustbowls in Kent and typhoons in Glasgow. Proliferating skin cancers. The Sahara, already swiftly advancing through Africa, now breaking into a gallop.

'The seas will rise and drown us!' Lady Divina called in her curious, carrying, fluting voice. 'And the nuclear fuel we have dumped at sea will break from its concrete casing and poison the whales. Our high streets will stink with dead fish . . . '

'Oh, shut your fucking gob, silly old bitch!' a male voice further down the corridor now began shouting – Major Bobbno, ex-Inniskillen Fusiliers, Sandhurst boxing champion, decorated in the First World War, recalled to the colours in the Second.

'Defeatism in the face of the enemy, rank cowardice!' yelled Major Bobbno. 'Take that man out and shoot him. It's not a soldier, it's a bleating sheep!'

Matron Trump hurried into Max's room. 'Oh, come please, Mr Fox! I'm having trouble restraining the Major. He's fallen on one knee and will not move. He has his light-weight hand-reacher to his shoulder and he's working those plastic jaws like mad. He has hit Nurse Daly with it, and I fear he's broken the magnet.'

Down the corridor Major Bobbno's voice barked stentorian commands . . . 'Ready, aim, fire!' This order was followed by a series of loud clicks and Major Bobbno became the firing squad shouting at the top of his voice, 'Bang, bang, bang!'

Cledwyn Fox looked darkly at Albert Turberville. 'You're causing a disturbance,' he said evenly. 'I must ask you to leave.'

But Albert stayed where he was, firmly planted, his House of Commons stance as when ordered by the Speaker of the House to withdraw – mutinous, stolid. 'Give me one good reason why I should? I pay for my father-in-law to be here, remember? Damn near five hundred quid a week.'

'I could give you a number of reasons, Mr Turberville. But one will do. You're standing in a large pool of urine.'

Max smiled.

One afternoon Fox watched as Albert thrust rather fat legs from his Jag, smoothed down the crumpled back of his blue suit, and cornered the little nurse-aide Imelda.

'Where in Christ's name is he? Tell me, you silly girl, or I will see to it that you go the same way as Imelda Marcos.'

'He's gone out,' she kept repeating helplessly.

'Where to?'

'We don't exactly know.' Mr Fox came up quietly behind them. 'Imelda, Lady Divina needs changing. I'll deal with this.'

'Are you telling me that my father-in-law is wandering about London? And unattended? You don't know where he is? What kind of authority are you?'

'We are not an authority, Mr Turberville, this is a nursing home. I've told you before. Your father is what is known as a "wanderer". That's why we've wired him up. I shall soon be fitting him with an electronic tracking device – once I can decide on some part of his person where he won't know about it. When he finds a homing device, he rips it off.'

'He should be confined.'

'What would you like us to do? Lock him in his room? I tell you this is a nursing home, not a prison camp.'

'A pity,' Albert Turberville had replied.

Now what on earth, wondered Cledwyn Fox, did he mean by that? But there was no time to go into it because Matron Trump bustled in and announced that old Maudie Geratie was 'just leaving'. And then Dr Tonks popped in and said, yes, Mrs Geratie was going 'and going quite splendidly quickly too. I'm very, very pleased with her.' And when Matron suggested it was really Dr Tonks who had done most of the work in getting old Maudie this far, Dr Tonks demurred and said: 'No, no. She's done most of it herself.' Dr Tonks, in his white coat and his belt, rather like a cartridge pouch, where he carried his ampoules and syringes. 'My ammo,' he called them.

'You don't seem to keep your patients for long,' Albert suggested rather sharply. 'They're out and about all over the shop.'

Mr Fox pulled at his lower lip, a movement he invested with gentle scorn. 'You don't understand. This elder is not going for a little walk. She's dying, Mr Turberville. Leaving. They do it regularly in Serenity House.'

Then as if by magic Jack appeared. Albert noted that he had a Mouse head tucked beneath his arm. The eyes were black, the nose bulbous. Black lips were parted in a rigid smile to show a poisonously red tongue. A furry black scalp beginning with a pronounced V swelling into big looping black ears. 'Hiya, Mr Turberville, sir.' Jack greeted his new landlord.

'Jack's a marvel!' Mr Fox said. No-one in Serenity House is ever quicker to the bedside of a departing elder than our Jack. You know about old Maudie, don't you, Jack?'

The boy lifted a thumb. 'On my way, captain.'

'I think he must have a nose for it,' said Mr Fox. 'Often he seems to know an elder is on her way before the elder knows herself!'

Jack looked at Albert and winked. Then the boy donned his head and sped lightly away to watch over the departure of old Maudie.

Jack had become an indispensable member of the staff of Serenity House. It was as if he had always been there. He wore the white uniform and took much pride in it. 'If only Marta could see me now,' said Jack as he preened in front of the mirror. Night Matron was especially pleased with his progress. 'He has energy, strength and no qualms whatsoever,' she reported to Cledwyn Fox, who beamed at the news and slept like a baby in his bed at nights. He was worth at least two members of staff.

No one knew where Jack went when he clocked off. It was vaguely understood that he was 'putting up' somewhere. It could not have been far away for it was observed that he walked to work. He had no social security number, no bank account, no address, no apparent friends. True, Edgar the chiropodist had invited him to a meeting to protest against Economic Monetary Union, and had spent a fortune on perfume for the occasion. Then Edgar had failed to turn up at Serenity House for a full fortnight and when he did appear he sported the ghost of a black eye and his pink lapel button – Eurobugger – And Proud of It! – had been badly dented. Jack and Edgar did not speak again after that – but no one noticed. Everyone thought he was simply brilliant. A triumphant addition to the cast of Serenity House.

Cledwyn Fox saw Albert to his car and he did not mince his words. 'May I speak to you, man to man?'

That's rich, Albert thought.

Cledwyn Fox had a good idea what Albert was thinking and it only made him angrier. Homophobic bastard, he said to himself. To Albert, he said: 'If you're unhappy with the facilities at Serenity House, I'm sorry. I want your father-in-law to be happy. I respect Mr Montfalcon. He's a gentleman. But I have to consider our elders. And my staff. Your visits are disturbing them. Some of our frailer guests are showing symptoms of distress. Serenity House, Mr Turberville, is like a heavily loaded ocean liner. Not as young as she used to be. Not as – shall we say – balanced? If we're going to make waves, then we should leave the ship.'

'Are you asking me to take Max away?'

'I will do anything to keep Serenity House on an even keel.'

'Like throwing an old man overboard?'

'Mr Turberville, I'm in complex negotiations with colleagues abroad to form a loose association with similar eventide refuges on the continent. Naturally my business partners wish to see a calm, happy ship. Like any institution we have rules. And if an elder is disrupting the lives of others, I can ask the elder's child to remove her.'

'Or him.' Albert was suddenly terrified.

'You could always take him home, Mr Turberville. As you're so concerned about his tendency to wander, take him. You could keep a close eye on him at home.'

Albert remembered how sorry he'd felt for Max when he found him wrapped in string, with only his blue eyes moving to tell Albert he wasn't dead. If only Elizabeth had gone on to kill her father. Driven out of her wits by the old man's cunning intolerable ways, his saintly daughter does for him. It happened more often than people liked to suppose.

Instead, Albert had saved Max. He made Lizzie see sense. He'd made other arrangements. And where had it got him. Erica Snafus in the House tea room: 'I hear Superintendent Slack's team have almost completed their enquiries in Poland. He wasn't joking when he promised to hit the ground running. They'll be home any day now. They'll want to talk to your father-in-law. If you ask me, Albie, the net's closing. Don't worry, your secret's safe with me. What's the matter, Albie? You look as if you've been kicked in the balls. What a surprise! Never thought you had any.'

CHAPTER FIFTEEN

Fee fi foh fum . . .

Jack and Innocenta kept to separate rooms in the big house on Highgate Hill, though Innocenta secretly wondered how long this would last. Jack had built a new wall across his room, of empty polystyrene boxes from the Green Dragon. The place smelt heavily of soy sauce. He did not like people sneaking up on him. 'I'd burn someone sneaking up on me.' Innocenta had laughed because she was sure he was joking. Wasn't he? Any day now she must tell Max she had taken Jack home and given him a room and was keeping an eye on him like mad.

Elizabeth interrogated Albert nightly. 'What do they say he's done?'

'I've told you.'

'Tell me again.'

'Your father went back to Germany off his own bat, in nineteen thirty-eight. Until that time he'd been a student at Oxford.'

'But he's British!'

'He was once. Then he wasn't. Then he was again. He's had three lives.'

'Does he have another six to go?'

'That's cats, Lizzie. He's had it. They're close behind him and they'll get him. The net's closing. They'll be banging on the door of Serenity House before long. As soon as they're sure that Maximilian von Falkenberg who went back to Germany and your father are one and the same. Unless he has the good sense to pop off.'

'Why did he go back?'

'His parents lived there. And apparently he felt a sense of duty towards his country. Anyway, once back in Germany he dropped out of sight. Until nineteen forty-one. Then he appears on the staff of the Nazi University in Poznań, Poland. The Germans had invaded Poland and their scholars were trying to prove that parts of Poland were German or had been long before they were Polish. This meant doing all sorts of research into the earlier settlements, as well as genetic and biological investigations into the differences between the races. Scientifically it was a lot of tripe. Nazi delusions about racial purity. Apparently that's what he did. A year later, in nineteen forty-two, he leaves the Reichsuniversität, and goes to work in some unidentified concentration camp in Poland. In the medical research block.'

'Where he did these things?'

'According to the allegations, yes.'

'Killed people – right? How many people?'

'No one knows. They don't even know precisely what he was doing. He may have been involved in experimenting with recessive genes governing eye colour. The eyes of prisoners were used for this research. He was also interested in the different shaped heads of the so-called pure Germans. He investigated the difference between the shapes of heads of Germans, Slavs and Russians. They say the prisoners were killed. Using phenol injections. Whether he killed them or not – isn't clear. Apparently this stuff was injected straight into the heart. Death followed minutes later.'

Elizabeth wasn't satisfied. 'You still haven't said how many.'

'For Christ's sake, Lizzie. Stop going over this.'

But she refused to give in. Albert would go over it again. 'They don't know how many, Lizzie. Anyway the figure is likely to be pretty much academic. Around four million are said to have died in Auschwitz alone. How many he killed personally is not an issue. Tie him to one murder and he's guilty.'

'Go on.'

'Around nineteen forty-three he disappears again. We don't know why. Next thing he's heard of fighting Russians on the eastern front. This puzzles the investigators. Some think it must be a kind of punishment. He can't have volunteered because a posting to the eastern front was virtually a death sentence. So to request a posting would be the same thing as asking to commit suicide.'

'Perhaps he went there to measure heads, kill more people?'

'No. By that time most Jews in Russia were either dead or they'd fled. Max served on the eastern front as an ordinary soldier. He saw action near Minsk, and then when the German armies began falling back, he retreated with them. Captured by the Russians we think he spent the next three years in a Russian prisoner-of-war camp.'

'How many?' Elizabeth's voice rose to that high quaver pitch that made Albert cringe.

'Only he knows that. Don't ask me Lizzie. The Russians let him go in 'forty-five and he returned to Berlin. There, for some reason, God knows what, the Americans took him in tow. Maybe they saw him as a prize of sorts.'

'Why didn't the Americans arrest him? Why didn't they charge him?'

'Nothing to charge him with. Perhaps to them he was an ordinary soldier released by the Russians. Or maybe he was useful. Perhaps he had information. Who knows? At that time the Nazis were no longer the enemy – it was the Russians. Camped in their half of Germany. Max was in American hands for about eleven months. The next thing we know, he's in Britain. The suspicion is that there was some kind of deal done between the American and British Intelligence Services. About two hundred thousand people arrived in this country after the war. Unlike other immigrants from the war zones, your father was never screened. Why not? Never vetted. Never questioned. He did not enter the country illegally. He just appeared. The change of name is nowhere validated, yet his claim to be Max Montfalcon can't be disproved. Either you accept there were two Maxes – or this thing was covered up. From one day to the next it seems Maxillian von Falkenberg became Max Montfalcon. That's what they are saying. That a German became an Englishman. On what your father likes to call the Mountbatten principle. Remember?'

'How could I forget?' said Elizabeth. 'Battenberg into Mountbatten. He was always a great admirer of Lord Mountbatten.'

'One or both Maxes had been English from infancy. To all intents and purposes. He was schooled here. He was at university here. It wasn't all that difficult. Yes, he became an Englishman so like the real article you can't tell the difference. Once upon a time there was a German who turned into an Englishman.'

'From Harwich,' said Elizabeth. 'Have you got any sense out of him?'

'This last time I saw him I thought I just might break through. Then they had a drama. One of the old biddies began dying. Everyone flew around like mad. The old people were terribly upset. It seems Jack was in the vicinity and whenever Jack is close, someone dies. He asked me if you enjoyed trying to kill Max,' her husband revealed. 'I said he'd have to ask you. Then he asked me if you'd killed anyone else. He seems to think that's what people do.'

Was the idea, then, something they picked up from Jack? The way one picks up flu, or meningitis, from close exposure to the agent of infection?

She asked him if he thought Jack 'might'?

Instead of saying 'might what?' Albert said that Jack might see to it that 'progress wasn't impeded'.

'It would be a considerable relief all round,' said Lizzie. 'Not least for Daddy himself, I'm sure. Will you speak to him?'

'The sooner the better. We'll take him for a drive somewhere we can talk privately. We'll sound him out.'

Instead he made a speech: 'I'm rather worried about my father-in-law. I don't think he knows himself how much he's suffering. Thing is, when death comes for Max Montfalcon, I'd be very grateful to anyone who didn't get in the way.'

'How grateful is grateful?' asked cunning Jack.

'Of course this would have to be stricly between ourselves . . . if we – um – made some arrangement. Innocenta wouldn't understand.'

'Cross my heart and hope to die,' said Jack. 'Anyway, you nearly popped him yourself,' said Jack, turning to look admiringly at Lizzie in the back seat.

*

After his drive with Albert and Lizzie he felt really good. He slipped into the house. He really was as quiet as a mouse, was Jack. He surprised Innocenta leaving his room. Didn't say anything, did Jack. Smiled wide and bright. Ran his hand around Innocenta's neck and said, 'Well, babe, still looking for that chessboard?' Increasing the pressure of his grip, until tears of pain welled up in Innocenta's eyes.

How very happy Jack was! To have all this and to have it for real. Jack needed to watch people being killed. He didn't mind much how it was done, as long as he got to watch it being done. Regularly. Snuffed out. He needed it as much as his diet of Chinese food.

True enough, most snuff movies were still in the silent age. But rapid miniaturisation was bringing big advances within the reach of even the most modest killers and soon one would expect to see the age of the talkies arrive in snuff movies. So the wise killer got himself one of those nifty camcorder jobs. There were lobbies prepared to defend to the death Jack's inalienable right to watch real people being done to real death on Marta's Panavision back in the trailer in the Tranquil Pines Mobile Home Park, back there in Orlando in what now seemed to him to be almost prehistorically early times, where the more advanced video chains were already supplying a useful service to grateful customers.

Now Jack was in England. He wasn't watching snuff movies, yet he didn't feel too bad. How to explain that? Sure, from time to time, he'd get a little bit of news from home. Some guy killed a load of people and was eating parts of them. He kept their livers and hearts in the fridge. But he didn't really miss it. Point was, he didn't *need* the other, not now that he had Serenity House. Serenity House and the elders supplied his every appetite – except for Chinese. They cried, they died, they loved him.

Now he was being asked by people he barely knew to put Grandpa to bed for them. All this way to get so lucky. All those years consuming the product, and Jack was being offered a franchise. He felt damn proud.

But not yet. Not yet. Jack knew something in his heart and in his head, knew from a long way back, knowledge he got maybe from Marta and her stories of human fat that fed the fires in the flaming pyres of Hungarians. Or perhaps even further back, tales he had heard at the knee (over long white leather boots) of his real mother who had run away to join a country and western band. From the tales his mother told him he knew a single, serious, fairytale truth: you do not kill the giant while he continues to lay golden eggs. Or should that be the goose that laid the golden teeth? Well, whichever.

He was still waiting to see what Max had left in his cupboard. There was more to Max then met the eye. And Jack had grown greedy for more. Max's big cupboard was like heaven, everything good came from it. He thought from time to time of Mr Kaufmann's face back there in the Kissimee Flea Market when he produced his treasures. 'Well, Jack, and what have you brought me today?' Sure he had had a good offer from Mrs T to pop off her old man. But there seemed no good reason why Jack should not get all he could for Mr Kaufmann from that cupboard, then pop the old man and collect the reward from the Englishwoman. That was only right. Jack was out to improve himself. Poor boy makes good. That was the American way. You can bet your – what was it? – seven-league boots on it!

It was all very satisfying. Not once since his job began at Serenity House had he felt the need to run a video through his head. Jack watched Max. Watched him from the second-floor window as Max practised on the front lawn, trying to remember how to run. Watched Max on the closed circuit television screen from the little locked room on the third floor. Scotch and a teacup. A few drinks. A tear or two. He watched Max leave the table and go to his cupboard and he saw Max lift this flask to the light and there, swimming, were what Jack thought at first were small fish. Perhaps swimming marbles. He moved in closer.

Neither fish nor marbles. Swimming in a bottle of preserving fluid were twelve human eyes. Max had put his own eye close to the glass – resting his cheek on the table and staring at the swimming eyes. Max laid his head down again on the table and pressed his eyes to the glass. Jack stared at the eyes staring into Max's eyes, and life seemed very good indeed. Jack had not heard about the American Dream. But who needed to hear about it when you were having it?

Then he'd see Max reach for his cigar box, heavy with stained molars, grinders, incisors. Solid with something that glittered – gold! He'd roll them on his bedside table like the croupier in some smart casino. Ivory dice, golden nuggets. And what was to come next from Max's cupboard, with the superior locks, beside his bed? Six round skulls. Heads! Sightless eyes and fixed smiles, tumbling from a leather bag on to the Formica of Max's table, and rolling free. An ivory bowling alley. Oh, boy.

For his part, Max watched the boy watching him though, in all the months Jack had been working in Serenity House the two had exchanged hardly a word. Max became increasingly agitated about security. He got Edgar the chiropodist to go to the local blacksmith to change the locks a second time on his old oak cupboard, for very advanced technological marvels which the locksmith assured him only a safe-breaker could get past.

He was increasingly convinced that someone was going through his things at night. Locking his door was out of the question. It was against house rules. Staff must have access to elders at all times. Old people might be young people who have lived for a long time, as Mr Fox never tired of claiming, but they had to be looked after. A nice balance had to be struck between the elder's rights to privacy and the nursing staff's need to tend to their charges.

There was another reason why Max could not go unobserved. The hours of darkness see most deaths, particularly the small hours after midnight. As if, at this time, the spirit is at its lowest ebb. The staff of Serenity House knew this and were trained to be ready for it. Just as they knew that deep depression is something the elderly frequently endure. They often take action. A spate of hangings a few years earlier had deeply embarrassed the management. Suicide rates actually increase with age, shooting up after sixty-five, hitting a peak around the age of seventy-four. Who would have thought it?

'Not the world at large,' Cledwyn Fox taught his carers. 'The world thinks the long-lived are no more a part of it. It's inconceivable that they should make love or kill themselves. But they do it with just as great a passion as younger people.'

Dying was an ever-present reality among the elders. They did it in the way younger people catch colds. Of course, in death, as in so much of modern life, science helped to set the standards. As Dr Tonks, who had spent time studying the forms of dementia, liked to say: 'My ideal patient is playing golf in the morning, dead that afternoon.'

How often they fell short of the standards set by science. Try as they might, most of the elders in Serenity House took a long time dying. Some had been doing so, by slow painful degrees, for years. Others had been known to take weeks over it. A death, rather like making a soufflé, or composing a poem, or having a baby, always takes its own time. Long or short, always it seems to take for ever. And even when it comes with the suddenness which the medical profession increasingly recommends, it is never over and done with in an orderly, professional way.

Jack was very much present for the death of old Maudie Geratie. She began fading on a Thursday afternoon and was put to bed by the day staff. When Jack clocked on she was unconscious, clammy to the touch and breathing noisily. This symptom is one which carers are warned about but the reality is still sometimes very distressing. Jack, however, was a model of patience, tact and bravery. He sat beside her and remembered not to talk too loudly, and least of all to talk about the dying person. For although they may often appear unconscious, they can hear what is being said. And it must be an added agony for the dying to hear that it's all over bar the shouting. Maudie was a little feverish and talked, in a slurred way, of her long-lost love Arnaldo, the baritone. It was all rather beautiful, and just before she died, she opened her eyes and looked imploringly at Jack. She didn't say anything, perhaps she couldn't say anything. But Jack felt he knew what she wanted. And without a word he went out of the room and came back carrying his Mouse head. A small light danced in Maudie's eyes, much the same light that was to be seen there when she caught sight of Edgar the chiropodist's nose-ring. In any event she died smiling, did Maudie Geratie, with the Mouse sitting beside her.

Jack, as he had been taught to do, set a screen around her bed. Then he called Night Matron and together they washed her, and remembered to close her yes. 'So many people forget that,' said Night Matron approvingly, 'and it sets the relatives off so terribly to see the departed staring back at them. Poor things. Not that they can help it.' When they had finished, Jack turned off the radiators, opened the window and left the room, locking the door behind him.

The following evening the toast of the Stroke Club took to the floor: Jack Mouse and Imelda Duck doing a lively foxtrot. Wasn't everybody having a lot of fun?

But you always get a party pooper. Just as the elders were clapping in time to the music of Joe Loss, played rather loudly on young Agnes's Sony, who should stride into the room – waving his arms, treading down the sides of his old leather slippers – but Max Montfalcon.

'I've been robbed!' He pointed a finger at the Mouse. 'The rat did it. I smell a rat!' He reached out and threw a punch at the Mouse and promptly fell over. He lay on the ground still flailing away. Of course the dancing had to stop. 'I'll tear him to pieces. I'll rip the living flesh from his bones. I'll send his skin to the tanners and his bones to the grinders. I'll feed his flesh to the pigs!'

Thank heaven for Night Matron. Tough as an old boot, perhaps, and certainly not everyone's cup of tea, but pure gold in a crisis. Single-handed she lifted Max into a nearby wheelchair instructing Imelda in a firm voice – 'Off with your head, girl! Blanket for Mr Montfalcon, and then beddy-byes. Don't stand there goggling – jump to it!'

Matron wheeled Max back to his room. He smelt heavily of whisky. Not for nothing had Night Matron grown up across the road from the public bar of Meikle's Hotel, Salisbury, Rhodesia, all those years ago, when drinking yourself into a stupor was the outward sign of inward male colonial uncertainty. It tended to be followed by a lot of shouting.

Max Montfalcon was, Matron decided, as pissed as a newt. Matron's professional eye noted that his incontinence had been unable to cope with the dual strains of anger and alcohol. 'Upsy-daisy, Mr Montfalcon.'

She lifted him out of his chair, slung his arm around her neck and helped him over to the bed, where he sat heavily. She rang for little Imelda and when the girl arrived, ordered: 'Squeegee and bucket, chop-chop!' She pulled off his wet nightclothes. He sat there, pale and silent, as she helped him on with a fresh pyjama top. It was only when he lifted his eyes to hers that she realised how angry he was. His look was the dark, baleful, bruised stare of a wounded buffalo. Imelda returned with sponge and basin and began swabbing.

'It smells,' Max said in a puzzled and rather distant voice. Then he lifted his nose and sniffed the air.

'What does?' Expertly she eased him out of his trousers and handed them to Imelda.

'Monosodium glutamate.'

'Is he drunk?' the girl whispered. 'Is Mr Montfalcon really drunk?'

Max seized Matron's arm. 'Can't you smell it too? It's still in the room.'

'What is it you smell – gas?' Matron asked him.

'What?'

'Is it gas you smell?'

Max lifted large stricken eyes to her. 'What gas? I was sitting here at my table, perhaps I dozed off. But I had them with me, right here. And now they're gone. I can't find them anywhere.'

'What has gone, Mr Montfalcon?'

'My bottle. He's taken my bottle. And my bag and my box.' Max clung to her hand like a child. 'You must get them back for me. Please, you must help me. My bottle and my bag and my box. All gone!' And he began to weep, iron, rusty sobs.

Night Matron lifted a significant glance at the half-empty bottle of whisky. 'Your bottle is exactly where you left it. Over there on the table. But there's no more for you tonight, Mr Montfalcon. You've had quite enough. I really don't know what I shall say in my report. You know that house rules forbid drinking in the rooms. Where did you get it from? There, Mr Montfalcon. That should hold you for a while. Now, into bed with you. Sufficient unto the day is the evil thereof. You're going to get two of my little bombs, I think you need your sleep.'

But Max sat there stubbornly, lips pressed tight, shaking his head.

'Oh, come on, Mr Montfalcon. Look, if I have one, will you have one? We'll put them in a spoon, see?' Matron pretended to feed herself from the teaspoon. 'One for Matron – and one for Mr Montfalcon! Mouth open – that's better! And now some water to wash it down. Into the mouth, over the gums, look out, tummy, here it comes!'

Max swallowed. Some water ran down his chin and Matron wiped it. Then he allowed her to push him back gently on to the pillows and tuck him into bed. 'It's of no worth to anybody else.' Max spoke slowly but clearly. 'Towards the end, things were finally falling apart and von F had a Polish assistant. One remaining of sixteen, you must remember. That's how it all went you see. In the beginning he had just one. Poor Marta. Later had sixteen assistants on his Block. One by one they dwindled. However hard he tried to help them. Until, in the end, he had just one again.'

'Poor Marta?' Night Matron looked sympathetic. 'When I was a little girl my nanny was called Marta.'

'Some hung on. Nordic longheads amongst the sixteen lasted longer. Blood Group A was also a help. East Baltic and *Ostisch* elements dwindled fast.'

'*Ostisch?*' Matron looked puzzled.

'Easterners,' said Max dreamily. 'Urslav types, those who transgressed the biological boundaries.'

'We'll hear more of *Urslav*s tomorrow,' said Matron, 'time now for beddy-byes.'

'The waste was everywhere. Good material dwindled. Tailors, plumbers, vital craftsmen. Von F pointed out that executing craftsmen actually harmed the war effort. It did no good. The man sent to fetch the eyes was one of the last remaining among von F's assistants. He was a Nordic longhead type. Blood group A. Still, he was nervous. Someone interested in genetic research in the genes governing eye colour had ordered him to prepare a sample.'

Matron began taking off his jacket. 'Of what?'

'Fresh material, he was told. Six of each. Half a dozen brown, half a dozen blue. But all he could find were six brown and five blue.'

'One short?' Matron unlaced his shoes.

'One blue short.'

'Well, he did his best,' said Night Matron.

'Von F found another to complete the set.'

'All's well that ends well.' She slipped his incontinence pad into his underpants.

'In the end they were never used,' said Masx. 'The Institute for Racial Hygiene changed its mind.'

'Typical,' said Matron. 'A lot of fuss for nothing.'

'But the man was absurdly grateful. He presented the collection to young von F. The poor fellow was convinced von F had saved his life. What he didn't know was that no one could save his life.' Max began weeping. His tears rolled off his cheeks and burrowed their way through his wispy chest hair.

'But he tried. Didn't he?' Night Matron led Max to his bed. 'That's the main thing. Now off to sleep, Mr M. And let's have no more talk about thieves. Nobody is stealing anything around here. Not while I'm in charge. Not in Serenity House.'

'Then where are my eyes?' Max demanded from the darkness.

She did not reply. She heard him, of course, but she chose not to answer. 'In your head,' seemed altogether too obvious and sarcastic a thing to say.

CHAPTER SIXTEEN

Problems

They always came for him at night. That was to be expected. They came from God knows where. You had no control over them. But you fought back, threw them out. Still they returned. Some came in the forms of smoke, flames, wheels, screams. Some came wearing striped pyjamas. Worst were arithmetic dreams from which, somehow, you never seemed to awake. You always seemed to be wrestling with numbers. Solving problems.

Ten thousand problems in a single night. And when you woke in the morning and picked up your copy of Fowler and went down to breakfast with the others, something followed you, like a smell.

Edgar the chiropodist tried to explain it: 'One's got no responsibility for one's dreams, Max. They come and go. Can't blame yourself for those.'

That was true. Dreams will not stand up in a court of law. After all, if we were all judged by our dreams – who would escape the gallows?

Sheer numbers. Confusion and technical problems. One who was not there could understand how difficult it was. Even one who was there could understand it. Young and old problems. Old ones were sent away. It might take no more than five minutes. That was all, at the ramp. Someone nodded. 'You left, you right.' Young problems were sometimes solved by mistake. Wander off among the old or pregnant. And look like one of them.

You got to recognise this and attempted, tried very hard, to warn those arriving not to assume anything. You did not perhaps say as much to them but wished it very devoutly on their behalf. You longed to say: 'Look – you are all problems here.'

For example, it was a mistake to assume that all intellectuals were destined for treatment. Indeed, around about 'forty-two, it became policy to preserve wherever possible scientific personnel, including doctors, nurses, engineers. Skills were in short supply.

Then there was the business of the trucks. A profound misunderstanding. Those selected for trucking to the depots were assumed by some, such was the contagion of fear and hysteria which gripped the new arrivals, to be heading for some better place. In fact the opposite was the case. Yet you had to stand by sometimes and see otherwise perfectly healthy, highly skilled problems, well deserving of preservation, chasing after the trucks as they pulled away carrying the old, the halt, the lame, the young and the pregnant problems, and literally forcing the officials to take them aboard.

It was argued by some that finesse was not required. After all, everyone would ultimately be selected. Whether early or late. So that meant that no special grace attached to avoiding the primary selection. But all of this was to ignore the vital necessity of smooth organisation. How to keep large numbers moving? It required co-operation, organisation, calm and obedience. Far better then the aids to tranquillity. The little houses with their white painted wooden fences that stood before the treatment centres, the air of orderliness – indeed, one might advance the paradox that the greater the chaos, the more was quiet order needed.

Before then you had the unnecessarily upsetting procedure of allowing girls, often Slav girls, to whisper what lay ahead, even as they stripped brooches, rings from those arriving. You could see how this disconcerted them. They would sniff the air as if there was something to smell. And they would look up into the night sky and go berserk. It reminded you of an escape from a slaughterhouse when demented calves run bellowing into the street and must be caught and restrained, often with what looks like unnecessary force.

It was a secret. You knew that. Because everyone knew it. There was no safer way of keeping a secret than to make sure that everyone knew it – but never spoke of it, because, after all, it was a secret and one kept a secret.

To be sent left was to go very quickly. Perhaps no more than ten minutes would elapse between choice and treatment. So the crowds had to be kept moving. With thousands of problems arriving all the time, of every one thousand five hundred, on the bad days, up to twelve hundred could go left, at the flick of a thumb. Often those on duty would whistle. A little Chopin waltz one remembers as having been much favoured. The cries went out all the time for 'doctors' and 'twins' and the Red Cross vehicles waited, their engines turning over, exhausts sending up a little blue smoke into the cold night air.

The Red Cross vehicles and the white coats you wore had a consoling effect. Newly arrived problems yearned for medical succour. From the moment of arrival doctors were vital at all stages from the first selection through to the solution. A doctor would be briefed on the policies which helped to determine the difference between those who went left and right. A doctor would make the choice as the fresh batches arrived: he would, of course, ride the Red Cross car to the ramp where the train stood; he would assess the nature and number of the treatments required; he would have to complete forms after the event; and finally he would be present for the necessary extractions which procedure laid down should always follow the treatments.

As things became more complicated, sometimes one yearned for the old days. In the old days there had been a true air of orderliness. And it was kinder both for the new arrivals and for the supervising officials. One was human, after all. One strove for clarity, for a sense of direction, for careful but not noisy control. A big door opened into the undressing area where there were seats. Each seat had a number. There were even tickets for clothes left behind. The notices were large and easy to read, since often those in the cleansing area were not in their first prime and, in any event, their spectacles would have been removed for safekeeping. They would be directed, those selected, in notices written in several languages, towards the showers. The cleanliness of the place was amazing. It gleamed like a mirror. Not a speck of dust was to be found. One thought of this as being in the best scientific tradition. To remain efficient under the worst conditions – and the ash was everywhere – is a form of scientific integrity. Is it not? One would like to think so.

But still things became ever more problematical. Staff struggled valiantly to be both humane and efficient. The questions most discussed by personnel of all ranks and expertise. How were you to handle the increasing numbers? What limit should be set? And, as it seemed likely, no upper limits were to be permitted, how was one to keep the process running smoothly? How to avoid a backlog when literally thousands of problems remained, naked and unaddressed? And the machinery broke down. Difficulties in keeping up standards of hygiene can easily be imagined.

Expertise, accomplishments, these were the governing factors of your life at that time. Even the non-qualified members of the administration realised this and they would make suggestions, often very useful ones, such as ways of keeping the ovens at a regular temperature, despite wild fluctuations in the numbers being treated. There was a modesty about these people that one deeply admired. They would preface their ideas with disclaimers: 'As a mere non-specialist, I stand correction, but it seems to me that the substitute of human fat for benzene would be a useful step.'

Complications. And, to be sure, exactly the same question of qualifications applied during the selections at the ramp. Only trained medical people were to be involved. Surely? And someone had put forward the argument, quite clearly: if you were not a doctor it meant you were technically ill-equipped to do this sort of work. One protested. Dentists did not perform appendicectomies. Nor, therefore, should anthropologists perform these selections.

One's point was taken and one was transferred without ado to the anthropological section on Block Ten.

Long ago and far away. Why then does one continue to dream? To dream, specifically, of Leon Garfinkel who must be dead now these many years. It happened one morning that one saw him in a work detail of what must be described as something like marching skeletons. There was always something terribly dispiriting about a work detail marching past with military rigour when most of its men were barely able to put one foot in front of the other. Those with some spirit threw out their thin and bony chests and flung up their arms and looked almost jaunty. This had the advantage of distracting attention from the slow members of the detail who drooped, their bony nakedness compounded by sagging, swinging scrotums.

But there was Garfinkel! Dear old Garfinkel, from Leipzig! How many long hikes had one taken with Leon as a young man, the two of them dressed in parkas, shorts and rucksacks, as they travelled the Eastern territories of the Volhynian Germans. *Wandervögel* – wandering birds – making a good ten miles a day on a couple of apples, orange juice and a slab of chocolate. Interviewing the peasants near Woeadimir and Rozyyszcze about such matters as their use of folk costume. Dear Leon, with his dark eyes and quick bright manner, was by far the best at getting unwilling peasants to answer one's questionnaires about communal politics. What days they were! And, later at Leipzig, Leon had been by far the most brilliant student of his generation. His thesis: 'The Linguistic Shifts in the Terminology of Sorbian Bee-keepers' drew from no less an eminence than Professor Reche the accolade – 'masterful'.

Suddenly there! Marching naked across the compound in a company of Mussulmans. It provoked the huge and headlong feeling: 'This cannot be!' You were determined to find and save the friend of your youth, that delightful boy and comrade of the *Wandervögel* days.

But it wasn't easy. It meant visiting all the blocks and there putting the same question: 'Where is Leon Garfinkel?' Alas, the men on the blocks were debilitated or stubborn or stupid, for not a soul appeared to know him. Instead they said things like: 'There is no Leon Garfinkel here.' Or worse, they liked to joke and say: 'We are all called Leon Garfinkel here.' Or they were just deliberately unhelpful and vague and replied: 'Garfinkel is a very common name. Why waste your time?' Or they asked the most nonsensical questions, such as – 'Did the Garfinkel you are searching for have boils on his abdomen?' Everyone knew perfectly well that all men in the condition of those marching skeletons were likely to have boils on their bodies, scars and scabies . . .

The puzzlement you had felt was explained by a fat, bearded Capo, as you were leaving one of the blocks: 'For God's sake, doctor, do you really think anyone will answer you when you walk into the blocks calling for Garfinkel? What do you think they imagine you want with him? You being a doctor, from Block Ten?'

How was one to explain to the likes of that Capo that the missing Garfinkel had merely been a friend of one's youth. How was one to explain, indeed, that one was not that kind of doctor? It seemed to be widely understood that if one worked in any capacity in Block Ten then one was one of *those* doctors.

And so they went these dreams. They took on the form of an unfolding discussion with someone he could not see. He did not invite them. He did not understand them. And yes, he was quite certain that in the morning he did not remember them. All he knew was that he awoke about four, always about four, and lay there listening, as he did now, to the steady drip of rain in the laburnums and felt glad to be English.

And so to breakfast. And sitting there, toying with an egg, feeding it not into his ear but in very small and neat movements straight into his mouth, sat Max Montfalcon in the early morning listening politely to Lady Divina warning about the latest ozone depletion.

'Blame the Americans! The gases that we send up into the atmosphere eat away at the ozone ceiling over our heads. What do we have to do to convince them? With our fridges and foam, our air conditioners and our motor-cars, we are making war on ourselves!' She lifted a bird-like claw, clutching a piece of toast and waved it over her head. The toast flew in an arc and hit Major Bobbno who was sitting opposite her, in the middle of the forehead. 'Nice shot, son!' said the Major.

He retrieved the piece of toast and ate it approvingly. 'The army needs lads like you.'

Max propped his Fowler against the salt cellars. He always did when talk got round to the environment.

'Look,' said Night Matron, 'Mr Montfalcon is reading his Bible again. What is the lesson this morning?'

179

'Camouflage,' Max said. 'The great thing about Fowler is that he loves plain speaking. He's very down on people who say "one"' when they mean "I". He has a name for it. He calls it "the False First-personal One". What he does is to show up how the disguise is exposed the moment you begin to mix the "I" and "one".'

'Give us a "for-instance"' cried Beryl the Beard, who was very interested in disguises.

'Certainly.' Max turned to pages 402 and 403 and gave out the following: 'Fowler says in a rather wonderful example of the false first-personal one – "I had known in the small circle of one's personal friends quite a number of Jews who . . . " '

'So have I,' said Major Bobbno. 'For some reason I never understood, the Irish battalions were full of 'em.'

CHAPTER SEVENTEEN

The Joy of Passing

How do you catch a mouse? Especially if you're not very quick on your pins. Cunning helps. And craft. First set and bait your trap. Then watch your mouse very carefully. Watch him as he visits the bedsides of departing elders. Watch him as he sets out for meetings of the Stroke Club and the Ballroom Dancing Sessions. Try a variety of little temptations by way of experiment. Keep an eye on him. Keep all your eyes on him. But remember, you're an old man, living on the second floor of a not very distinguished old-age home in North London. The authorities have taken to keeping you under electronic surveillance. But he is a fleet young rodent. Not only is he quicker on his pins than you, but he has four to your two. And you have a limited means of assaying which bait the rodent is likely to take and even fewer ways of knowing which will prove to be the definitive solution. For it must be lethal, your stratagem. We're not pissing around here. These old English houses are sadly prone to vermin. Serenity House is no exception. Switch on the lights late at night in a kitchen and scurry, scurry go the little feet, carrying off the last of your supper, your final fragments, the remains of your life. The plague, you remind yourself, was spread by rats. What do you do? Well, driven beyond endurance, you call in the exterminator.

Time was running out. It had come to the ears of the elders that Mr Fox was contemplating the unthinkable. He was planning to sell out. This was the reason behind his series of trips to Cologne. Max had learnt of it from Edgar the chiropodist.

The information came to Edgar via his cousin who knew a woman in Bruges who happened to be travelling in Cologne. There she met a man who mentioned to her that he was negotiating with an Englishman over the sale of a premier London eventide refuge. He represented an outfit called Age Without Frontiers.

At first the term 'Englishman' had fooled a few people. Edgar was removing a rather painful splinter from Max's left foot when he divulged this information. 'What have we been doing to ourselves, Mr M?'

'Chased a thief down the stairs in my pyjamas,' Max growled. 'He got away.'

'My cousin's friend from Bruges worked out that this man in Cologne didn't understand the difference between an Englishman and a Welshman. We can expect to see a further blurring of regional differences as more and more countries merge their identities in the Euro Smog.'

'In the man from Cologne, what we've got is a prime example of German arrogance: England's full of Englishmen. That's an end to the matter,' said Max. 'I do not intend to live under a German regime. Of course, I can only speak for myself in this. But I'll be very surprised if there aren't great misgivings right through the house.'

And he was quite right. A small delegation from the Stroke Club had put the elders' worries clearly: 'We won't be living off black bread and sauerkraut, Mr Fox. The elders think it's only right that you should come clean about the future of Serenity House. They ask if you have a hidden agenda?'

Mr Fox reacted angrily. He had not attempted to deny the charge. He had lifted his sharp chin, pursed his lips and said he would be issuing a full statement at the appropriate time.

It appeared on the noticeboard a few days later:

It is with particular pleasure that I can tell all staff and elders that Serenity House is to enter into a loose association with the Cologne-based enterprise Age Without Frontiers.

Since certain regrettable rumours are circulating in the House, let me make it clear what our new association will not give rise to:
– changes in dietary arrangements;

– arrivals of numbers of German elders;

– alterations in timetables (the so-called 'German work-plan');

– faceless bureaucrats in faraway Cologne deciding how British elders should spend the evenings of their lives;

– increasing numbers of German staff.

As I am sure all staff and guests will know, I abhor the negative and so am delighted to confirm some of the benefits to which our new partnership will give rise:

– considerable advantages in the management of day-to-day expenses (food, bedding, drugs and equipment) through the practice of economies of scale, especially in the funerary and cremation fields;

– considerable economic clout in an increasingly competitive age-market via the benefits of our partnership with similar eventide refuges in over a dozen countries across Europe;

– the assurance of local autonomy of each of the Houses owned by Age Without Frontiers; and the right to continue to enjoy their own beliefs, diets, customs, creeds, last rites, etc.;

– the possibility (and I do believe this is a real first!) for elders to move freely between Houses in all member countries. Spending, say, the winter months in the Spanish House, spring in Greece, and autumn in our very fine House in the French Alps. In each of our refuges elders will enjoy full residence rights as well as access to all amenities including Stroke Clubs, Ballroom Dancing, Foot Care, Funeral Clubs, etc. Freedom of movement and abode would be guaranteed in an Eventide Charter and elders taking up residence in one of our other houses would not have to convert their own currency but would make use of a monetary unit specific to the refuges in the scheme. Though still in its early stages, a name has been put forward for this special currency: the 'Wisdom'. Thus a member would carry her stock of Wisdoms between different Houses, exchanging them for goods and services.

It should have gone down wonderfully well. It was meant well. But within a few days the first signs of revolt were to be seen when graffiti, written in a shaky scrawl, began appearing on the walls of Serenity House: COLOGNE-ISATION? NEIN!

'Very funny,' snapped Mr Fox and ordered out Imelda with sponge and bucket to remove all traces of the offending message.

'I find the German reference particularly insulting,' Mr Fox told Night Matron. 'When will people begin to realise that making Germany the scapegoat won't solve our problems? Any more than the Americans will get places by blaming everything on the Japanese.'

The trouble did not end there. For his part Max kept well out of it. Except, that is, for a discussion with Edgar the chiropodist about the unionising tendencies of the Weimar Government of Gustav Stresemann in the late twenties. 'The German and French were talking about forming an association even then; Stresemann and the French foreign minister were as thick as thieves.'

'Was this after the evacuation of the Rhineland?'

'Indeed it was. Nineteen thirty or so. By closer economic union, the Germans hoped for commercial stability and larger markets.'

'And the French no doubt hoped to lock Germany into political federation?' Edgar shot back. 'What else is new?'

Max nodded. 'From Weimar to the Treaty of Maastricht. Nothing has changed. It was and is a German racket.'

The Stroke Club meeting was packed. Even the three sleepers were there and special arrangements were made to accommodate the Five Incontinents with little Imelda on catheter patrol. The Reverend Alistair woke up for long enough to say that the Bible clearly stated that tribe did not prostrate itself before opposing tribe any more than lion lay down with the lamb. Josh Malherbe said that back in his wine importing days his relations with Bordeaux had been very strong. But it was a far cry from keeping good business ties to rushing headlong into the arms of a German holding company. Major Bobbno said he had fought Germans in two wars and the only language Gerry understood was having his balls nailed to the wall and he appealed to Brigadier Montfalcon to back him up. Max did not respond. He sat in his Gazelle, his hands under his Kumfee Thermalux cover, and thought about ways of killing mice.

Finally a consensus was reached demanding that Mr Fox call a referendum and allow the elders of Serenity House to register their feelings whether for or against the *Anschluss* he proposed.

Mr Fox objected to the word *Anschluss* because of its regrettable historical associations. 'As the end of the century approaches,' said Mr Fox, 'we have the chance of going forward towards the year two thousand, enriched by our association with a chain of like-minded eventide refuges reaching across the continent of Europe. Or going it alone. The train is about to leave the station. Will we be on it? Or will it leave us behind? I am determined that the elders of Serenity House will not only be on that train bound for the future, they will be in the driving seat!

'Let me give you some idea of the problems we face if we listen to siren voices urging us to miss that train. Between nineteen eighty-seven and two thousand and twenty-seven, the numbers of those aged sixty to seventy-four will rise to ten and a half million. There will be another five and a half million people over seventy-five. And elders over eighty-five will climb in number to well over a million. On retirement, according to recent studies, a man can expect to live to 78.4 and a female elder to 81.2.

'How are we to care for our seniors? The Government already faces diminishing resources. More and more elders scrabbling for crumbs from an ever-smaller cake. If life expectancies continue to rise, and I'm afraid they show every indication of doing so, then elders across Britain face a bleak time of it. I dread to think of Serenity House early in the next millennium.

'As to the question of a referendum, I have to tell you that I see no need. Management has gone into the question of joining Age Without Frontiers. Management has a duty to manage and I have decided that this is a purely administrative decision.'

They heard him in silence broken only by the Reverend Alistair's soft snores and the occasional liquid spatter as one of the Incontinents lost a catheter and Imelda had to rush to the rescue.

*

185

In fact Mr Fox was not entirely sanguine in his expectations of the coming association with Age Without Frontiers. His conversations in Cologne had alerted him to the rather disagreeable realisation that Serenity House had some way still to go if it was to compete with the facilities offered by some of the continental eventide refuges. Serenity House suffered from a shortage of skilled staff. A legacy perhaps of Cledwyn Fox's unwillingness to invest in training programmes. The fabric was old and infested with vermin, cockroaches and mice being especially troublesome; repairs to the roof were long overdue. Profit generated consistently fell short of running costs.

The elders, too (fond of them though he was), left a lot to be desired. Although fees at Serenity House kept pace with inflation (close to £500 a week and rising) several guests had failed to meet that pace, fallen behind with their payments and showed little sign of catching up. Serenity House could no longer carry passengers. If only the human dimension of Serenity House could be made to measure up, the other things could be adjusted.

What was needed was a totally new regime. Many of the unprofitable elders would have to give way to a new breed of guests. Higher fees and a reasonable rate of turnover was essential. Elders would have to understand that Serenity House did not owe them a living.

It was a real problem and one to which Mr Fox did not see any speedy solution. Though he did mention it to Night Matron and she promised to give the matter some thought. She also promised to speak to Dr Tonks. Dr Tonks was full of modern ideas.

Night Matron, as people later came to realise – even if the realisation came to some too late for them to appreciate it – made a significant contribution to solving the problems facing Serenity House. She introduced the concept of the Living Will.

She will always be remembered for it. (Indeed, as things turned out, she was also very likely to be charged for it, indicted and tried for it. But that all came later. When many of the eye witnesses were deceased. When the survivors either had a hundred stories of what had happened and who did what to whom – or they couldn't remember.)

But let it not be thought that Night Matron came easily to the concept of the Living Will. She told Jack: 'We are all potentially immortal, but you have to earn immortality. Not all of us are up to it. Sadly. Christ came to bring life more abundantly. It says so in the Bible. All we need is to be in touch with our cells. Immortality. Not in the next world, but now.'

Matron, however, was a realist and there were clearly many people in the world not in touch with their cells. Such cells were, as Matron explained, 'in fact already dead'. What was one to do then with these lost souls? Her answer was the Living Will. 'It's a wonderful idea, Jack. I think it comes from your wonderful country. The clear recognition that nothing is gained by prolonging a life no longer worth living. I think everybody should have one.'

And by the time she'd finished everybody did.

She began by designing her forms, set out in plain, clear English, and big bold text for those with failing eyesight. Eventually, she hoped, braille copies would be available upon request. She composed her Will on the office word-processor. The heading was in confident bold capitals: 'My Medical Testament'. The preamble in definitive bold lower case: 'My Medical Testament sets out and directs my desires regarding medical treatment should sickness prevent me from speaking for myself. I sign this testament, being over the age of eighteen and of sound mind, and with a full and healthy understanding of the consequences of my wishes.'

Matron's Living Will specified the elder's wishes in the event of serious brain damage, or facing a variety of incurable conditions, examples highlighted in discreet italics. Terminal cancer to emphysema. Advanced Alzheimer's to Parkinson's. And/or – here was the skill of the thing –

> any such life-threatening diseases which in the opinion of my GP and several qualified consultants is diagnosed as a threat to life and irreversible, then I solemnly declare that I wish for:
>
> 1. Heart shock machine
> 2. Breathing machine (ventilator)
> 3. Chemotherapy
> 4. Major surgery
> 5. Pain control
> (Delete whichever is inapplicable)

In the event of irreversible coma *I wish/do not wish* that attempts be made to resuscitate me.

'I've kept the language dead simple. No jargon about cardio-pulmonary resuscitation. The elders know what a heart shock machine is. They understand a breathing machine. So make your choice and Bob's your uncle,' said Night Matron. 'A child with a Biro could do it. The beauty of my form is that it isn't a legally binding document. No need to bother with lawyers.'

Matron's Living Will looked like being 'Flavour of the month', said Mr Fox. Everybody wanted to try it. She assembled half a dozen interested elders in the television room and did a trial run with pencils and paper. Several key workers helped to assist elders whose arthritis prevented them from scoring through the various forms of treatment they did not want.

From this little test group, it became clear that some minor adjustments to the form were in order because, faced with a clear either/or choice for, say, ventilation, guests like young Agnes and the Reverend Alistair simply could not make up their minds but sat there with their pencils in their hands, squabbled over the pencil sharpener, or doodled aimlessly all over the forms. Or they put their hands up and asked to leave the room. Some, like old Beryl the Beard, burst into tears and wouldn't say why she was crying. Young Agnes asked impossible questions: 'Excuse me, Matron, but can I have the – you know – heart resuscitation one – but without ventilation? Or if you have the heart machine without ventilation does that mean you're disqualified?'

To which Matron replied, rather curtly perhaps: 'For heaven's sake, Agnes. We're talking about the last hours of a human life. This is not a game of bingo!'

In the end she had to redesign the forms for those amongst the elders whom she called, privately, but with some heat, 'the dodos, the ditherers and the defunct. Got to give them some leeway.' On the new forms, after each of the terminal options on offer, instead of a straight deletion for terminal services not required, Night Matron allowed a straight choice: 'Yes/No/ Don't Know . . . Circle as required'.

Dr Tonks was exceptionally pleased with the Living Will. He

came along to talk to the elders. In fact the geriatrician made a little speech: 'I'm jolly pleased and proud to see how you chaps are all facing up to your responsibilities. You know, we doctors can only do so much. We're not infallible and when one of you is wheeled in, after a fairly testing stroke, or an especially tricky heart arrest, we look down at you and wonder. You can't tell us what it is you want. How very useful then – no, I lie – how positively liberating it is for chaps like us to be able to call up your Testament on the VCR, right there in the theatre, and know in a flash just how you feel about the whole matter. Yes or no? Stay or go? What we're after is not just life for the sake of it but a longer life lived well.'

In conclusion, Dr Tonks told them all about the Nirvanatron.

'A state of the art instrument progressive patients facing departure might find really interesting. I hope so. It comes, of course, from the great US of A . . . ' This was accompanied by a smile and a wave at Jack who stood at the back of the room. Jack smiled and waved back, showing that he did indeed body forth in his compact person all that was best in America.

'Now we get a lot of understandable questions about the Nirvanatron. People ask: "Does it hurt?" and "Does it take long?" and "Is it expensive?" To all these queries I can give a definite "no!" If the Government were not so shortsighted as to have forbidden import of the Nirvanatron, people would be able to try it for themselves and many ridiculous rumours would be scotched.

'The Nirvanatron is a box with tubes, valves and a couple of bottles. Simply lie down. Or sit, or kneel, if you prefer. One tube feeds in the soother, sodium pentathol. A few minutes later you're feeling good and happy and high as a kite. The other tube does the rest. A solution of potassium chloride slips into the bloodstream and shuts down your heart. You do need a trained person in attendance to ensure proper intravenous connection. But then it's over to you.

'We can truly say that the Nirvanatron is partially patient-driven. But I'm certainly not saying it's the only way. I sometimes think we specialists concentrate too much on technologies of departure and not enough on the leaver's own cocktail of desires. So I'm making myself available to anyone who wants it, my personal copy of the latest how-to book from the States. In my humble opinion, the best departure-zone guide yet. *The Joy of Passing* has been on the best-seller lists for months; it canvasses the best methods, equipment, ingredients for patients about to enter the DZ, lavishly illustrated.

'Mr Fox will have my copy of *The Joy of Passing* in his office whenever anyone feels like consulting it. Thank you and good luck.'

Mr Fox held up a hand as the elders mulled about the exit in a clashing traffic jam of wheelchairs, sticks and Zimmer frames.

'Remember, my door is always open.'

Matron said in a mood of fine enthusiasm, 'If any eventide refuge is the first to use the Nirvanatron, you can be sure it will be Serenity House!'

'Bless you, Matron,' Mr Fox said gratefully, 'perhaps elders will understand a little better why I'm so passionate about this link with Age Without Frontiers. Serenity House must face the next century with the latest and best for all our elders. Those arriving, staying and departing.'

'Bless *you*, Mr Fox,' said Night Matron.

The very next day the Reverend Alistair awoke briefly, went into the laundry cupboard and pulled a plastic bag over his head.

'It's a surprisingly pleasant way to go,' said Dr Tonks, 'despite a lot of fearful imaginings. I think *The Joy of Passing* is going to prove a wonderful boon.'

Chapter Eighteen

The Great Escape

Early one misty morning, Max could be seen in the garden of Serenity House. His left leg was thrown out before him, his right arm behind him. He was hoping to remember something of great importance. He was wishful to learn. ('Wishful' says Fowler, 'is a word used as a way of avoiding the synonym "anxious to".') Max refused to regard himself as feeling particularly anxious. He was jolly well going to learn, that was all. Though exactly what it was he was learning he could not quite remember. He'd been out in the garden every morning since Innocenta had called in tears.

The news was grim.

Albert and Elizabeth had been shrieking about a certain Superintendent Slack. (Was that shrieking or freaking? He always had trouble understanding Innocenta when she lapsed into the jargon of the young.) 'You know, the policeman in charge of the hunt, Grandpa.'

'I'll be ready,' said Max. 'I am in training. Come and see me, my darling. It's time we went rat-catching.'

When Max decided to move on Jack, Innocenta came to his rescue. She thought the success of their plan turned entirely on her. This was true up to a point. Beyond that point Max did not enlighten her.

A petrol-blue beret, apricot silk scarf, blood-red suede boots. To Max, Innocenta looked very beautiful when she called with the news, though she did look rather shaken up. It was quite impossible, as she sat opposite him, for him to do anything but love her.

'Well, what do you have to give me?'

'By about eleven, Jack was the best pickpocket on the Eastern seaboard. I still find it hard to believe. By twelve he was carrying a gun and holding up shopkeepers. The following year and he was in a detention centre. Two years later the Juvenile Court was told he had been arrested thirty-five times. He escaped from the detention centre and robbed an old lady in a lift.'

'Knocked her down,' said Max. 'Ripped the rings off her fingers. Took her purse. Sexually molested her.'

'Raped?' Innocenta asked. Max's weak eyes could make out tears on her cheeks. She sniffed loudly.

'It seems not,' said Max. 'But only because there probably wasn't time. He was sent to a corrective centre in Florida. That's where Marta got to know him. She has a good heart, Marta. She took him home. Tried to sort the boy out. Innocenta – there's something you've not told me.'

Innocenta blew her nose. 'I've been keeping an eye on him, Grandpa. Staying close, like you said I should.'

'Does he know you're here?'

'Daddy and Mummy took him out. They went off in the car. Something's brewing there, for sure. I took him home, you see. Back to your place. I told them that you'd agreed. Stay close, you said. Didn't you? And they'd thrown you out of your home. So I was taking what was yours, anyway.'

Max leaned back. 'Bravo!' Innocenta got up and walked to and fro, from his cupboard to the door where his dressing gown and pixie cap hung. 'When he was at work one night, I found things in his room. Syringes. At first I thought, oh yes, he does serious drugs. Except they looked pretty tatty, those syringes. I also found a pair of pincers.'

Max touched thumb and forefinger to his temples. 'Like this?'

'Just like that.'

Max leaned further back in his chair and flexed his leg muscles. Things were improving. His incontinence exercises were beginning to pay off, and so were his limbering-up routines. He could turn much more quickly now. Turn and thrust. In fact, Night Matron, coming upon him in the corridor, wheeling, thrusting, feinting, had turned quite pale and it was only when he clutched his knee and fell over and she had him safely belted into a wheelchair that she calmed down enough to tell him he'd scared her half to death. 'We're not as spry as we used to be, Mr M.' And Max had looked properly contrite, thinking to himself that as long as he was a tenth as spry as he used to be then someone was in for a big surprise.

If Innocenta had not been so self-absorbed she would have noticed how her grandfather, usually so very slow, so rickety, now left his chair with a sudden graceful movement, like a fallen tree rising in slow-motion. He crossed to her as she leaned on his blue table, close enough now to see the bruises on her neck which the apricot silk scarf did not entirely hide.

'Those parcels, my dear. They're mine. And there is something else. A blue carpet bag. Find them, Innocenta, bring them to me.'

'I'm scared, Grandpa. He'll hurt me.' She touched the bruises on her neck. 'He found me in his room yesterday and took hold of my neck. I couldn't breathe. I think he'd kill me.'

'Both of us,' said Max, 'without hesitation. Unless we get him first. Get my things. The parcels, my carpet bag. And I promise you we'll escape. To another place.'

'And then? Do I bring them to you?'

Max smiled. 'That would be fatal. When you have them, get out of the house. Find a phone and ring me. I'll tell you where to go.'

'Somewhere we'll live happily ever after?' Innocenta wiped away her tears. 'Like in the fairytales?'

'Something like that,' said Max.

Seated in his wheelchair, unmoving beneath his Kumfee Thermalux cover, Max waited – the frozen man. He was waiting for Innocenta's call.

When it came it was as bad as anything he might have expected. Innocenta's voice was curiously calm, deliberate. Thick with sleep or pain. The parcels had been where she'd last seen them. The carpet bag had given her slightly more trouble. She'd located it at last, beneath Jack's bed.

'I was just reaching for it, Grandpa, when he hit me. I know it was him, though I never saw his face. He wore his Mouse head, all the time.'

He had taken the carpet bag, placed it on the bed and forced her to kneel above it. He had drawn her legs apart. He had roped her hands together, using, she said, a large roll of waxed string from the kitchen. Max thought he recognised the string. He had torn her orange robe. He had ripped and scattered the beads of her *mala* across the room. Then without bothering to do more than loosen his belt and lower his jeans he had rammed himself home into her.

When Max asked if he had said anything, Innocenta replied carefully, 'No. He didn't say anything. But he whistled.' He whistled a tune she had recognised because she had once had a friend in the Inland Revenue who performed it at Christmas concerts. It was called 'The Whistler and his Dog'. Did Max know it perhaps? And Max replied gently that he did indeed know it. Would he whistle a few bars, then?

'Yes,' said Innocenta when Max obliged. 'That's it.'

'Are you hurt?' Max demanded.

Innocenta replied that she was bleeding. But she wasn't really hurt. 'What really hurts is that I didn't get your things. Now we can't go away. I had my bag packed, Grandpa.'

'Good,' said Max gently, 'because it may be of very good use in the days ahead.'

And then, speaking very calmly, he told her what to do.

The ground was muddy underfoot, the grass sodden and defeated. An ankle-high mist hung around the drainpipes of Serenity House. It lay upon the roots of the laburnums like soapy water.

Now and then Max would come to a stop. He would throw out his right arm and place his left leg as far behind him as possible and then he would count to ten, take a deep breath and with a great looping hop, like a wounded cricket, he would reverse arm and leg. He would do this twice, three times, and then hold on to the fence to catch his breath. He felt he was undoubtedly improving his technique even if he did not appear to be moving.

'What this place needs,' muttered Max to himself, 'is a camp orchestra.' There was nothing better to exalt and energise, to urge the body on. To organise the capacity for labour in mean-ingful patterns. 'That's how it was done,' Max panted. 'Oh, yes, it *was*! We played them out each morning and we played 'em home at night. Those that came home. That's how we lived every day.'

Strange! Apparently something was not working. If only he could remember what it was. Max wore his blue blazer and a long red knitted scarf, tubular and skinny, wound twice around his thin neck and hanging down below his waist. His cap was an egg-yolk yellow, a parting gift from old Maudie Geratie, RIP.

The boys across the road, now on their way to school, paused in stifled delight at the spectacle of the tall, thin old man in yellow hat and red scarf who, slowly and painfully, with a stabbing, sharp mechanical action, like scissors in slow motion, changed the position of his legs and arms with immense effort.

Just then who should come by but Detective Chief Superin-tendent Slack, jumping nimbly from his Honda. Neat in salt and pepper suit, Superintendent Slack was in fine form. His team was absolutely first-class, beavering away in Poland.

'Morning, Mr Montfalcon,' Superintendent Slack felt good enough to allow himself a little jest. 'Or should I say – Mr von Falkenberg?'

Max saw a thin man who looked rather like a ferret. 'I beg your pardon?'

'No need. Stopped by in the hopes that you might be ready to talk to me about von Falkenberg, and the life before Harwich.'

With creaking precision Max reversed arm and leg. His scarf ran like a banner from neck to ankle. His pixie cap had fallen over his right eye. 'There is no life before Harwich.'

'What do you remember about young von Falkenberg?'

'He's dead,' said Max.

'Yes,' said the policeman. 'This many a year. Strange how much we know about this young man. His schools and universit-ies. His time at Oxford. His return to Germany. His rather peculiar scientific interests. What we don't know is what hap-pened to him. After the war. From one minute to the next young von F ceases to be. In his place there appears one Max Montfalcon. If von Falkenberg is dead, the question is – did you kill him? Along with all the others? Is this how our German frog became an English prince?'

Edgar the chiropodist drew up in his little van with the angry banner: fl-EEC-ed! Followed by little Lois Chadwick with her portable hair-care salon.

'You a new boy?' Lois asked Superintendent Slack. She watched Max slowly reversing his arm and leg. 'Heavens above, Mr M! What do you look like?'

'We've been discussing English princes,' Max spoke slowly – slightly out of breath, but definitely improving.

Lois giggled. 'Get Mr M on the subject of the Royals and you'll be here all day. Him with his nose always buried in *Fealty* or *Homage*. You're an incorrigible old monarchist, Mr M – that's what you are. Must fly. Byeee!'

'English princes and German frogs,' Max told Edgar. 'This gentleman's just wondering how German frogs can turn into English princes.'

'Piece of cake,' Edgar assured him, nose-ring glinting in the early light. 'Wonder no more. Look at Prince Albert.'

Superintendent Slack began to feel somewhat tense. He warned Max quietly: 'Time's running out, sir. The fairytale's almost over. My men are in Poland and Germany, sifting the evidence.'

All over Serenity House windows were opening as others began taking an interest in the conversation in the garden below.

'I say! Who are you?' A stern, imperious female voice called high above their heads. 'Yes, man, you! You don't think I mean Mr Montfalcon, d'you?'

Superintendent Slack looked up to see at a window at the very top of the house a woman with long unkempt grey hair, wearing a pink dressing gown.

Firm and polite always, was Mr Slack. 'I'm a policeman!'

'Are you now! Well, young fellow, you could not have come at a more auspicious time. Did you know that there is amongst us someone who has killed and tortured many people? And I can identify him?'

'Can you indeed, madam?' Superintendent Slack reached for his notebook.

'Whomsoever he brushes against dies!' thundered Lady

Divina. 'I shall be pleased to supply evidence in private. Your name and rank, sir?'

He had to shout very loudly but in the end she got it.

'If you could give me his name,' Superintendent Slack persisted.

'He is the Angel of Death.'

'I see.' Superintendent Slack replaced his notebook.

'And he's a thief, too,' said Max. 'A sneaking, cunning, greedy, thief.'

'I shall come along to see you soon for a private discussion,' Lady Divina promised ominously. 'Now not another word. As you can see, our walls have ears.'

It wasn't so much that walls had ears, Superintendent Slack decided. It was rather that windows had heads. They stuck from almost every opening on the face of Serenity House. Like a rather large advent calendar.

'A policeman!' Night Matron, still on duty though it was high time she clocked off, pulled her head in smartly and closed her window. 'This might be a bit bloody embarrassing. Who knows what Lady Divina will tell him?' She turned to where Jack lay on the floor of her room studying the Living Wills of the elders. 'I wonder who might like to take dear Lady Divina for her walk?' Matron wondered gently. 'And a wash?'

'Sure could do with one,' said monosyllabic Jack, 'but first I gotta make it for Beryl. Today's Beryl's big day. When I done Beryl's big day – I'll do Lady D. I owe her one, Lady D.'

'Would you, Jack!' cried grateful Matron. 'That would be such a load off our minds.'

It was Beryl the Beard's big day. The boys gathering on the corner paused slyly as they glanced up at the window where she would appear. Then came the time-honoured invitation from the infernal little carol singers: 'Oh, B-e-r-y-l! Show us your beard, please, Beryl!'

What happened next, generally, was this. At an upstairs window there would appear, faintly at first, like a vision or a mirage, the features of Beryl. For she would bring her face forward slowly out of the gloom, until her nose touched the glass and all the unwanted feminine facial hair of ninety-two-year-old Beryl was plain to see. It ran down the sides of her long jaw in wispy tangles and across her upper lip in a dark hedge and around her chin in soft grey curls. It never failed to reduce the boys to awe-struck delight. And their laughter never failed to make Beryl cry and cry as she stood in the window, her tears running down her cheeks and disappearing like liquid rabbits into the bush of her beard.

But not today. True, Beryl did not resist the siren call from the schoolboys in the street below. And, yes, she slowly approached the window. But today something was different. Today Beryl the Beard was without her beard. A miracle? A sudden loss of hair in the night? An impostor? No, the answer was a new Beryl, a born-again Beryl, a good-as-new Beryl! The answer was a four-letter word: Jack!

For the boy, in a very real sense, appeared to have found his vocation. It was he who coaxed Beryl into paying a visit to the beauty salon in Highgate High Street, who consulted with the beautician about the right combination of treatments for Beryl's hirsute jaw-line. A judicious mixture of the razor, depilatory creams plus a bleach to tone down the dark stripe of her moustache and blend it into the flesh of her upper lip.

And so to bed. Beryl, now beardless, tucked beneath the blankets, with Jack sat beside her to tell a bedtime tale called: 'See Florida – and smile'. With Jack a journey to the Kingdom of Dreams, to the Land of Nod. She held his hand. He adjusted his head.

'Ready, Beryl?'

'Ready as I'll ever be.'

'Hold tight, then. Here we go.'

They would start in the Comfort Inn, mid-way between Orlando and Kissimee, keep going south on the Orange Blossom Trail and hit the Gatorland Zoo and the Tupperware headquarters and museum. Head east down Sand Lake Road, past the pink and green Sheraton, hang a left on Orange Avenue and end up just fifteen minutes maximum from the Tranquil Pines trailer park.

Due west along Highway 4 lies the Magic Kingdom. It's fun, it's easy, it's convenient; it's marvellously placed for a holiday, hideaway, assignation, ambush. Beryl and Jack, fugitive, fantastical pair, just two more tourists who have flown into the Florida sunshine. It was beautifully warm for March with mean daily temperatures in the low seventies. Flown into Orlando airport on a flight out of Gatwick, England. They admired the alligators in the airport moat. They had hired a car from the Alamo Rent-A-Car, a nice grey Buick with rich port-wine upholstery. They found the Comfort Inn all its name implied. She wore pink shirts and a T-shirt which read: 'Life's Uncertain – Eat Dessert First!' He wore light blue jeans and dark blue espadrilles with a canary yellow golf shirt and a sea-blue baseball cap. You wouldn't have recognised them.

'Is it like Lourdes?' Beryl asked. 'Where they heal people?'

Jack thought about it. He had no idea where Lourdes was, but he said: 'Yeah, like Lourdes – but with rides.'

A fine place, Florida, for the young and the young at heart, and the young who have lived a long time. Those who believe in fairytales come to Florida, to Orlando where there is space for dreams and fantasy and invention. This is still the new world. It is perhaps the only new world left in the New World. In the old world the old just get older. But here they train at Jimbo's Senior Gym and even the most frail can increase their muscle mass by up to twenty per cent.

'Keep pumpin' those pecs. You're looking swell!'

'Thank you, Jimbo.'

'You're welcome, Mrs Beryl.'

In the old world, fairytales, like the old themselves, get a bad press. Full of nasty giants and poor kids, bad kings, weak fathers, greedy brothers, paranoid stepmothers, ugly witches and loquacious toads who ask you to do the most disgusting things.

In Florida you can hug King Kong and get away with it. Even his breath is banana-flavoured. Nobody needs to be ashamed of being, well, senior. Everyone lives in the land of once-upon-a-time, where all the rides end happily. Where the customer co-operates in the sting. Where fortune favours the well-insured. Where they vacuum the streets and disinfect the phones.

And so it was that Beryl went to sleep with a smile on her beardless face after what had been a very big day.

And the elders of Serenity House added another form of departure to their list. Some called it, 'Doing The Mouse'.

*

Up in his office, Cledwyn Fox heard the news with gratitude. He wrestled with problems. He'd had a rather scary meeting with Mr Gunther in Cologne. Mr Gunther told him that although Age Without Frontiers saw Serenity House as a positive addition to its portfolio, problems remained. It was top heavy. Mr Gunther pointed a finger at his forehead.

Mr Fox retorted that his staff were doing what they could to address the problem of top-heaviness. His staff were working at full stretch. Often they improvised. They were short of decent equipment, yet always they went forward with a will.

Undoubtedly, replied young Mr Gunther. They were doing well. But they would have to do better still.

Alone in his office now, seeing below him in the garden Max Montfalcon engaged in a strange set of callisthenics, Cledwyn Fox had to admit the substance of Mr Gunther's merciless analysis. More and more people born. And living longer. Present population increase was about two per cent a year. At this rate the living space available to each of us by late in the next millennium was reduced to a few yards. Fifty billion by 2100, and a century later, 500 billion. Project the figures into the third millennium and the space available to each human being had shrunk to one square inch! Even if you could shoot them into space, you would have to expel around 10,000 an hour, for ever, to make much difference.

Artificial prolongation of life beyond its natural term was simply no longer sustainable. Hard choices would have to be made. The Tonkian principle of a short life but a merry one. A certain individual freedom was fine, but in the end, only large-scale intervention would deal with the problems. Mr Gunther had liked the pictures of the Nirvanatron, though he was rather scathing about shoddy American workmanship. He thought they could do better in Düsseldorf.

The air of anxiety, Mr Fox observed, had begun to communicate itself to the elders. Small signs of insurrection were to be glimpsed. Wanderings increased. A directive from Cologne urged electronic 'nursing' among the wandering demented be adopted throughout the eventide community. So he took steps to monitor this activity.

Other symptoms were more difficult to treat. Major Bobbno, on the advice of Dr Tonks, had signed on for a course of male hormone injections. The theory was that 'regular doses of the hormone improve circulation and stoke up the heart,' said the doctor.

Unfortunately it had another, fiercer effect on the old military wallflower. He leapt out of cupboards. He frightened the younger nurses. He planted himself in corridors when anyone female was passing. With solemn staginess, he threw away his Zimmer frame and, swaying dangerously, would cry: 'Look out, girls – Bobbno's on the run!'

Only Max Montfalcon seemed calm. His callisthenics were clearly doing him good. On the day he completed his training he felt ready. Rehearsed. Forward planning. That was the secret of military success. Chocks away! The day had come: J-Day.

He sat in his room listening to the cries of the Incontinents. He heard Bert calling for help. In an act of liquid defiance the Incontinents had destroyed their boilable knickers. They had razored their catheters. Bert was calling Jack to help him remove the ruined yards of good carpet. Max smiled and went to his cupboard.

The old bastard was waiting for him as he turned the corner, a sopping mass of carpet in his arms, unprepared for the force of Max's attack. He was wielding a *Glockenschläger*, a fencing sword used by the old German student fraternities and named for its bell-shaped guard. A gift from young von F. Max wished he had been using the very old weapon, the *Stossdegen*. This had unsharpened blade edges. It made an ugly wound when skewering your opponent's arm or rump. It caused very nasty internal bleeding, did the *Stossdegen*. Which was why it was outlawed after the grisly death of a student at Göttingen in 1767.)   Taking up von F's old duelling sword reminded Max of what it was he had really been doing in the muddy garden. Not learning how to run at all. That's why the movements of the feet took him nowhere. He was trying to remember the fencer's *glacé* stance: left foot stationary and only small steps allowed with the right. All so long ago he had not only forgotten it but had forgotten ever remembering it.

A certain Glanning had accused von F of being 'non-Aryan'. Satisfaction was demanded, and given. A sharp lesson for the slanderer. No one trifled with the family honour of Max von Falkenberg.

Jack's right arm took the thrust. The carpet he was carrying saved him from further damage. His cries and Imelda's screams alerted the staff. They had trouble disarming Max. 'Put it down, Mr Montfalcon,' Bert kept shouting, 'or someone will get hurt!'

Someone was hurt. Jack lay on the floor and the blood that ran from his arm seemed to Max to have a slightly greenish tinge to it – 'Beanstalk blood'.

He let them take him away. He gave up his sword. Honour done. Tomorrow was the first Tuesday of the month. Day of diversions in Serenity House. Max was happy. He had seen something in Jack's eyes. That was all he needed.

And Jack, what did he think as he lay there bleeding? Well, first of all he felt hungry. Yes, sure, he also felt hurt. But, strange to tell, what he felt most badly was homesick. There was one other thing he felt as he lay on the wet and reeking carpet and watched what might have been his life's blood draining away – until Matron staunched it. What was it Jack felt? Jack opened and closed one blue eye. Then the green eye. His lips blew a pensive bubble of spittle. There was blood in his hair. But he got it at last. Sure thing. He felt as mad as hell.

CHAPTER NINETEEN

Pat Dog Day

First Tuesday of every month was Pat Dog Day in Serenity House. The Friends of Serenity House arrived by mini-van with Petal the Corgi and Denis the Rottweiler. Little and large, the dogs were led between the beds of the elders. Everyone had a turn – in the old days – from young Agnes and the Malherbe Twins, to Beryl the Beard, and even the semi-comatose, like the Reverend Alistair, Margaret and Snoring Sandra. In the case of the three sleepers, their hands had to be guided to Denis's broad and ridged forehead. Or into the thick, warm fur of Petal's pretty golden nape.

Now, the ranks of the elders had thinned considerably. But tradition endured in Serenity House, even if Denis and Petal did the rounds in no time at all.

Pat Dog Day greatly impressed Dr Tonks. 'It reduces blood pressure, stimulates interactional relationships in people who may have no one to love and pet. Studies were conducted in the States with men in gaol. Prisoners related far better to others when put on a pet programme. I'm all for it!'

For once he was more or less alone in his enthusiasm. Mr Fox, who detested dogs, locked himself in his study on Pat Dog Day. Even the dogs disliked it. Denis the Rottweiler gave a perplexed frown when elderly hands descended on his brow and his bloodshot eyes focused hungrily on the fluttering fingers. His neck muscles inflated like bicycle tyres and he began to growl somewhere deep in his throat. Denis had been muzzled ever since Major Bobbno had a go at him with his hand-reacher.

'Take that, you big black brute! Down, sir!' Petal the Corgi had a habit of shaking herself irritably after each patting session and scattering far and wide a snowstorm of fine fur.

'I find dog hairs between the sheets for days on end!' Day Matron lamented.

At the end of this unusually brief Pat Dog Day, Denis and Petal were locked in the luggage depository to await the return of their owners.

Max, for his part, ignored the visit of the dogs. He refused to pat them and returned to his room content to note to himself: 'Camp authorities ordered dog patrols stepped up after recent escape attempts.'

He was having increasing difficulty telling the difference between sleep, waking dreams and fragmentary memories. Surely the driveway of his old prep school, at Churtseigh, curved left past the big house and down to the woods where those lovely cedars stood? Perhaps seven in all? But now he wondered if indeed that driveway had not curved to the right? One wished to consult with young von F. He would certainly have remembered.

Max watched his diet. No meat. Certainly not. One was well aware that thievery was always a problem in special treatment facilities. Meat was regularly stolen by the very people who were supposed to guard it. No wonder some doctors were forced to use human flesh instead of animal tissue for their cultures. The flesh of inmates pressed into the service of science. A terrible thing, but hardly surprising, when the guards were stealing the meat supply.

No meat then. Fruit and chocolate – and patience. For ever since his steely encounter with the boy Jack, Max had been formulating his little plan. He had seen something in Jack's eyes. Something, that is, besides the intricate network of blood-filled canals which reminded him vaguely of old photographs of the canals of Mars, back in the days when eminent astronomers still believed in life on Mars and scorned the idea of man-made space-flight; and supported their scorn with the numerate speculations by which scientists like to bolster and dignify their prejudices. That he now knew Jack's head – or capitation unit he would call it – to be as devoid of intelligent life as the canals of Mars, did not prevent Max from drawing a sudden and brilliant conclusion from the gleam, or say at least from the small, muddy, rather dirty light, doomed and dull, which appeared in Jack's eye when they met in the corridor after the stabbing incident and Jack turned tail and fled! *Fear* . . .

Jack would follow Max to the end of the world because he very sincerely wished to kill Max Montfalcon. Like Americans sincerely wished to be very rich. He would follow him because he was sure the old man had something to do with the recent disappearance of Innocenta. He would follow him because otherwise how would he know the old bastard wasn't lying in wait for him? Ready to do him in. Once bitten, twice-shy Jack!

Over at Greyacres Lizzie Turberville would say to her visitors as they sat drinking tea in the room above her father's old apartments: 'What was that? Did you hear a sound?' And she and her guest would place their teacups silently on their saucers and listen carefully. And if they were very lucky they would hear, seemingly a long way off, a kind of scratching, as if there were mice behind the skirting boards. Or sometimes the murmurous sound of a voice humming low and long and soft, like a distant singing sea. And the guest and Lizzie would lift knowing eyes to each other and nod over their teacups. 'Yes, there he is,' their looks said. Jack. Of whom they'd heard from Lizzie but never seen. Somewhere down below, in Max's old apartment, rolling his dice across the green baize, staking everything on another win like this one. Or pressing his eyes to the columns of eyes, which so dreamily eyed him back, and looking forward to more delights in the room of the tall old man with the locked oak cupboard and the disturbed nights.

Wasn't it a coincidence, her Living Will filed away in the office of Matron Two, that Lady Divina should one evening, quite of her own accord, leave her room at about nine (dressed in her pink dressing gown and a long white chemise upon which were embroidered several blue sheep grazing beside a red haystack set about with green daisies) and make her way to Bathroom Three, on the second floor? She carried a sponge-bag and a shower cap. (This item was to prove an unexpected boon.)

At approximately nine fifteen, having run herself a deep warm bath, Lady Divina had stepped out of her gown, removed her chemise, pulled on her shower cap (thank heavens) clunked on to her pink bathability chair and sank slowly beneath the waters.

Who knows what had made Lady Divina set out on this journey without warning and without proper nursing attention? She who had declared wild horses would never get her into a bathroom or shower ever again? A mystery: a miracle. A blessing in disguise, said Mr Fox.

Still locked in the luggage depository Denis and Petal lifted their heads and howled when she was found which, Matron Two said, was very touching, her being such a friend of nature.

Lady Divina lay several inches below the surface of the water, still ensconced in her bathability chair, looking, except for her shower cap, a little like an elderly Ophelia. No resuscitation was possible, although Matron tried artificial respiration for a while, simply because that was what she was trained to do. Lady D's Living Will required that everything be tried but it was too late to try anything.

Cause of death, as Matron had correctly predicted, was not drowning, but heart failure. How lucky that Lady Divina had kept her hair so beautifully dry by tucking it up neatly within her shower cap. All they had to do was put on her nightdress, slip her back into bed and send for Dr Tonks. One could always depend on Doctor Tonks. 'A beautifully clean departure,' he said, with his puppyish smile. 'Smashing stuff!'

Running scared, was Jack. And hopping mad, his arm throbbing under the bandage. Popping grandad, that's what his head hurt for. Getting him a piece of beef. And doing what you got to do. Right? Home would be easy. Home would be Guns 'n' Gold on Orange Avenue. A good piece. And bingo! Another one bites the dust. How many a year – twenty-four? twenty-five? thousands. What was one more?

But this was England. The old boy was crazy. Jack was

jumpy. He didn't feel too good. He was off his food. Was there something in the water? He should never have drunk the fucking water. England was an old country. It had old water.

A call one night, around nine, Max, soft in voice, almost apologetic: 'Lizzie? A bit of a problem. Are you there, my dear? Can you hear me? The police have been here, Lizzie. For some silly reason they're interested in my old war mementoes. Don't ask me why. Of no possible interest to anyone except me. But they want to see them, Lizzie. Embarrassing thing is that I can't find them. I'm sure I'd brought them when you and Albert so very kindly arranged for my transfer to Serenity House. In my old carpet bag. Remember? The blue one? Well, I don't have it any longer. Can't find it anywhere. Unless of course, I never brought it with me. Left it behind. No – not my place. *Your* place, now, Lizzie. Remember? Would you have a look for me? Should be easy to spot. The old blue carpet bag – and two small parcels wrapped in pink tissue paper. Possibly in my chest of drawers. You know the one. It's a bore I know. If you'd rather not, just say so. Then the police can do the looking themselves. After all, that is their job. Isn't it?'

It did not take her long. Innocenta's room had been stripped bare. It was as if she had never been there. In fact Lizzie began to wonder if she had not imagined the whole thing. Jack's room showed only slightly more signs of human habitation. A line of empty polystyrene boxes built diagonally across the room and the pervasive, slightly mildewy odour of old prawn crackers. In the chest of drawers she found the parcels. Beneath the bed was the old blue carpet bag.

The micrometer screw in its leather case and the two syringes meant nothing to her. At least not at first. But what she found in the blue carpet bag made her scream and scream until her daily came flying downstairs to find her hysterical, surrounded by pink parcels, a cigar box, a leather bag and what looked like a bottle of boiled sweets.

When the shaking had stopped she phoned Albert.

'I don't believe you,' her husband said. 'Eyes?'

'And heads. Skulls. Albert! Bare and grinning skulls. And a box of teeth. Still with their fillings. This is what the police must be looking for. What are we going to do?'

'Do? For Christ's sake, Lizzie! We're going to get rid of them. Take them back to the old bastard!'

'But how did they get here? Do you think Jack took them?'

'What does it matter? Perhaps they grew legs and walked. Perhaps Max came one night. Just get in the car and take them round to Serenity House.'

'Jack says Daddy stabbed him with a duelling sword.'

'Believe that and you'll believe anything. Your father might have been up to that sort of thing in the past, Lizzie, but his killing days are over. I don't believe Jack. It's damn Americans all over. Hot air.'

'Daddy says the police have been around to see him.'

'I'm not surprised. The superintendent in charge of operations has already put on a fine burst of speed. All over the country certain elderly gentlemen of – what shall I say? – European extraction, from the Ukraine, the Baltics and Belorussia, are waking to a loud knock on the door. I warned Max, but I don't think they'll cart him off yet. Not till they get the Polish reports. Allegations are one thing. Proof may be more difficult to come by. That's why we must get these things back to their rightful owner. We may be the family of a mass killer, Lizzie, but do we also want them saying we hid his loot?'

'I'd still like to know how they came to be in his old apartment?'

'Who knows?' Albert replied gloomily. 'Perhaps he got someone to plant them there. Maybe the old bastard was trying to frame us.'

She sat facing her father in the same little reception room in Serenity House where, what seemed years ago, she and Albert had left him when the grand bargain failed. Once again Max sat with the blue carpet bag cradled in his arms.

'I put on my coat. See? I can go out if I wear my coat. You always said so.'

Yes, he had worn his coat, the horrid green hairy coat she so disliked. And that appalling pointed yellow woollen hat, yanked over his ears. His face was pasty, grey, and he was blinking furiously, a shining drop of moisture hanging from his nose, a few flecks of tobacco clinging to his lower lip. He had not shaved. And all that she could think of saying was, 'I shouldn't be here.'

Max sat in his chair, his large hands in his lap, holding the bag. She had loved those hands as a child, their broad palms and long tapering fingers with shining nails. Max had always been very particular about his nails. The only man she'd known who had a regular manicure. He went to Herr Otto Kelner, who ran a small salon in Euston. Otto Kelner . . . Her father kept his own manicure set above his shaving mug in the bathroom. A soft black leather case in which reposed in snug scarlet velvet beds his clippers, trimmers, scissors, nail-files, emery boards and cuticle creams. Otto Kelner, a German – only now did the significance of this occur to Lizzie. She hugged herself and shivered.

'Is it true what they say? That you were one of those doctors or scientists in the camps? That you were responsible for making people go to the gas chambers? That you stood by the ramp when the Jews arrived in cattle trucks. Is it true? And these injections? With – what was it? – phenol? You injected them with phenol, that's what they say. Sometimes as many as thirty or sixty a day. Week after week. Tell me!'

Max stopped shaking his head and looked up at her. 'Not on Saturdays. Not on Saturdays or Sundays.'

'Why not? Why not on those days? Are you saying that you had the weekend off? You could all go home, to your first wife, Irmgard? You never told me about her. Your wife before Mummy. Is that what you did on Saturdays and Sundays? You went home to Irmgard?'

'One is asttempting to measure, to compare, to make notes. But one had no say in the choice of material. One simply took what they gave one. As for saving anyone. Well, what does that mean?

'All I remember young von F saying is that when he began work in the Hygienic Institute on Block Ten he had just one assistant, a complete fool named Behrens. When he left there were seven. Did he save anyone? As these few treasures signify, he did not. He kept them to remind himself of his failure. When he died they came to me.'

'Why did people take the weekends off?'

'It's perfectly normal. Time with their families. Or maybe they go to the football. Even doctors and nurses need some time off. The staff will occasionally dwindle to just a handful – Matron, and a little skeleton staff. Even Mr Fox slips away for a weekend, from time to time.'

'Mr Fox? Daddy, what are you talking about?'

'He has a cottage, I believe, somewhere in Wales.'

'I'm not talking about Wales. I'm talking about Germany.'

Max got up, walked to the window and peered cautiously into the street. Then, appearing satisfied that he was not under surveillance, he turned on his daughter his sweet, untroubled smile, a smile so genuine she had to guard herself against falling beneath its charm.

'We must remember, Lizzie, the incredible strain. Especially when people are dying. Everybody is trying so hard to work in impossible circumstances. Everyone feels a sense of responsibility. It's pleasing the doctors that patients care about most. Let a couple of GPs arrive for an inspection and everyone tries to stand up a little straighter, to cough a little less. The Incontinents – and we all have a bit of a drip problem, Lizzie – try to discipline their bladders as best they can. Little miracles occur. What one wants above all is to avoid medical disappointment.

'Between you and me, this puts the dying in a pretty uncomfortable position. When Dr Tonks asks them how they feel, they know that he doesn't want a straight answer. They want to give him the answer they hope he wants. The wrong answer is fatal. A little movement of his hand to the pens in his top pocket and they live or die. Red means life – blue and they are finished. A whole series of supplicating, mute little signals of the eyes. The dying try to signal to Dr Tonks that they're making the best job of it they can. People are always trying to placate their doctors. They try to do it by getting well – if that's what the doctors expect. Or they apologise for taking such a long time to die, or doing it so messily or so painfully. And all the time they're hoping of course to be told that perhaps they don't really need to die. But no one's left Serenity House alive, ever. We all go down the ramp.'

He got up then and to her horror crossed the room with his carpet bag. He tried to lay his head on her lap. 'Save me, Lizzie! Don't let me die! I've got my coat on – take me away. Please!'

She pushed him away. She ran to the door. She never looked back. Her father's voice reached her as she fumbled for the car keys. 'Watch out for Jack, Lizzie. He's going to want to kill somebody. Soon!'

Mr Fox summoned Saul Tusker's boys from Doves to collect Lady Divina at the ramp. Surprisingly, Mr Tusker found himself unable to do so. ''Fraid this is an American job,' Mr Tusker said. 'We're being gazumped by the damn Yanks!'

'What on earth are you talking about?' asked Mr Fox.

Then Mr Middler arrived. Backing up to the ramp in a big white Jeep with red decals on doors and bonnets, a cruciform design combining the latest in Red Cross imagery and the sensation of speed and efficiency.

Mr Middler, all in white, a black string tie with brass clasp in the form of a charging buffalo, with a pristine skull cap and PVC boots, pulling off his skull cap, scratching his grizzled locks and saying, 'Jeez, buddy, have I got the right place, is this Serenity? Where's the power points?' Then seeing Mr Fox at the foot of the ramp, striding forward, hand outstretched: 'Jesse Middler, Eternity Inc., Cola, South California. Pleased to meet you.' Looking at his inventory. 'Where's our member? Lady – would I be right in pronouncing her name Dee-vee-na? Is she a real lady? Wow! OK. Let's go. No time to lose. Would you have our member stretchered down the ramp?'

'Your member?' Mr Fox enquired politely.

'Sure. Signed up to Eternity, oh, a year back, I guess. We stretcher said Divina to the collection vehicle. Give her a preservation spray. Short term but enough to keep things humming till we get to the depot at Gatwick Airport. Ready to fly.'

'You fly her out of the country?'

'Not immediately. Once in the depot at Gatwick we begin the cryogenics. The member is injected with preserving fluids.

Then frozen. It takes about three days to freeze a member adequately. Once frozen we slide the member into a tube.'

'Into a tube?' echoed the fascinated Mr Fox.

'Yeah. A steel tube. A bit like a Thermos flask, but made of stainless steel. Then it's off to storage in Cola, South California. Liquid nitrogen, in a special rack, against the day when we've got the technology to rouse our members for repairs.'

'How long would you say it will be?'

'Depends on how good we get at cell-repair. It's coming along in leaps and bounds. Reckon in thirty, fifty or at the most, say, a hundred and fifty years we should be able to fix most things. Or clone a whole new you from a single cell. So if we can't fix what's left behind, we'll take a little bit and make us a replica. This is a promise in our policy: Eternity Inc. won't unfreeze you until we're good and ready to fix you. So, what's to lose? It's a better bet than prayer. And, hell, for immortality, it's cheap at the price.'

'What is Lady Divina having done?'

'Just her head, ol' buddy. Neurosuspension. We do what we call a capitation job. There's a good deal to be said for it. You still get all the grey matter. All the essence of the person. If you take a mechanist or behaviourist position, then everything there is is in the head. Right? If you see what I mean. And the price comes down. Around thirty-five thousand dollars per neuro-suspension against one hundred grand for a full body job.'

Mr Fox wondered if she'd told them about her Alzheimer's? On the other hand – would they care? If they had a century or two to play with, and nothing really to interfere with the storage process. Except for, say, nuclear war. So she would wait, hoping for a cure for her Alzheimer's, or a new body by cloning. But, above all, she would wait out the threat to which she had given most vocal expression, stored away down there in the giant Thermos flask in the vaults of Eternity Inc., in Cola, South California, solid in her envelope of liquid nitrogen. No matter what happened to the ozone layer, Lady Divina would be safer than most on the globe from sunstroke, from the overheating earth, like a blue egg, frying.

Mr Fox waved Mr Middler's white collection vehicle out of sight, on his speedy way to Gatwick Airport, rooflights revolving,

klaxon going. He walked into Serenity House, now quieter than
it had been for many a good year. He sat down at his desk and
thought. 'Hell! That was a good couple of weeks of work.'
He was about to ring for a list of recent departures when St
Margaret Drive was suddenly crowded with more revolving
lights and sirens. For a moment he thought that Mr Middler
had come back. Perhaps he had forgotten something.

But these were blue lights. And men in blue. And Chief
Superintendent Slack banging on the front door of Serenity
House and demanding entry.

And that was when the roof fell in on Cledwyn Fox.

Superintendent Slack had a warrant for the arrest of Max
Montfalcon. Reports from Poland were deeply unsatisfactory but
Slack was not to be held back by the dithering of incompetent
subordinates. He was taking Max Montfalcon in for questioning.

Superintendent Slack, in pursuit of guilty men, came down
on Serenity House like a wolf on the fold. That his fugitives
were doddering, deaf, senile, toothless, incontinent and forgetful,
that they were liable to take leave of this world without per-
mission, was a fact that had haunted Slack. Once the War
Crimes Bill passed into law, he had pledged to press and country
that he, Trevor Slack, would 'hit the ground running'.

As supersonic speeds are measured in Mach units, so Trevor
Slack had, once upon a time, in a jerky way, when he'd thought
of movements measured at the speed of light, considered a new
scale of such celerity. Star travel would be measured in 'Steins':
Einstein, Zweistein, Dreistein – each Stein being the equivalent
of ten light years.

Alas, the brain rots. Though Trevor Slack had never been
known to exceed the alcohol quota – twenty-one units weekly –
allowed for the best preservation of mental health, though he
had never in his life inhaled tobacco smoke, or indeed any other
noxious drug, though he ran a mile each morning and exercised
each evening, yet, do what you will, the brain rots. Cells falter,
fail and float away much as the skin flakes and drifts. It is a
progressive, incurable human condition. He might have thought
of this now, as he hit the ground running and moved up to
the speed of light. He might have remembered the old man's
unaccountable amusement at their last meeting. He might have

been a tiny bit prepared for what he found – or what he did not find in Serenity House. He might have – but the death of the brain intervened. Alas and alack, he had forgotten about the death of the brain.

And so when Cledwyn Fox reported absolutely no sign of Max Montfalcon, he simply refused to believe him. 'There are recent cases, in France,' said Superintendent Slack, 'of clergy hiding war criminals. I hope you're not doing the same. I have a search warrant, I'll turn this place upside down.'

And he went at it with a will. That old and rather fragile Victorian house felt the force of Slack and trembled. Roof tiles fell to earth. Bits of plaster showered the Superintendent and his team as they moved from room to room.

The residents of Serenity House, whom he had been counting on to help him track down Max Montfalcon, proved a considerable hindrance. Most of them were dead. Worse still, his investigation into the strange disappearance of his quarry turned up alarming evidence that the departed elders had not died naturally.

The staff, the survivors of this carnage, were confused. They made instant reference to someone called Jack. Such charges! Drowning patients in the bath. Injecting them with tranquillisers in massive doses. Among the most grisly executions (for that is what the newspapers were soon to be calling them) was the alleged method of disposal whereby poor Reverend Alistair's tongue was depressed with a tongue depresser and water forced down his throat. The Reverend Alistair, Snoring Sandra and Margaret had all perished in this fashion. Yet, most remarkably, these weak, semi-conscious patients had actually fought their attackers, as evidenced by skin beneath their finger-nails.

Night Matron accused him of having administered fatal injections of insulin and Valium to elderly patients or having conspired with others to do so. The Superintendent asked why she or her staff had not attempted to stop him? She refuted the imputation with vigour. 'All I ever did was to bring relief where there was suffering. Joy where there was discord.' And she quoted the latest American statistics to show that anti-cancer treatments in the very old seldom do anything to prolong life. A waste of time. 'My conscience is clean. God is my judge.'

The little nurse-aide, Imelda, confessed to having seen this Jack taking several patients for what she called 'the swimming cure'. In the swimming cure, water was forced into the lungs while someone held the tongue and nose of the patient. All cases of the cure had proved fatal.

Certain surviving elders also made reference to a member of staff named 'Jack'. But records at Serenity House showed no trace of this person.

Some elders, it is true, were more positive in recalling a boy with one green eye and one blue, and yellow hair. Major Bobbno, for example, swore that 'this fellow Jack combined the cunning of a Pathan with the hygienic habits of an African warthog. We used to see him around the camp in the mornings, banging on his mess tin with a spoon. A superior gait he had. Stiff. Polish, I suspect!' And here Major Bobbno paused to demonstrate, throwing out his legs and tucking his hand-reacher under his arm. 'He was particularly vicious', Major Bobbno added, 'with the Russian prisoners. Poor swine!'

Other members of staff disagreed in their evidence. Day Matron, for example, dismissed the very idea of Jack's existence. 'Hysteria!' she snorted. 'It's not uncommon in institutions of this sort. It happens in much the same way that women kept confined will begin to menstruate at the same time. You also get spreading hysteria in small communities operating under strain. As far as I am concerned, there never was a boy. He did not have green eyes or blue eyes or red eyes. Or a black moustache. He didn't ride a broomstick.'

Superintendent Slack's chill realisation came at last to be unanswerable. Max Montfalcon had done a runner.

In the days that followed Dr Tonks was to announce that he was 'stunned' in one of the tabloids. In another he was 'shocked'. In a third – 'unrepentant'. While not condoning any alleged mistreatment of aged patients, he asked: 'Do you think I want to live on in that fashion, my bowels leaking, my head dead, my family anguished? Hell, no!' At least he did not rave like the others did about the mysterious Jack. When Slack asked about the boy, Dr Tonks replied: 'I do not believe in Jack. I am a scientist.'

*

Lizzie Turberville was found stripped down to her black lace French knickers, hanging from the branch of an apple tree in the garden of her house in Highgate. When she was found, she looked, thought Sergeant Fyffe – one of Superintendent Slack's team of officers, thirty-five he was, blond and something of a connoisseur – to be something out of a surrealistic painting by Dali. Or was it Max Ernst he was thinking of? Or Magritte? It was the black bag over her head that so disturbed him as she swung silently on the creaking apple bough. It was a touch, that black bag, both menacing and seductive.

In fact the bag was also cosmetic. For the face of Lizzie Turberville had been hit so many times with a blunt instrument, probably a hammer, that it was perfectly unrecognisable. The sheer ferocity of the attack suggested that the killer had had some further psychological problem with his victim. Lizzie Turberville had died from a double knife-thrust to the heart. The attack on her head had come later. Had been gratuitous. It was an assault as ugly and as senseless as any Sergeant Fyffe had seen in his career. It was as if the first blow, which probably broke her nose and cheekbone and lifted an eye from its socket, had merely enraged the killer. Driven demented perhaps by the terrible look of asymmetry it gave to that once calm and smooth face, he had rained blow after blow until nothing was left that remotely resembled human features.

The bag, of black velvet, German manufacture, some time in the early forties most probably, and possibly meant to contain jewels, had been dropped over her battered skull and the draw strings closed and then fashioned into a neat bow which she wore on her neck like a pathetically formal bow-tie. It was the bow-tie that had made young Sergeant Fyffe hesitate between the artists Magritte and Dali and, finally, come down on the side of Dali. It was the playfulness of that tiny chilling detail of the bag that decided him. And, then, to be sure, there was the fact that the pubic hair of the victim had been skilfully shaved. Not all of it, but exactly half of it, the right-hand half of it.

All in all it looked like a pretty exotic murder committed by someone with very serious sexual hang-ups. 'A pervy bloke,' was the way Sergeant Fyffe put it, though not in his report. Had he known something about the way things are in America,

Sergeant Fyffe and his superiors, who puzzled over 'The Body With The Bow-Tie' as the papers called it, would have recognised it as a carbon copy of one of a series of murders carried out in the video *Girl Crazy*, which had its origins in a wildly popular rap song by a group called Make Mine the Widow which contained in it the lines: 'Gonna slice that thatch/Right off your snatch.'

And if, in the unlikely event, the young and artistic Sergeant Fyffe had been familiar with any of this, he would have suspected the killer to be carrying, somewhere about his person, the shaven pubic hair of his victim. He wouldn't have been at all surprised to find Jack wearing a small brown leather pouch under his shirt. For Make Mine the Widow punched into the stinging rhythms of their song, the refrain, 'And gonna wear your dreck/Right around my neck', but none of this was ever likely to see the light of the English day. No one in the police team hunting down the killer of 'The Body With The Bow-Tie' knew the first thing about American culture.

Carpet bag on his lap, Max sat in the back of Mr Middler's speeding ambulance beside the recumbent body of Lady Divina, still wearing her pink plastic shower cap.

He reflected with a certain wry amusement on Lady Divina's head, resuscitated, opening its eyes and lips upon a brave new world and another century, another millennium, and finding it still wanting. Hotter than ever. The Great Lakes of Canada dropping and still dropping. Tropical cyclones hitting every other week the vanished Maldives, now sunk like Atlantis; malaria in Dorset, ringworm and river blindness in darkest Wales.

Max chuckled in the darkness. 'Won't they be sorry they woke her up!'

'May I see your tickets, please, sir – madam?'

A tall old man with thick grey hair that took on, in certain lights, a faint blue tinge. He was dressed in what looked like an ancient green overcoat which revealed a glimpse of white and pasty calves ending in short white socks and ancient leather slippers. He also wore a long, lolling, yellow pointed woollen cap and a red tie, the knot huge beneath his Adam's apple. He carried an old-fashioned carpet bag. Next to him sat a girl. Great silver circles around her eyes, a chalk-white face, hair no longer red, but black. For yes, it was Innocenta. And, here was an interesting thing, though lustrously thick, raven black, the hair also sometimes took on a hint of blue.

I cannot seem to go back to the place I came from, Max reasoned, because I can't remember where I came from, but I can, at least, go back to the place he came from. And so they found themselves standing among hundreds of Orlando-bound passengers in one of the lengthy queues snaking back from the check-in desks where, in the dim distance, the girls of Northwest Airlines sat smiling. Security guards moved along the lines checking passports.

'American airlines are terrified someone will get in with a gun. Or a bomb,' said Innocenta.

'If they carry Americans in number, I suppose they have to be,' her grandfather retorted.

Dark, deliberate, diligent, the security man scrutinised their passports.

'Do you have any other form of identification?'

Innocenta gave him her driving licence. Max handed over a seamed and threadbare card, made from grey paper. It was covered in a spidery purple script in a language the young man did not understand.

'What is this, please?'

Max stood up very tall and smiled his dreamy smile. 'What does it look like? That is a fine example of the card carried by German students who belong to one of the fencing fraternities. The student corps. What you have there is an identification document of a *corpsier*. That is to say a young man given over to self-observation, self-answerability and self-control. A young man who undoubtedly knew the taste of cold steel, who had fought in real combat, known as the *Mensur*. A young man who probably learnt to fight with honour and dignity using a rapier with a guard shaped in the form of a bell. They called it the *Glockenschläger*, *glocken* meaning bell. Although the *Mensur* was forbidden under the Weimar Republic, students still engaged in it. In the same way as they kept on drinking. And running after women. That's the way the world over.'

'That's interesting, sir,' said the young security man, 'but it won't do as a form of identification. Even if you could prove that you were the young man who signed this card and fought duels with the *Glockenschläger*.'

'I think I made a mistake,' said Max. 'Between the young man who signed this card and believed in the honour of his fraternity and his country and the elderly man who stands before you now there is no connection in the world.'

'Then why did you give me the card, sir?'

'I really don't remember.' Again Max smiled his rather vacant smile. 'Here, take my pension book instead.'

Three times Max failed to pass through the metal detector. He tossed his pen into the receiving dish beside the electronic archway. He put in it his silver lighter, his coins, his watch and his two gold rings, but still the machine shrilled its protest whenever he stepped through its regarding eye.

'Do you happen to wear metal arch supports?' the attendant asked in desperation.

Max shook his head but took off his shoes. He walked through the arch in socks. 'Hallelujah!' the officer said. 'You're clean, mate.'

Innocenta bought him a pair of white tennis shoes. Except tennis shoes, as he remembered them, did not have gold and purple arrows on them. Nor orange laces, which Innocenta advised him to leave untied. 'They're made to be left undone, Grandpa. I'm sure that's better for your feet.' She showed him how to inflate them. 'Press here. It's a built-in pump. You can put as much air as you like into the shoe. They take on the shape of your foot. Good! Now you're walking on air.'

Max followed her to the plane. He was indeed walking on air. His new shoes were very comfortable. Running shoes, Innocenta said they were. Their huge blue tongues flapped when he walked, like the tongues of thirsty puppies.

Cledwyn Fox's attempt to ingratiate himself with the police by revealing the existence of an electronic tracking device in the

heel of Max Montfalcon's right slipper (I've fitted all my wan-
derers with them') did, at first, cause not a little joy. For in no
time at all the transmitter had been located and had established
Max's presence very precisely. Superintendent Slack made the
drive to Gatwick in just an hour and a quarter which, allowing
for London traffic, was not bad.

Max's badly trodden slippers were still lying beside the metal
detector bleeping pathetically like a lost child. But the owner of
the slippers was eighteen hours gone, and at that moment, for
the first time in his life, about to step into a Jacuzzi in the Days
Inn Motel just off the Bee Line Expressway, twenty minutes
from Orlando airport, Florida.

And the moon shone down on Serenity House, dark, locked,
seemingly deserted. Gleamed down upon St Margaret Drive
and the cul-de-sac of Lord John Road. It filtered through the
windows and painted the wheelchairs lined up neatly in the
hall. It fell lightly on two discarded papier mâché heads, of the
Duck and the Mouse, which had rolled like abandoned footballs
beneath a forest of Zimmer frames, the moonlight like a ghostly
fire in the cold fireplace of the downstairs parlour. The house
seemed to creak and mutter. Somewhere behind the skirting
boards mice scurried. The survivors had been found temporary
accommodation in the Church Hall, while investigations continued. Somewhere in the very bowels of the house, two dogs
began to howl, as if they could see the moon, which assuredly
they could not. Forty-eight hours' incarceration in the luggage
depository had had an inevitable result. The animals had begun
to eat the suitcases piled on the great luggage mountain, the
hill of leather bones. Their toothmarks showed in the old hide
as they bit and gnawed at Max Montfalcon and Maudie Geratie
and Lady Divina. Petal and Denis, forgotten since Pat Dog Day,
raised their voices and howled to be taken home.

CHAPTER TWENTY

Kingdom Come

The incoming contingents still arrived by train. Nowadays a monorail. One marvelled at the many modifications and improvements to the system. One was free to arrive individually, by car, coach, or even on foot. Flagged into place by peach-shirted perimeter guards. Leaving one's vehicle in the spacious parking areas, each designated by a large friendly animal or cunning dwarf. A useful aid to memory and one was grateful for that. He parked in the area guarded by a droopy-eared dog. Then, like everyone else, he took the train to the imposing entrance of the facility. One had seen attempts made at deception, but nothing compared with this. Friendly turnstiles, an air of excited bustle suggested a market, or fairground, together with the colour and exuberance such feast days inspired in simple people. Yet the same unobtrusive, steely discipline, required to keep large numbers of people moving, was very much in evidence, to anyone who knew the signs. NO EATING, SMOKING, DRINKING, PLEASE REMAIN SEATED AT ALL TIMES. Excellent. No sign of panic. Guards carefully placed, never letting the newcomers out of their sight as train after train drew up to the ramp and the arrivals stepped on to the platform to be artfully funnelled towards the camp itself. Control of numbers, obedience at all times (whether voluntary or enforced), that was ever the secret. Fences high but discreet. Once inside, no exit except through the turnstiles. The fences probably reinforced with concrete foundations to prevent burrowing. The appearance of normality, even optimism. The fake station was wonderfully achieved. One believed one was on a real train bound for a real destination. Platform tickets, ostensibly offering new arrivals the choice of a stay lasting, perhaps, three days. It seemed one remembered similar soothing deceptions in other facilities long ago. A complete station, with waiting rooms and timetables. A clock whose hands were frozen at six. Six in the evening or six in the morning? No one ever knew. But never anything on this scale. The turnstiles clicked behind one.

An official guide appeared and announced an orientation tour. She wore a dark blue riding helmet, short blue skirt, white knee-length stockings and she carried a riding crop. Her name was Magda and she came from Munich. How very excellent. Dear old Munich! What happy memories of bicycling along the banks of the river Isar that bisects that elegant city. Magda waved her riding crop and offered a history of the facility and its achievements. It promised to be a fine warm day. Magda, no more than twenty, smiled beneath her riding helmet, showing teeth entirely beautiful.

'We will have time off for snacking, yes! Ach, I can see some of you are senior citizens. If I go too fast just call me and Magda will hear you.'

Guards everywhere. Different coloured uniforms, no doubt keyed to function. Perhaps also coded for rank. Smiling was evidently compulsory. Magda marched them first into the camp cinema to study the life of the founder. Once inside the auditorium the big doors closed behind them. HURRY UP, FOLKS. I WILL BE KIND TO YOU. THE DOORS WON'T. This from the elderly guard. Remote control was everywhere favoured. The engines that drove it all, he reckoned, were probably buried deep beneath their feet. He craned to see signs of chimneys but these appeared to have been carefully hidden.

The founder of this world, one learnt from the film in the auditorium, or briefing room, was a product of the Depression. After active service in France during the Great War, he had returned home determined to build an empire that would straddle the globe. Where everyone would be happy, healthy and tremendously organised. Millions across the world were to revere this man and speak his name with awe. The film ended, the dangerous doors opened to the sunlight. Magda led them safely from the theatre before the doors could be unkind.

'Just keep your eyes on my riding crop,' she smiled, 'and everything will be fine!'

The elderly guard at the door smiled. Everyone smiled. CAN YOU ALL MOVE FORWARD? THIS HALL HOLDS 591 PEOPLE. PLEASE HELP US TO FILL IT! They were to be shown a film on human conception, probably as a means of educating inmates in eugenics and the need to preserve ethnic distinctions if one was not to end up, as they had done in Poland, with the human material hopelessly disordered, a racial haystack full of ethnic splinters. Or should that be needles? KEEP YOUR HEAD AND ARMS INSIDE THE CABIN AT ALL TIMES. STAY CLEAR OF THE DOORS. THE DOORS OPEN AND CLOSE AUTOMATICALLY.

All day, and deep into the night, the trains arrived at the ramp and out poured the eager thousands. One was struck by the numbers of the ill. Wheelchairs, probably discarded, lined the fence when one arrived. There were numbers of blind and lame. It was unlikely they would be staying long but clearly the camp authorities were determined to ensure that they made the best use of the time remaining to them. Surprising numbers of foreigners. A good deal of Spanish spoken. Certainly many *Mischling*. Numbers of mulattos and what Fowler called 'half-breeds, halfcastes, Eurasians, hybrids, mongrels, quadroons and octoroons'. One watched a fat man with an artificial leg photographing an even fatter black man. Photographs were clearly encouraged. This would never have been permitted in his day: the penalties for taking photographs had been very harsh. Presumably with the intention of educating inmates about the danger of vermin, life-size replicas of mice strolled the pathways and waved at the inmates. Infestations of vermin were always a danger. One remembered the lice. Here, health concerns were well to the fore. There were no Mussulmens to be seen. A great relief.

In its way, one could not but respect the magnificent obsession to define the Indo-Germanic race. The need to measure size of brains and skulls. The preoccupation with the pathological features of skull formation. Even as one's researchers went forward, the human material on which those researches were based was diminishing. What was this? A remarkable copy of the Crystal Palace and, in the washrooms, they were playing 'Eine Kleine Nachtmusik'. Fascinating to observe how the original German concept of special treatment centres, though now much overlaid with modern advances and psychological insights, was still the solid basis of the entire enterprise. Inmates were now better clothed and fed. They were healthier. He saw not a gun, a stick, not even a whip, except for Magda's dainty riding crop. Yet the result was a ten-fold increase in obedience and a whole-hearted willingness to follow where the camp authorities decreed. Exceptional cleanliness everywhere. Paths swept, grass clipped.

There were shops, canteens, recreational areas, educational exhibits, lakes in which no birds swam and obedient trees. Even a fine camp orchestra. The musical side of things had been wonderfully handled. Optimistic melodies were piped from speakers hidden in bushes and trees. If only such ideas had been in place in the place where one had been! How much unnecesary suffering inmates and staff would have been spared. Here was a Japanese privet. Tall enough to conceal one from Magda's sharp eye. *Japonicum Lingustrum*, ABUNDANT CREAMY WHITE FLOWERS IN SPRING, NATIVE TO JAPAN AND KOREA. Thank you, Magda from Munich, soon to go on to a new facility being built even now in far-away France. Good luck and God speed!

To step now into the Magic Kingdom, that enchanted place where all the world lies bright beneath a broad blue heaven and a sun whose benevolent eye falls on man and mouse with equal warmth. And here, as in all good fairy tales, was an enchanted castle, blue and white turrets, fluttering pennants, a moat, a keep, a close, a portcullis, a gift shop and a secret lift. Yes, the observant might have noticed the secret lift. It lay behind the medieval dining hall, hidden by a thick disguise of padded leather. It was used to transport cast members, wearing animal disguises, from the shows they gave three times a day at the foot of the fairytale castle up to their changing rooms. Such castles deserved a good story. And the story was this.

Once upon a time, in the Comfort Inn, on the Orange Blossom Trail, there lived an old man named Max and his granddaughter, the dark-haired Innocenta. They were happy. If he looked at her a little sharply in the mornings, it was because she felt a little off-colour, something she hoped he had not noticed. But, of course, he'd noticed. He knew the signs. This was an unexpected development. But not inexplicable, biology being what it was. A little Jack in the cellar was beginning. *Hans im Keller*. What was to be done about that?

But first to step into the lift and be carried high above the camp. What a view! Far below, the waters of the moat. Far below, the toot-toot of the cheery little train that bustled about the camp carring inmates to their appointed tasks. YOU ARE UNDER TV SURVEILLANCE THROUGHOUT YOUR RIDE. And here on the battlements one rested, and waited, for the appointment one knew he would keep.

For one had not been idle since one's arrival. How well one got to know the road between the Comfort Inn and Jack's deserted caravan as to and fro one plied. Past the Amber Keg Sandwich Shop and the Good Shepherd Medical Clinic, past Magic Motors Used Cars, and the All Bug Control. Visiting the Medieval Lifeshow; admiring the imperious falcon and the ravenous hawk feeding off gobbets of raw meat. Watching the alligators consuming sections of chicken. Stopping for a cup of coffee and a blueberry confection in Wolf's Bun Shop. How can you go to Florida and not live a little? A spot of window-shopping at Big Bob's Used Carpets; some cash from the dispenser at Ye Olde Banke Shoppe and then on, for a brief pause at Fat Mansy's Guns 'n' Gold – 'All weapons to be unloaded before entering.' There to be introduced to a lovely little something, no less a beauty than the Tec-9, an assault pistol, 32-round magazine, less than three hundred dollars. This model specially coated to leave no prints. Self-defence? Yessir! And then on past Freddy's Famous Steaks and Wendy's Facial Surgery, past the Aardvark Video.

How big were the billboards! 'Orlando, a water-conscious community.' And then, just beyond, an even bigger billboard, 'People against pornography', hang a left into the Tranquil Pines Mobile Home Park.

One had left a note upon the door of Jack's old home there. Something of value would await Mr Jack Robinson should he present himself in the appointed place at the appointed time. And yes, pat, he here came, stepping quickly from the lift. For this is Florida, right? Where fairytales come true. This is King-dom Come where all we pray for will be granted.

'Hello, Jack,' says an old man to the boy in a Mouse head, 'remember me?'

One had learnt something after all from the stories Jack told the departing elders in their final bedtime tales. The Mouse had barely time to lift its paws. In the old world Jack might rob the poor giant blind. Of his goose, that in a steady auriferous rain of riches, drops eggs, heavy and golden. Of his few wartime treasures. Of his peace of mind. But in the *new* world those frail, forgetful beings, the old, those dispossessed giants, may at last turn on their tormentors and blow them to Kingdom Come.

And walk away. Slowly, it is true, but erect. While nothing of this drama high in the Castle ramparts above their heads is heard by the dancing dogs, ducks and chipmunks in the square below, who continue to sing that repetitively but somehow mem-orable melodic affirmation which recognises that we will endure the worst of everything, if given sufficient sweeteners. Enough sugar makes the most bitter medicine palatable. PLEASE COLLECT YOUR BELONGINGS AND THEN STEP CAREFULLY ON TO THE MOVING PLATFORM. Out now through the magic turnstiles where one is promptly stopped.

For one agonising moment one wonders whether possibly the body upon the battlements has been found, blood upon the crisp white shirt front, bubbling between the black lips, polka-dotting the yellow bow-tie. But no, it was merely a bureaucratic enquiry. One was leaving the camp, was that right? Indeed one was leaving. And did one intend to return? Certainly one did. At the very first available opportunity. One had not enjoyed oneself so much in half a century. Very well, would one please proffer one's wrist. No, not the left wrist, it must be the right wrist. And then, scarcely believable, the thing which showed that however modern this facility, some things do not change! One's wrist is stamped with some invisible but indelible number. To show one has spent time in the camp. Cold and quick on the right wrist. There, with a backward glance at the new contin-gents arriving every few minutes on the special trains, one located one's grey Buick from Alamo Car Rental, in the section represented, for the ease of illiterate newcomers (had one not seen hordes of those arriving in the old days?), by a large dog with droppy ears which reminded one very faintly of Denis the Rottweiler. One's driver was waiting. And his glance could not but take in that she still looked off-colour. What was to be done about that?

It was a difficult choice to make. Scientific instinct was strong enough still for him to think wistfully of the loss of human material which a termination would lead to – a rare opportunity to study the foetus of a girl who had mated with a monster. But there was no place for sentiment. One would have to take steps. Quite soon. And so one drove away smiling, as the happiest endings insist, into the sunset.